THE BOOK OF
CALLING

Tania Donald is a Melbourne-based author and artist. Her first novel, "Haunted Heart," was published by Penguin in 2011. She holds a Ph.D in English Literature and has written for theatre, radio and cabaret. She is also the author of the "Haunted Heart" sequel, "Fantôme Fatale."

The Book of Calling

First published in 2014 by RAVENSIN

ISBN 978-0-9876087-6-5

RAVENSIN PUBLISHING
Melbourne, Australia.

Tania Donald

THE
BOOK OF
CALLING

TABLE OF CONTENTS

"Demons are like obedient dogs;
they come when they are called."

Remy de Gourmont

CHAPTER ONE
Paris: 1890

I met him at The Silver Key, a gloomy little bar in Montmartre. It was the last place that I had seen her. I was having a bad week, and had found myself drifting around the places that I knew she used to frequent, hoping that fate would bring us together once more – as if that would make any difference.

I'd waited in her favourite café, Claudine's, earlier that afternoon, searching the faces of people bursting in from the rain as they shook their umbrellas and laughed with the relief that shelter brought them. But I found nothing except my own gnawing emptiness staring back at me in the ghostly reflections of the swinging glass doors, and in the distorting curves of the little silver teapot that I cupped between my icy hands.

Restless, I had drifted through the windy streets, battered by the heavy raindrops and feeling as grey as the darkening sky. I had known longing before, but never like this. I had known sadness, but not this kind of despair. I had played at love before, but now love was playing with me.

I did not notice him at first, as I sat in the crowded bar, trying to numb my aching heart with a succession of cognacs and staring always at the door. Perhaps he had been waiting too. But gradually, out of the corner of my eye, I had sensed him studying my face before I turned to remark him

1

He bowed his head to me as our eyes met, raising his glass in a melancholy toast: "To your health, Monsieur." I returned the gesture and as we both drank, he with his eyes closed and his head tilted back, I watched him. He was a good deal older than I: in his late sixties, I supposed. His mode of dress was elegantly refined and he appeared in every respect a gentleman. His silver hair was neatly swept back and an immaculately trimmed, triangular goatee emphasised his somewhat pointed chin. His complexion looked sallow in the golden gaslight and there was a weakness to his movements, a frailty in his posture that made me wonder if he had not been ill. He swallowed his drink and opened his eyes again: narrow, grey-blue eyes, full of thought and sadness. He raised his eyebrows at me and made an expansive gesture with his hand. "Another?"

I attempted a smile and made a little flourish of acceptance. He stepped down from his stool at the bar and clicked for the waiter, to whom he gave his order. There was something in his face that struck a chord with me: a suggestion of carefully contained distress, a hollowness about the cheeks, and in the eyes an uneasy searching look of longing that I recognised from my own mirror. His brow was etched with deep lines. He approached my table, walking with the aid of a silver-topped cane. I wondered what a gentleman such as he should be doing in a shabby bar full of artists, performers and ne'er-do-wells – perhaps the same as I was.

"May I join you?" he asked.

"Please."

"Permit me to introduce myself, Monsieur – Gildian Greene, at your service."

He leant on his cane and stretched out his hand. I rose and shook it.

"Nicolas de Bresson. Won't you?" I urged, gesturing at the empty chair.

"I took the liberty," Monsieur Greene explained with a thin smile as the waiter brought over his tray and began to set out glasses, slotted silver spoons, a sugar bowl and water jug upon the table. "It is, after all, the green hour – but then, I suspect every hour here is tinged with that bewitching shade."

I nodded and looked around at the absinthe ritual that was being performed all around us in every conceivable fashion from dainty refinement to louche drunkenness.

"I fear she is not coming, Monsieur de Bresson," Monsieur Greene said in a soft and sympathetic tone as he placed the spoon on top of his glass and sat the sugar cube neatly over the slots, which were shaped like sinuous flames. He looked up at me with kindly eyes.

"No. No. You are right. She is not. And even if she did … it is no use. She simply does not give a fig for me."

Monsieur Greene nodded slowly and poured cold water from the jug carefully over the sugar cube. In the low gaslight that glinted warmly off the brass fixtures around us, it almost looked like some magician's trick: the sugar dissolving and the cool, clear green of the absinthe clouding and swirling into milky opalescence. The rising perfume of anise and other herbs allured me irresistibly and I repeated the ritual in my own glass.

"I know what is it to yearn for someone," his low, steady voice consoled as I drank, "to be so consumed with longing that one would give anything to even catch a glimpse of her. Then, all one can do is to dream of how to win that heart that holds your own as its captive. But even dreaming does no good in the end, does it?"

"Yes, yes. That is just how I feel. I am her prisoner – and I doubt that she even remembers my name." I laughed bitterly and drank again.

"And it has been a long time, has it not? All the while, you had hoped that you would forget her, but your heart will not be so obliging as to let her go."

I nodded my head.

"The heart is like an intractable child," he went on in a soothing tone, "insisting it must have its way, regardless of the

3

danger or cost, regardless of the sorrow its senseless appetite inflicts upon you. And this terrible, impossible longing, and the shame you feel at being overpowered by your own feelings, you keep secret from those around you, do you not? You bear your burden alone. Believe me, I understand, Monsieur, only too well."

He clicked his fingers once more for the waiter as I drained my glass.

"Marchelline," I sighed, as the warmth of the spirit, and the sympathetic face of my companion began to ease my taut nerves.

"Her name is Marchelline ... "

On we talked into the night, though countless swirling clouds of absinthe and cigarette smoke until my head swam. Monsieur Greene was a most agreeable and consoling companion and ensured that my glass was never empty. As intoxication loosened my tongue, he drew out the story of how I had first seen Marchelline singing at Les Ambassadeurs; how we had had been introduced by a mutual acquaintance in this very bar in Montmartre and had enjoyed here the most lively and enthralling of conversations; how she had lingered in my mind; how I had returned to hear her sing again; how I had run into her once more at Claudine's, the little café on the Rue des Martyrs, and how we had talked then so easily, so thrillingly, for hours; how she had permitted me to kiss her hand then; and later, how I had heard of her close association with the Comte de Mortaine; and how my hopes, feelings and dreams of her continued to grow, long after they ought to have been extinguished by the painful reality of the engagement between them that many said was imminent.

I had last seen her here, at this very table, with her lover. If she recognised me then, she did not show it. Her haughty companion had merely looked me up and down and waved me away, as though I were just another stage-door Johnny.

I would never have talked so freely, nor for so long, but that Monsieur Greene had insisted I unburden myself of the whole sorry tale. By the time I had finished I was wretchedly drunk – so much so that I had begun to feel desperately tired and not a little unwell. The throng in the bar had thinned out, and weary waiters were wiping tables and glaring at us with impatience. I supposed it was very early in the morning as Monsieur Greene took my arm and led me out into the wet and blackly shining streets.

I must have dozed off in the carriage. I remember nothing until I came to myself a little later in an elegant, if somewhat old-fashioned, parlour. I was slumped in a blue velvet armchair and staring into a roaring fire. Monsieur Greene was pushing a cup of coffee into my hands and we seemed to be in the midst of the same conversation.

"I know how foolish it sounds," I heard myself saying in an apologetic tone, straining not to sound as drunk as I felt. "I know how foolish it *is* – only, when I saw her and spoke to her, I had the strongest feeling that here was the woman I would marry. I cannot explain it. You might dismiss it as some romantic fancy, but I felt so strangely certain! I have never felt thus before. I thought that it must mean something. I struggle to accept that I could be so mistaken."

"If only the power of your longing could summon your love to you," Monsieur Greene remarked wistfully. "If only you could find some way to touch her heart, as she has touched yours."

"Yes, yes, but it is quite impossible. The Comte – "

" – But perhaps it is not ... If I said there was a way – a secret, hidden way to achieve such a miracle – what would you say to that?"

"How? How could such a thing be done?"

"Not by any natural means. No. Nor by any means one might mention in polite society, or before one's priest. Not by such means as one might ever disclose to another living soul, for indeed that is a strict condition of the ... arrangement to

5

which I allude. But would you scruple at such a caveat if it meant that you might gain your happiness?"

"No, Monsieur, I would not – for you see the pathetic state of misery that grips me. My love for her has become a torment. I would give a king's ransom to free my heart from her chains – and I would give my life itself to win her."

Monsieur Greene merely nodded. He paused a moment in grave meditation, then hobbled silently to a tall bookcase in a nook at the far end of the room, whose glass doors were framed with sinuously carved rosewood and secured with a small golden lock. He drew a key from his pocket and opened the doors, reaching for a book on the topmost shelf. For a moment he seemed to hesitate and drew back his hand, then his doubt resolved itself and he proceeded to take down the book and returned with it towards me.

"Very few men have ever seen this book," he began. "Those who have possessed it have found their lives utterly transformed, as mine has been. I will show it to you now only if you will swear on your life never to disclose its secrets to any other – will you swear to that? This oath is no trivial matter, Monsieur," he warned, his eyes burning with intensity and his face drawn as he loomed towards me.

"Yes, I – I give you my word," I answered, taken aback but desperately curious to know his great secret.

"I myself once took such an oath and I do not take its breaking lightly. But I am growing old – my health is not what it once was. You are so young and I can see that you are a sincere and heartsick young man. I know where these sorrows can lead Monsieur, for men such as we, whose hearts are not fickle, but, once touched, close like a steel trap around that which they cherish. We cannot release that which we hold dear without lacerating ourselves and breaking our poor hearts in the process." He wiped away a tear and shook his head, as if trying to shake off some painful recollection. He knelt down before me. "This is The Book of Calling," he whispered, staring at the book with a most solemn aspect. He

6

held the book out towards me. With a thrill of fear that took me by surprise, I accepted the book from his hands.

It was bound in black-green leather of evident antiquity, with a sparse, irregular, curling pattern traced on its cover in worn gold leaf. An arresting and not altogether pleasant scent seemed to emanate from the tome – a coppery, metallic tang that made the hairs on my neck prickle. I flinched and for some reason I felt afraid to look within. I gazed up at Monsieur Greene, who now stood by the fire. He was staring into the flames and did not turn back to address me. "Go on," he urged quietly.

I opened the book and turned its yellowed and brittle vellum pages until I saw black writing in a very archaic hand. I adjusted my glasses upon my nose and began to read. The first letter of the text was large and illuminated in brilliant red, blue and gold. Around this great letter "K", tiny black devils and the most hideous, grotesque creatures of some medieval artist's imagination grappled and tore at each other.

Know thee,
I am the Book of Calling.
My secrets are thine
And thy secrets mine.
Blood and silence are the price of our bargain.
Thy will shalle be made flesh
Inscribed forever upon thee and me.

I shook my head. "Blood?" I asked, still feeling unwell from the drink and suddenly overwhelmed by confusion and unease.

"Turn the pages," he replied, still not looking at me, "until you come to the names."

The next page was densely covered in small script and seemed to set out some form of elaborate instructions. The page that followed it seemed to be some kind of key, with a long list of curious symbols down the left hand side and their

7

meanings at the right. I turned the page again and started at what I saw.

At the top of each subsequent page there was a name, underlined and written in large letters: letters formed in what appeared to be blood – although much darkened with age. Underneath this unusual heading each page bore other names written in smaller script but all alike in the hue of their dark red-brown ink. Alongside these smaller names were inscribed certain strange symbols. Some pages bore only one name and one symbol next to it. Others bore many names, accompanied by diverse symbols.

I swallowed as I came to a page set out like all the others but sprayed with gouts and smears of blood. There were other pages like it too – one so rigid and completely soaked through that any writing it might once have borne was obscured by the deep stain. There were indentations in this page: dints and criss-crossing score marks, irregular and suggestive of destructive anger on the part of their maker. I suddenly felt very unwell.

I hastened to put the book down upon a side table close to my chair.

"I … I am not sure. I don't know what this means," I said weakly, swallowing hard.

"It is exactly what it purports to be," Monsieur Greene said evenly, turning around to face me at last. "You write your own name in the book, then underneath it, the name of whomever you wish to summon to you. The various symbols cause different effects upon your subject, as you will see. I can assure you, it is quite real, and its effects are … undeniable."

I thought I heard some insomniac crow cawing as the wind picked up outside and the sounds of rain resumed with renewed force. I flinched and turned my head in fright at another noise behind me. Heavy, floor-length curtains masked a window, from behind which emanated an irregular weak tapping and scratching against the pane.

"There is no need to be alarmed," Monsieur Greene

reassured me evenly as he drank from his cup. "It is merely the wind moving the branches of the tree."

"Of course." I felt foolish. I was terribly tired and so horribly drunk. I believed that Monsieur Greene was quite sincere. He had shown me nothing but kindness – but the peculiarity of the situation was making me nervous.

"I know you will think all this quite unbelievable," he reasoned, as if aware of my thoughts as they were occurring to me. "I felt the same way when first the book came into my own hands." The tapping and scratching on the window seemed to increase, even as the sound of the wind died down. Monsieur Greene began to pace the room with some suggestion of agitation. I wondered if my scepticism about the book had angered him.

"I can only tell you that you are wrong to doubt it," he went on, raising his voice over the tapping and squeaking at the glass and the low whistle of the wind. "The oath I have broken to try to help you should dispel your misgivings, and the fact that I am giving the book to you: this most precious and rare treasure, inscribed with powers that man was never meant to know. Such powers are yours now, to bring your Marchelline to you – if you want them. But perhaps you do not." He moved to the side table and picked up the book protectively. The wind and rain rose again and the scratching and squeaking of the glass continued. "Perhaps I have misjudged you and the sincerity of your desires. No doubt some other chorus girl will soon take Mademoiselle Marchelline's place in your affections – perhaps it is time I arranged a carriage to take you home." Clutching the book to his chest he began to limp back to the bookcase.

I stood and followed him on unsteady legs, catching him and clutching his arm. "No, no, please forgive me – I meant no offense. I want to believe you, more than anything. You know how fervently I yearn for her – you alone – for I have confided in no-one else. But you must own that such things as you have suggested to me are far beyond the

9

commonplace. Such arcane knowledge exists, I am certain of it. What I dare not believe is that such forbidden power could ever be mine."

He looked into my eyes a long moment, searching my face for something. The wind and rain eased and, with them, the noise at the window died away. Monsieur Greene seemed to soften and relax, his face regaining that kindly aspect it had worn before.

"Very well," he said quietly. "But you understand, this is no trifling matter – I had to be sure." He pressed the book into my hands and went to fetch my hat, coat and gloves from another chair.

"You have been more than generous to me and I shall be forever grateful to you. Whatever else may happen," I said, looking down at the book, still unsure but desperate enough to try, "your kindness has consoled me greatly, and I thank you for it."

"It was nothing. One day you might do the same for another."

"Perhaps we might meet again?" I ventured.

"Perhaps," he replied uncertainly, "but I regret that I am not often in town – my life is a nomadic one at present."

"Well then," I said, clumsily fishing a card out of my case as Monsieur Green showed me to the door and clicked his fingers at the waiting cabman. "If the opportunity ever presents itself … "

"Indeed, it has been a great pleasure to make your acquaintance, Monsieur de Bresson. I wish you … all the luck in the world."

Tipping his hat as he approached us, and taking in my inebriated state with a knowing look, the cabman took my elbow and assisted me down the few steps onto the street where the carriage awaited. Still unsteady on my feet, I clutched the book tightly to my chest and climbed inside. My head was spinning and I craved sleep more than anything. I looked back at Monsieur Greene's house as the lamps in the parlour were extinguished. All was silent in the deserted street, save for the rhythmic clatter of the tired horse's hooves.

With some nebulous worry nagging at me through the haze of my drunken thoughts, the carriage drove me away into the early morning fog.

CHAPTER TWO

I awoke late that afternoon feeling absolutely wretched. As I lay in my bed – a tangle of thoughts and images flooding back into my consciousness – I wondered if the strange events of the night before were anything but a curious, absinthe-induced hallucination.

I rose, fighting a wave of nausea and seeking water to ease my terrible thirst. As I moved blearily to the water jug, I was assailed by a scent that struck at my raw sensibilities. I nearly gagged. It was the same coppery smell I had perceived in Monsieur Greene's parlour – it was the stale odour of blood that filled the pages of the Book Of Calling. I rushed to the window, squinting as I drew aside the heavy blue curtains and threw open the sash. Swallowing hard to suppress my rising sickness, I let the cool air soothe my head as I rested there, leaning against the window frame, with my eyes closed against the light.

Surely, Monsieur Greene had been playing some morbid practical joke on me; that was all. Perhaps my maudlin self-pity had provoked some cruel mischief in him. I despised myself for a pathetic, lovelorn fool – I could hardly blame *him* if he found me worthy of ridicule after all that I had told him. No doubt the book was some gruesome fake contrived for such gulls as I. What else could it be but a ghoulish joke?

I steeled myself with some deep breaths of fresh air and marched over to the open bureau where the repugnant book lay. I had thought to dismiss it at once and laugh the whole

12

matter off, but as I reached out to take up the book a hot scorch of fear in my gut arrested me. Some instinct stayed both my hand and my blithe dismissal of the book. Soberly, I sat down and put on my spectacles, leaning my throbbing head on my hand. Passing over the first page of writing with its cryptic talk of blood and secrets, I read on.

Take care that thou knowest what thou shalt do, for, once done, my work cannot be undone. He who shalle be called can never be released save by the giving of this book, and thereby thine own fate, into his hands. Seek neither to destroy me, for harm to me shalle be harm to thee.

Deep in the hours of darkness, takest thou four candles, and set them around thee at the cardinal points in certaine order: North, West, South, East. Light the flames, and then with a red chalke, seal the circle, intoning thrice the names of the diamon: Shedu, Shabriri, Asmodai, Azazel. With a blade of silver, passed widdershins through the flames, offer thy blood to the diamon through each of their fires. With a quill made of a raven's feather, then give thy blood to me in binding compact through thy name. The under-lining of it shalle set the seal thereon.

Thence the work of Calling may beginne…

I sat back in my chair and took off my glasses: disbelief struggling against hope and a cold, half-formed fear. What if it was real? What if it were *possible*?

Later that evening, I found myself walking slowly toward the grand and imposing façade of the Hotel de Crillon. I had told myself I must stay away. I had promised myself that I would never return to Les Ambassadeurs while Marchelline still sang in the café-concert there. But the yearning I felt compelled me – as if my own name had been written in a magical book and it was *I* who was bewitched and called to her. I simply lacked the strength to fight the impulse tonight. I had to see her once more, and I despised myself for the weakness of my heart.

I paused outside to smoke a cigarette: anonymous in my evening clothes amongst the throng of elegantly dressed ladies and gentlemen milling and assembling around me. I watched couples passing me by: men of my own class, no better, no worse than I, with lovely, smiling women on their arms, arrayed in colourful satins, frivolous hats and velvet evening cloaks. I exhaled a long sigh of smoke and crushed the stub of my cigarette under my heel.

Securing a table some way back from the stage I ordered a glass of wine. How my head still ached. Around me the outdoor theatre space was quickly filling with revellers eager to make the most of the evening's clement weather. A sea of black gentlemen's hats, and the gay and colourful chapeaux of their escorts, soon obscured my view of the orchestra. The stage, and the tall columns that framed it, glowed white like a beacon in the darkening night.

I have, from the earliest days of my youth, been a solitary creature, but seldom had I ever felt so alone as I did then. My heart sank as I noticed a tall, striking figure making his way through the crowd to a table reserved very close to the stage.

Upright and imperious, the Comte de Mortaine strode forward, his silk top hat lustrous in the radiant, white light of the lamps the hung overhead. He held a small bunch of blood irises in his hand and dropped it carelessly onto the table. He looked about him, proud and unsmiling, as he unbuttoned his astrakhan fur coat and cast it down upon a chair. He smoothed down his thin black moustaches and tugged sharply at the front of his tailcoat before he took his seat.

I wondered what it was that Marchelline saw in him. He was handsome, certainly, but had I not been called so often enough? His countenance was stern, forbidding, whilst I, when not in my present state of melancholy, saw in the glass an open and convivial aspect, fair and amiable. I had talents:

14

as a composer and pianist I had achieved some little success in my twenty-three years and was hoped by many to have yet greater achievements ahead of me. But he had a title, and the privilege and connections to which an aristocrat is heir. He could make her a Comtesse.

Now I recalled the conversation I had shared with Marchelline in the café; the things she had told me of her childhood in the roughest streets of the city. Her talents and fierce determination had lifted her out of that brutal poverty. Why should she not seek to rise as high as she might? How could she resist marrying into the nobility if she had the chance? It was only natural that she should wish to secure herself as far away as possible from the squalor and deprivation of her unhappy beginnings. Whatever other attributes might be mine, I could not elevate her to the summit of society as he could.

All at once the stirring of the orchestra dissolved my reverie and the chattering, laughing crowd fell silent. Music swelled in the evening air, now suffused with warmth by the gathered throng and the many great, round, white lamps above us. However expertly played, the gay, romantic theme of the orchestra sounded hollow and mocking to me. All around, I saw women's faces illuminated by smiles of delight, and I felt my jaw clench hard. I was relieved when applause replaced the music.

I barely took in the buffoonish master of ceremonies as he ingratiated himself with the audience. I could not listen to his facile patter, and watched with mounting impatience the indifferent opening acts. There was only one phrase that I was waiting to hear.

"And now Mesdames and Messieurs, I have great pleasure in presenting to you the Nightingale of the Tuilleries gardens, Mademoiselle Marchelline Rossi ... *La Rossignol!*"

The piano began to play and there she was, the *Nightingale* herself, tripping lightly out through the long, red velvet curtains and onto the stage. She was radiant in a ruffled,

15

crimson dress, her pale pink skin glowing in the footlights as she swept, laughingly, to the front of the stage. Two red roses were arranged in her chignon of curling chestnut hair and a simple black velvet band ornamented her slender throat. I felt myself colouring as she smiled so dazzlingly and inclined her head to the audience who received her with such warmth. The rest of the orchestra took up the exceedingly lively waltz and Marchelline gave a knowing smile and began to sing, with a twinkle in her eye.

> *Well my sweetheart and I, we went walking,*
> *Out in the country one day*
> *'My dearest,' he said, 'here's a sweet little bed*
> *A pillow of flowers for your pretty head.'*

Despite the exquisite prettiness of Marchelline's high, trilling voice, which did indeed warrant comparison with the nightingale from which she borrowed her stage name, her light-hearted song only plunged me deeper into despair.

> *'Come lay down beside me,' he beckoned,*
> *'Away from the world's prying eyes,'*
> *But we weren't so alone as he reckoned*
> *In a branch high above us a birdy did cry –*

Marchelline spread out her arms to the audience, inviting them to join her in the chorus of the popular song. Eagerly they followed her.

> *Tra lalala, Ooh lalala!*
> *What did he see?*
> *Tra lalala, Ooh lalala!*
> *Up in that tree?*
> *Tra lalala, Ooh lalala!*
> *Nobody knows! – Tra la-la-la!*
> *But that birdy, my sweetheart and me.*

With her vivacious charm and beauty, Marchelline held the audience in the palm of her hand. As I looked around me I saw with a pang that amongst the sea of finely arrayed and rhythmically swaying couples sat another man: still, solitary, and with that same pained countenance I had seen in my own mirror. Further away, there was yet another. It seemed that I was far from alone in my infatuation with Marchelline.

How sweetly she laughed and smiled as she sang, lending innocent charm to the risqué lyrics that another singer might have made coarse or bawdy.

It was Heaven I found with my true love
I was feeling quite warm I confess,
'Don't be shy,' whispered Freddy, 'my sweet dove,'
Well, since no-one was looking, I took off my –

She paused, running an elegantly gloved hand along the frill at her décolletage before adding in a mock-guilty, confidential tone, "– *hat.*" The audience laughed, but I did not.

The Robin's a curious fellow
And would not return to his nest
As we lay on our sweet bed of flowers
He whistled and watched till a blush flushed his chest.
Tra lalala, Ooh lalala! …

She went on, once more inciting the audience to join in the merriment as she waltzed about the stage. But gazing out at us all from the little stage, Marchelline did not see my unsmiling face, nor the faces of the other men she held so unwittingly in her thrall. The only face her eyes sought as she sang her mischievous refrain was that of the Comte, at his table close to the stage: her deeply ruffled skirts swirling around her feet as she moved toward him in a gay little dance.

Nobody knows! Tra la-la-la!
But that birdy, my sweetheart and me.

17

Impassive, the back of the Comte's head revealed nothing of his response to her.

– Hear him whistle and squawk
I'm so glad he can't talk –
Oh, that birdy, my sweetheart and me! Tra-la!

As the song ended the audience erupted into enthusiastic applause. Without rising from his chair, the Comte flung the little bouquet of irises onto the stage, at Marchelline's feet. Bowing, she picked them up, her face illuminated with gratitude and joy.

How had I ever thought that she could be mine? All the men of Paris were hers for the choosing; what was I among this crowd but another self-deluded admirer? If I thought that she had ever been singing just for me, it was only because she was such a gifted performer. If I had believed that she had been as fascinated by me as I had been by her, it was only because she was charming and generous enough to indulge her followers with kindness.

I rose as Marchelline left the stage, weaving my way impatiently through the clutter of tables and chairs that stood between myself and the exit. The spiel of the master of ceremonies and the receding laughter of the audience rang hollow in my ears.

Out on the street once more and away from the heat of the crowd, the evening suddenly felt terribly cold. I walked down the Place de la Concorde, towards the river, assailed by the stale-smelling wind that jostled the leaves on the trees along the Port de la Concorde. What was I doing, letting my feelings for a girl I hardly knew overwhelm me and make me so miserable? I had my youth, my own talents, two fine houses and an income that left me free to pursue whatever ambitions and pastimes I wished. But all I wished to pursue was Marchelline. I wanted for nothing – except her.

I walked along the river's edge, trembling as much from the cold as from the agitation in my breast – the feeling that my heart was not my own. I stopped and my thoughts began to drift. I realized that I was staring into the fast-flowing water as it glittered blackly before me. A rough gust of chill wind hit me and I felt myself wavering, balancing on the balls of my feet. There was a shriek at my right and I turned to see two young women, one laughing at her companion, who was chasing her hat as the wind blew it along the ground towards me.

I stepped back from the water's edge and, turning, stopped the hat with my foot. The red-faced young lady laughed and stopped running. She stood upright and puffed out her chest, straightening her gaudy dress and smoothing her hair with a smirk as she neared me. Stooping, I grasped at the hat and noticed how overburdened it was with ribbon, feathers and ugly cloth flowers.

"Oh you *are* a gentleman, Monsieur," the girl began, moving very close to me. "I don't know what I would 'ave done if it had gone in the water. It's me best one!"

I proffered the hat to the young lady. "It was nothing."

"So handsome, and all alone … ?"

Impatient, her friend yelled at her coarsely from up the way. "Come on, Marie! I'm not goin' into that bleedin' bar all by meself again – a girl's gotta 'ave some dignity!"

Laughing, the pink-faced girl snatched her hat from my hand and turned on her heel, running off after her friend. A movement caught my eye, as something fluttered down towards my feet. I knelt down and picked it up. It was a feather from the young lady's hat. It was long, straight and deeply black. I turned it to catch the light and it shone a lustrous jet-black tinged with blue. It could only be a raven's feather.

I sat at my piano, a near empty glass of cognac resting impatiently on the edge of the case. Beside it lay the raven's feather. My hands moved restlessly over the keys, trying to release into music the tumult that was tearing at my heart. I felt myself rocking slowly, my eyes closing as my feelings all at once crystallised into a mournful theme, to which my left hand provided an insistent and accusing bass counterpoint.

This might be her song, a song I might give to her to sing – if it weren't so utterly hopeless. Yes, my music might easily be a pretext to arrange some meeting, but such renewed contact would only inflame my heart and my infatuation. I stopped, and hastily notated the music onto the blank manuscript paper in the music rack. I thought a moment then added a title at the top: "Song to the Unrequitor."

From beneath the cover that darkened his cage as he tried to sleep, my African Grey Parrot, Maxim, gave an annoyed squawk. Unable to sit still any longer I stood, my legs pushing back the piano stool with a squeak. My agitated fingers grasped absently at the cognac balloon, and as I shuffled from the drawing room I realised that I held something else in my other hand. I did not need to look. I knew at once what that smooth, hollow, bluntly pointed shape was that I unconsciously rolled between my fingers. The feather tickled my palm as I turned it, pricking my memory with a notion that I could not seem to let go.

The house was silent, save for the ticking of the clock and the sound of my shoes upon the floor. The gas lamps were turned down very low. The servants had long since gone to bed in their quarters high above in the attic. They were sufficiently accustomed to my habits not to be surprised by any nocturnal noises I might make, if indeed they could hear them.

I knelt upon the bare boards of my bedroom floor, four candles burning around me. Within their compass of flame, the Book of Calling and I were contained by a circle drawn upon the floorboards in red chalk. At my left rested a small silver knife. At my right lay the raven's feather, its point sharply cut to form a writing quill. Before me, a small white bowl waited for my blood. In the silence of the night, my breathing sounded conspicuously loud and rapid.

"Shedu, Shabriri, Asmodai, Azazel," I intoned for the third and final time. My voice was a harsh whisper, and I wondered if it were loud enough to be heard by ... whoever might be waiting. I stifled a shiver as I heard the wind rising and the beginnings of rain tapping at the window panes. Rushing air whistled in the chimney and the fire in the hearth flickered and crackled.

I took up the knife and hesitated, not afraid of any pain or injury, but of what I had come to, and what folly my fixated heart might yet compel me towards. Surely this was madness – but I *had* to try. The book was the last straw of hope I had to clutch onto. Crouching upon the balls of my feet I cast the point of the dagger into the flame in front of me. Hunched, turning anti-clockwise as the book had demanded, I repeated the ritual through the other three flames. At the last I paused, knowing that to proceed further was to commit to a course that frightened me for what it might signify about the state of my own sanity.

I took a deep breath and, with one motion, I drew the tip of the blade from the flame and sliced an incision diagonally across the thumb of my left hand as I held it up in front of my eyes. I gasped at the burning pain, and, seeing the blood beginning to well, I dropped the knife and leaned out to let the drops fall into the first candle. Eager to perform this part of the rite quickly lest I burn my bleeding hand, I focussed my attention on dripping the blood directly onto the flame, as at first, trembling as I was, I had only succeeded in dribbling it down the side of the candle and onto the floor. Now I turned again to my left, shuffling, bleeding, listening for the quiet sizzle of blood in fire, that I might turn again and again till at last it was done. The smell of my own burning blood filled my nostrils.

Dizzy, I stopped, reaching for the empty bowl with a shaky right hand and catching my breath as my throbbing,

21

scorched thumb pulsed its thick red drops into the porcelain bowl. The rain beat harder at the windows and the wind rose still higher, whistling its fury through the tiny gaps in the casement.

Having collected enough of the crimson liquid in my bowl, I pulled a handkerchief from my pocket and bound my thumb tightly. I opened the Book of Calling, flicking quickly through leaves covered with names and signs and stains, until at last I came to a blank page. Kneeling low over the book, I took up the raven's quill and dipped it in my thickening blood.

"Nicolas de Bresson," I inscribed carefully at the head of the page. As I wrote I had the most curious delusion – as though, out of the corner of my eye, some shadow moved. I looked up, and saw nothing but the dancing lights and shadows of the fire's making. I filled the nib again and drew a thick line underneath my name, imagining again this illusory movement of a dark shape in my periphery, fancying now that red eyes burned in the form and stared towards me. But of course, when I looked up, there was nothing to see. Doubtless, I glimpsed the glowing reflections of the candle flames in the mirror upon my dresser, and my inflamed nerves had done the rest.

The casements rattled as the wind increased its howling. I shivered, feeling suddenly very cold. Then, strangest of all, I fancied that the low, moaning roar of the wind, with its inharmonious shrill overtones, somehow formed words in my mind. My eyes closed, involuntarily, and the windy, wild, inhuman voice seemed to ask, "Who is to be called?"

The breath left my lungs and I shook my head, not believing my own senses. I dipped the quill once more and scrawled beneath my own name in a shaky, spidery hand, "Marchelline Rossi." And even as I wrote the words it seemed that the spectral voice outside wheezed and moaned them too in its slow, inhuman intonation, distorted with jarring harmonics.

"And how shall she be called?" the voice of the wind seemed to ask then, surging and halting, at one second as loud as a roar and the next as quiet as a whisper. The flames of the candles began to bob in a strange, infernal rhythm. Scarcely breathing now, I quickly turned back to the page of symbols and made my choice. It was the first symbol depicted and the most simple of them all: an arrow circling anti-clockwise, back upon itself, which the key interpreted as "The Sign of Calling and Summoning." With the last drops of my blood in the little bowl, I filled the quill and made the sign next to Marchelline's name.

I suddenly felt overwhelmed with fear and foreboding and rushed from the circle, lighting the gas, turning it up high, so that light might dispel the restless shadows from the room and from my mind. I hastened to close the book and blew out the candles. I pulled another handkerchief from my drawer and began, vigorously, to scrub away the red chalk circle and the drops of blood and wax that spattered the wooden floor. I replaced the candelabra upon the overmantel, wiping them and the candles they held until all were unsullied and bright once more. Last, I cleaned the little bowl, till no trace of red remained.

I unrolled the rug back over the spot where I had done my work and then I threw the red-stained handkerchief into the fire. No evidence remained of my mad interlude, save my injured thumb and the book itself. This I took up and locked inside my bureau.

Exhausted and troubled, I retired to my bed, where the violence of the gale, and the tempest of my own thoughts, did little to lull me to sleep.

Chapter Three

I awoke the next morning feeling sobered and chastened. My head had finally cleared from my bizarre fugue of the day before. I could find no explanation for my mad behaviour other than that I must still have been drunk when I did those ridiculous, blasphemous things. Absinthe was not something I customarily drank and Monsieur Greene had plied me with so much of the foul stuff, its strange delirium must have lingered in my mind. It seemed that the drink's notorious reputation was, indeed, well deserved.

I had been spending far too much time on my own of late, brooding, letting my heart and my imagination run wild, and indulging myself in foolish, melancholy fancies. Clearly, if things were so hopeless with Marchelline that I had attempted black magic to win her, it was now time to take myself in hand and make a serious effort to forget my infatuation and get back to the work of composition. At least music was in my power to control, and I was always happiest when I was being productive.

I looked out of the window and was cheered a little to see a blue sky. Perhaps the tardy spring was now properly beginning after all. Down on the street below, traces remained of last night's storm: little puddles shining here and there, and leaves and broken bits of branches littering the road. But above, all was sweet tranquility, as nebulous grey-white clouds made their slow progress across the azure sky. A coarse guttural sound intruded upon my reverie and I scanned the scene to find its source. Atop the street lamp sat a glossy black raven, crowing his slow, sardonic laugh. As he turned to survey the street I noticed that his tail was missing one of its feathers.

I had arranged to meet my dear friend and musical colleague Paul Petit for a late lunch. We had so often talked of collaborating on a composition; I resolved to make this project my new preoccupation. Paul's sunny disposition could only be a good influence on me now when I needed cheering and conviviality. I had hesitated on the telephone when he had suggested that we meet at Claudine's, but wishing neither to explain why, nor to allow my movements to be curtailed by my ridiculous infatuation, it seemed simpler to agree.

How different the complexion of the world seemed when I emerged into the daylight. Sunshine, a clear head and an invigorating walk made me feel more like myself again. I had lost myself so easily and on the basis of nothing more substantial than a beautiful face and voice and some pleasant conversation and fanciful dreams. As I strolled along the Rue des Martyrs I turned my thoughts to what sort of music Paul and I might create together, searching my recollections of the interests we shared, and wondering how best we might blend our common influences. Then I froze. As though some heavy chill crashed down upon me, I felt myself instantly glued to the spot, the blood turning to ice in my veins. Directly before me stood Marchelline, a look of confusion and something approaching fear upon her face as her eyes burned into mine. If either of us had taken another step forward we would have collided – so close were we. A puff of her breath shocked my cheek with its warmth.

I felt myself colouring. "I d–do beg your pardon, Mademoiselle," I muttered quickly, stepping out of her way. Marchelline shook her head slowly, as if straining to remember or understand something just beyond her grasp. How utterly sublime she looked in her dress of red and black striped silk with its high frilled neck. A little red hat ornamented her chestnut curls. It was adorned with a tiny stuffed finch, its feathers gloriously red, with patches of black and golden yellow. A striped parasol hung from a red ribbon around her wrist.

"You ... ? I seem to remember, or did I dream? But, I know you, do I not, Monsieur ... somehow?"

"We have met, Mademoiselle Rossi. We have a mutual friend in Paul Petit." I gestured towards the painted glass frontage of Claudine's, where I assumed Paul waited inside. "You were kind enough to converse with me here, and at The Silver Key where we met once again. It was quite some months ago now."

"Of course, of course, now I can place you." She smiled, but the cloud of unease would not leave her pretty brow. "A musician, no? It is ... Monsieur Vuiton, is it not?"

"De Bresson – Nicolas de Bresson," I said, with a thin smile and a slight bow of my head.

"Yes, yes," she murmured, now biting her thumb through her glove and seeming ever more bewildered.

"Is – is something the matter, Mademoiselle?"

Marchelline rubbed at her brow as she struggled to collect her thoughts. The little bird on her hat shook with her movements. "It is rather odd," she said at last, her hands now clasped together before her chest, her fingers fidgeting restlessly. "I haven't the least notion of what I am doing here." At last she gave an exasperated laugh and raised her prettily curving eyebrows at me. "I must be going mad, Monsieur," she joked, shaking her head.

"It is a lovely day," I ventured nervously, "No doubt the blue sky drew you out, as it has all these other sun-worshippers." I looked around at the crowded street and the scores of people congregating to talk and drink on sidewalks that had for months been near empty.

"Yes ... yes." She nodded absently, searching my face for something. "Well, I must not detain you, Monsieur de

26

Bresson, if dear Monsieur Petit is waiting. Would you be so kind as to pass on my best regards to him?" Speechless, I could only bow.

She smiled at me. "Well, goodbye."

"Good day, Mademoiselle Rossi."

She nodded her head to me, and as I turned to enter the dark glass doors of Claudine's, I saw in their reflection that for a second Marchelline went to follow me, her hand reaching out momentarily as if to arrest me with some word. But instantly, she stopped herself and walked on up the long and narrow street, shaking her head.

Rushing into the darkness of Claudine's, I covered my face with my trembling hands, wincing, screwing up my eyes, trying to catch the breath that seemed only able to enter my lungs in shallow gasps.

"Nicolas!" Paul's friendly voice called out to me, "Over here!"

Seeing that I had little appetite, and doubtless showing a friend's concern for my preoccupied silence and bad colour, Paul suggested that we take a stroll up the hill to observe how the construction of the basilica of Sacré Coeur was progressing and to take the air in the gardens. It seemed that half of Paris had the same idea.

It was not long before we were standing amid the crowd on the high first balcony of Sacré Coeur, staring up at the gleaming edifice with its rows of layered, curving arches and its great rounded domes reaching almost to the clouds. Its white travertine was luminous against the blue of the sky.

"How beautiful," I remarked, "even if it does remind me more of some grand Roman temple than a Catholic cathedral."

"The real miracle will be if they ever finish it," Paul joked. "But look here Nicolas, this is what I wanted to show you." He put his arm around my shoulder and turned me around to look out over the balcony at the vast city sprawling away to the horizon in all directions before us.

"There," Paul whispered at my ear, as I leant with him on the stone railing, "call me a heretic, but I would rather look down there where life is, than up in the sky, as the basilica urges us to do – and not just because it hurts my neck." He nudged me in the ribs. "In each of those buildings, on every street, in every arrondissement, there are people waiting to be entertained by music – our music – people by the thousands. There are beautiful girls waiting to fall in love with you. There is music, food, wine, art, pleasure: wonders to be enjoyed." Paul gestured behind us at the great church piercing the sky. "That is the realm of dreams and phantoms," he whispered, "of martyrs, saints, holy spirits: the ghost stories Man tells himself about the kind of ghost he hopes to become when he is dead, and the ghost stories with which he consoles himself over those he has lost. But down there, life waits. It waits for you, Nicolas. It is easy to get trapped up here," Paul went on, tapping at his temple, "especially for those of us with an imaginative soul. It is a pleasant place to visit – it is beautiful – but down there is where we can truly be alive … no? I've been worried about you of late. You are not yourself. Moping about forever alone in that silent house, it is not good for you. I've been having such a grand time of late, meeting people, enjoying myself – I only wish the same happiness for you. And a man of your talents ought to share your gift with the world."

I smiled and nodded. "Of course you are right."

"Then let us make music and take it down there, to the cafés, the nightclubs, places of enjoyment and life," he went on, "not the stuffy concert hall or the opera house where a man daren't so much as sneeze. What do you say to that, hmm?"

"Yes, yes, it is a marvelous suggestion," I replied, allowing myself to feel inspired by his enthusiasm, and trying to forget my strange encounter with Marchelline. It was a coincidence and nothing more – it had to be. If she lived in Montmartre, she might pass Claudine's every day. It meant nothing. It could not mean anything, and I would not let any

28

imagined significance take root in my imagination. She did not remember me. I meant nothing to her: that was the only fact of significance that I should keep in mind.

"And we needn't limit ourselves to a song here or there – we might try and write a whole show," Paul ventured, nudging my arm and walking away from the gathered throngs now milling around the basilica's façade.

"Yes," I agreed, following him to the top of one of the twin staircases that seemed to stretch endlessly down to the base of the hill. "We might create a cabaret with a theme – a musical theme as well as a narrative one."

"We might find added inspiration in creating material for a particular performer or an ensemble," Paul speculated as we descended step after step.

"Had you anyone in mind?" I asked, a little nervously.

"Well, why not Bruant or one of the top men? Although I suppose he has regular songwriters that he employs – he is a bit of a specialist, now I come to think of it. I shall make some enquiries."

"Yes, I don't know how it would come across, chaps like us writing songs about the poor and that type of gritty subject matter that Bruant favours. Even satire – I'm not sure it is really my style."

"Well," Paul reassured with a breathlessness I now shared at our exertions, "he is not the only star in his constellation. Perhaps some other star is rising, and seeks new music such as ours to set it glittering all the brighter."

Relieved to be approaching the large open landing at the base of the stairway I lifted my eyes from their concentration upon the stairs. Here fashionable society was seizing its chance to promenade in the sunlight. But there, a still point in the midst of a crowd caught my eye. The figure I saw made me start and stumble, so that Paul had to catch my arm as I tripped.

In a black and red striped dress with a little red hat stood Marchelline beneath the shade of her parasol, at the

29

centre of it all, looking about her in great confusion and worry, as though she were a lost child.

"Steady on, old man!" Paul chided, "and we haven't even started drinking yet! I say! Look over there! I think that's *La Rossignol* herself. Let's go and say hullo."

I tried to catch Paul's arm to hold him back but he had already broken away from me. I stumbled after him, as he called out to Marchelline.

"Why what is this? A nightingale lost in the city?"

Marchelline turned at the voice, but her eyes looked straight past Paul and fixed upon me. She flinched and started towards me, then stopped herself, shaking her head once more, her face darkening beneath the parasol that she drew closer to herself like a shield.

"Over here!" Paul cried, waving energetically as he reached her.

The terrible look on her face softened as she saw him and she smiled as they kissed hullo. A moment more and I was with them.

"Paul? But weren't you just at Claudine's? Where I ..." Her deep brown eyes were wide and searching and, as they turned to me, some shadow crossed her face. With a pang of horror, it struck me that there was the suggestion of fear in her countenance.

"Are you following me, Monsieur?" she asked me, her gaze burning into mine.

Paul laughed. "What? Are you joking? Of course we're not, you ninny! We're only doing the same as you and everyone else – enjoying this glorious day, the lovely basilica, plotting to take over the nightclubs of Paris with our music. Well, perhaps not everyone is plotting that. Is the Comte not with you today?"

"No," she replied, still struggling with some thought. "I came out alone. "

"Aren't you going to say hullo, Nicolas? Don't you remember Mademoiselle Rossi?"

Trembling, afraid, I could only bow, scarcely able to form words. A pain stung at my chest: a kind of burning ache that seemed to crystallize the torment of my nerves.

"It is the queerest thing, Paul," Marchelline murmured, "I came out today not knowing why, or even where I went, and twice now I have run into Monsieur de Bresson – and each time it has seemed to me almost as though … I were remembering a dream from long ago, or … that somehow I knew, without consciously knowing, in the moments before that – oh, I can't explain it at all. How silly I must sound. Perhaps I am coming down with something," she said, feeling her brow with her wrist that was bare above her glove. "I am not feeling at all myself."

Suddenly, Marchelline blanched, her nostrils flaring and her eyes widening in alarm. Her hand clutched at Paul's arm for support as her knees appeared to weaken. "That smell," she said weakly, as Paul caught her tiny waist to stop her from falling, " … blood."

"Blood? But there is no blood here, my dear," Paul reassured her as he clasped her supportively.

I moved forward, anguished and wishing to help but not knowing how. I froze as I wondered if the smell was still on me from last night – the smell of the book and of my own burnt blood. I hid my bandaged thumb behind my back, the agitated fingers of my other hand rubbing absently at the painful spot on my chest.

"There!" Marchelline said with horror, pointing at me as she turned her ashen face away.

Paul started, staring at me in concern. "I say old man, she's right. You *are* bleeding."

I looked down and saw that upon the glowing white of my shirtfront, at the spot where I had felt the pain, a small, wet, red mark was slowly spreading through the cloth.

Paul quickly left to escort Marchelline home in a cab. Shaken, I had wandered off, little caring where I went.

31

Automatically, my feet stopped outside a bar and I went in for a brandy to steady my nerves. It was only when the waiter taking my order kept staring at my shirt that I was reminded of the blood that had appeared there. I rushed into the bathroom, pulled off my cravat and undid my shirt studs. Whatever the injury was it was only small, no larger than my thumbnail. I wet my handkerchief and wiped away the congealing blood, flinching at the burning pain the wet cloth's abrasion caused me. Not believing what I saw, I wiped and scrubbed harder as I leaned in closer to the mirror. But the mark would not wash away. It was red, raised, like a burn mark or a fresh scar, and in places, tiny spots of blood continued to seep from the shape. It was an arrow, curving, anti-clockwise, back upon itself.

I frantically scrubbed at the mark on my shirt but only succeeded in spreading the red stain. In a panic I returned to the streets, rushing, sometimes running, as I scanned the shop fronts I passed by. At last I found what I sought and ran breathlessly into the post office. Clearly alarmed at the stained and disarranged state of my shirt and my wild countenance, the balding, middle-aged clerk eyed me with some suspicion.

"May I help you, Monsieur?" he asked, furrowing his high forehead with the utmost seriousness.

"Yes," I panted, trying to catch my breath, "if you would be so kind, I urgently need to find the address of a gentleman whom I recently met – for I cannot remember where he lives. His name is Gildian Greene."

The clerk bit his lip and thought for a second before pointing to a broad counter behind me, adjacent to the wall.

"Monsieur will find the telephonic directory and the post office almanac at his disposal."

I scoured the books, checking every possible variation of spelling, but I could find no trace of any Gildian Greene.

CHAPTER FOUR

By the time I arrived home, the brightness of the day was darkening into cool twilight.

I hastened to change my shirt, turning up the lamp and examining the mark on my chest with a magnifying hand mirror. It was still there, just as red and conspicuous as before. I ran my fingers over its raised shape and found that my fingertips were marked with little smears of blood. Now *I* could smell it too. The blood had not stopped but continued to seep, now very slowly, in tiny droplets here and there from the wound. I tore a little piece of blotting paper and pressed it to the wound until the blood held it in place.

All at once the cryptic words of the book came back to my mind. I pulled on my dressing gown against the chill of the evening and rushed to unlock the bureau. The pent-up odour of the book made me turn my face away. Hooking my glasses over my ears, I turned to the first page of tiny writing.

Blood and silence are the price of our bargain.
Thy will shall be made flesh
Inscribed forever upon thee and me.

Inscribed forever upon me … could it really mean … this? I flicked through the pages, inadvertently fanning the unwholesome stench into my own nostrils. I came at last to my own page, then turned one page back. Gildian Greene had been the book's last owner, and if he had used the book his

33

true name must be recorded therein. I felt certain that he had used the book himself. I did not doubt that part of his story.

"Solomon Henri" was the name recorded there. Underneath it was the name "Marie-Thérèse Charpantier" with several symbols alongside it. Beneath that, other names were written, "Jean-Baptiste Pétain, Jeanne Lafiite, Marthe Chabot, Esther Cécille." There were fewer symbols alongside these. Curiously, one name, Jean-Baptiste Pétain, and the symbols beside it, had been struck through with a single line.

Perhaps I could decipher what some of this meant by myself. But the only person who could answer my questions decisively was the man who had given me the book, by whatever name he now called himself. That very act of deception worried me. What reason had he to lie to me – unless he did not wish to be found? Unless he expected me to come looking for him. None of it augured well.

I knew I was not insane. I knew that Marchelline had crossed my path twice, the very day after I had entered her name in the Book of Calling; now this bleeding weal had appeared upon my chest. I could not laugh any of it off as coincidence or the product of my lovesick imagination. Little able to fathom what I had gotten myself into, I had even less notion of what my next action should be.

I jumped at the sound of Maxim screeching from the drawing room downstairs, immediately followed by the chiming of the doorbell. I wondered who might be calling at this hour. Hurriedly I hid the book back in bureau and pulled on a shirt, as I heard the sound of Paul's cheery voice chatting to the my butler Félix in the hall and then to Maxim. As I fixed my shirt studs I remarked my countenance in the glass. That familiar look of pained yearning on my long, slender face had been displaced by an expression of deep unease. My formerly smooth brow was contracted in an uncharacteristic furrow. Behind my glasses, moist hazel eyes searched their reflection for some reassurance, but found none. I smoothed back my hair and was surprised to hear music coming from the drawing room as I hastened to finish dressing. The melody instantly brought back all the wretched sorrow and longing of the night before and I rushed down the stairs to stop it.

"Paul!" I cried, wishing to distract him.

" 'Song to the Unrequitor?' This is really very good, old man," Paul said evenly, continuing to play as I entered the room.

"It's just an idea, really only a sketch, it's not finished – I only started it late last night," I demurred, taking the manuscript off the stand before him and catching my breath.

"Oh." Paul stopped, a little deflated.

"How is Mademoiselle Rossi?" I asked, trying to feign a casual air.

Paul frowned. "I've never seen her like that before. Perhaps she *is* coming down with a cold or something. She is usually so bright and gay – well, I'm sure you remember, from when you met her before." Paul looked at me from under his eyebrows.

"Yes, I do recall. A more vivacious young lady would be hard to imagine. Did you call a doctor for her?"

"What? No, she didn't want one. I'm sure she'll be fine. My younger brother Jacques is exactly the same – faints dead away at the merest sight of blood – even the mention of it can set him off. I don't know if it's superstition or some over-sensitive instinct, this violent aversion to blood."

"I was playing with Maxim," I said, trying to explain, pointing to the large grey parrot who was busily climbing about and chattering to himself in his tall and ornate, black ironwork cage near the window. I rubbed vaguely at my chest. "He bit me, and I suppose I must have scratched it while we were at Sacré Coeur and ... "

"Who says you can't train a bird?" Paul joked as his fingers moved over the piano keys once more, slowly picking out from memory the melody he had just played. He watched his moving fingers and his body swayed ever so slightly as he improvised and elaborated around the theme.

"Nicolas ... there is nothing going on between you and Marchelline is there?" he asked quietly.

"What? No! Why ever would you think that?"

"Oh, just an odd feeling I got when the two of you were together ... I don't know ... her unease – and yours ... the way she would not say why she was there – almost as if the two of had a secret that I had accidentally discovered."

"No!" I stated firmly, walking over to Maxim's cage and offering him some seed. "Of course, I admire her – very much. I could only dream of winning such a woman. But her heart belongs to the Comte de Mortaine, does it not? Why would she even look at me?" Maxim climbed the wall of the cage with his great clawed feet, bobbing his head excitedly and talking to himself. His huge curved beak grasped at the seeds, messily dropping as many as he ate.

"Indeed. It is well to remember the Comte. He is not a man one would be wise to cross, I think. Although from what I gather he does not hold himself to the same high moral standards he expects of his inamorata."

"Oh?"

"One hears whispers ... "

I moved to the fireplace to take a cigarette from the ebony box on the mantel. Distantly, I thought I heard birdsong: a high trilling call that was almost inaudible. As it continued, I fancied that its tune echoed the song that Paul continued to play. I shook my head, dismissing the thought as a flight of my overtired imagination. I listened again. I could not help it. In the still evening air the sound was approaching. Paul tilted his head, straining to hear it too over Maxim's ceaseless whistles and chattering. Paul's fingers came to rest and the piano music died, but the song outside went on, continuing the tune he had just been playing.

Maxim screeched, swaying and bobbing along his perch as he tried to look out of the window.

"I'm sure I know that voice," Paul remarked with some perturbation.

He rushed to the hall and was out of the door before my trembling fingers could finish lighting my cigarette. Anxiously, I peered through the net curtains, seeing a female figure walking along the street towards the house. Paul hurried down the front steps as the silhouetted figure moved closer, singing its haunting, wordless melody.

"You again!" he effused.

Into the pool of light beneath the street lamp stepped Marchelline, as if in a trance. At the sound of Paul's voice she recoiled. Her beautiful face was suddenly distorted by perplexity and she looked around wildly.

"Paul?"

"What on earth are you doing here?"

"I don't know... Where am I? I have that feeling again – as though I were somehow dreaming – awake and dreaming."

Some impulse pulled me to the door and as I stepped silently onto the threshold, Marchelline's face turned to me with a look approaching terror.

"*You*, Monsieur? *You* live here?" she hissed in a breathless whisper.

Paul's eyes flickered from Marchelline to myself, a blush colouring his cheeks.

"Perhaps it is time that I was leaving."

"No." Marchelline grabbed his arm. "I do not know what is happening, Paul. I am afraid."

We managed to persuade Marchelline to come inside for a drink to settle her nerves. Paul had once again offered to escort her home or wherever she wished to go, but, as ill at ease as she was, for some reason she did not wish to leave.

I could see Paul studying her as she walked gingerly into my hall. Paul had to direct her to the drawing room. Marchelline looked around, plainly unfamiliar with what she saw. She nearly jumped out of her skin at Maxim's sudden chattering, spinning around and clutching her heart with relief when she saw that he was only a bird.

"You have never been here before," Paul observed at last as I poured the drinks.

Now that she was here in my home – this creature who had for months lived with such vital intensity in my heart – I had no idea of what to say or do.

"Never," Marchelline replied, walking around the room, taking in my various paintings and ornaments, her hand gently brushing the broad, shiny leaves of the potted palm, and nodding slightly to herself, her face pinched and her mouth open. "But somehow, I remember it, as though from a dream – a dream I had forgotten I ever had until this moment. It makes no sense."

I approached her and held out a balloon of brandy. I could barely look at her, but she paused there, staring forcefully at me before she accepted the glass. Fearing what she might see in my eyes, I was grateful when she resumed her examination of the room. She stopped at the piano, grabbing at the manuscript that I had discarded on the case. Her eyes raced over the notes, her head at first shaking and then nodding vehemently.

"Where did you get this music?" she demanded, looking from Paul to myself and back again.

"I – I wrote it, last night, Mademoiselle Rossi."

"You wrote it? But I have had this tune stuck in my head all day – from the moment I first woke up – how?"

"My word!" Paul exclaimed with a shiver, and sank into a leather armchair. "This is most peculiar. Are you sure you are not ill, Marchelline? How very odd."

"Something is happening," she said to herself, more calmly. "Despite all her human frailties, my mother was a very wise woman with great knowledge of mysterious things. She was a *Zingaro Napoletano* – a Gypsy – by birth and tradition. What you might dismiss as superstition, she taught me to read as signs of the hidden workings of the world. Something is going on here – leading me to you both, and to this music I think – can you tell me why?"

I thought I would choke on my brandy, so terribly exposed did I feel. I was grateful at least that She saw Paul as part of whatever it was, and not just myself.

Paul scratched his head. "Well, you know I don't normally go in for superstitions and all that – but I can't help noticing Nicolas, that we ran into Marchelline just after we decided we needed a cabaret star as the muse for our collaboration. Now I play your latest song and *La Rossignol* appears again. I'm not so dim-witted that I can't see when fate is hitting me over the head ..."

"Perhaps," I ventured, attempting to feign a light-hearted air, "it was written in the stars." I gave a nervous laugh.

"What a wonderful phrase," Paul mused. "I think *that* would make an excellent title for a song, or a show. And its theme, of Fate or destiny toying with us – predetermined events that we cannot change – is certainly one to conjure with."

Feeling ever more nervous, I sat down at the piano and began to play, almost involuntarily, at first just choosing chords suggested by my previous piece, then improvising around another little melody that drifted into my mind as I played and spoke. It seemed to give voice to my agitation. "Yes ... those strange presentiments we sometimes have," I began, shooting a glance at Marchelline who stood at the far end of the piano, still holding the manuscript, and my heart, in her hands. "As if fate were allowing us to glimpse what might be – even if only to torment us with that possibility that it will hold forever out of our reach."

"Or to warn us against it," Marchelline said, putting down the music and walking towards me, her delicate red gloved hand gliding along the piano case. "My mother always told me that the dreams or premonitions that tantalise us most are the ones that hold the greatest danger for us – for we are too blinded by our own desires to heed them as the warnings they may be."

"Yes, yes, these are all fascinating thoughts – keep going, I shall return directly, if you will excuse me," Paul urged as he left the room. "And when I return I shall make some notes," his voice resounded from down the hall.

Alone with Marchelline at last, my heart swelled. How breathtaking she was. How right it seemed to see her here beside me – as though she belonged here, in my home. The book had done its work and brought her to me. Might not she now see something in me to stir her heart and make her forget that other? I drew a deep breath and tried to give the tune beneath my fingers a more romantic tone.

"But what of your presentiments of today?" I ventured. "They brought you here to listen to my music, and perhaps to inspire music that is yet to be written. That seems more like a promise than a warning to me." I smiled at her, trying to convey the tender warmth that was in my heart. I tried to express the best of myself and the sincerity of my yearnings in the music that poured out of me, in the hopes that it might somehow move her.

She came closer, studying my face. I caught the fragrance of her perfume and longed above all else to take her hand and kiss it – to hold her in my arms. Her lips parted and her cheeks glowed. For a moment it seemed that some conversation flowed between my eyes and hers – those deep brown eyes that I was already lost in.

"I have the most inexplicable feeling about you," she began, haltingly.

"You do?"

"I do not know you Monsieur de Bresson, but I see before me a countenance of gentleness and sensitivity. I see in your manner refinement, kindness and the fine feeling of a fellow artistic soul. You are utterly charming, talented, handsome, sweet … but I fear you and I do not know why."

"What? But —"

" — It is not Paul, it is not the music – it is you."

Stung to the very core, I felt hot tears fill my eyes.

"Whatever do you mean? I promise you I mean you no harm, I lo —"

" — I am sure you do not mean me harm," she effused, blushing, turning away and hastening to collect her things from where they lay upon an armchair. "And I mean no offence. You will think me mad, I'm sure, but I have not survived this far by ignoring my instincts, however inexplicable they might seem to others, or even to myself at times. When they speak I must listen – and they speak to me now as never before. Somewhere in this situation some grave danger lies for me – it may have nothing to do with you personally, but you are connected with it. Perhaps I might meet my death on the street before your house if I came here again. I do not know, but I cannot take that chance. All I know is that I must leave here at once."

I pulled off my glasses and wiped my eyes roughly as she turned away to the glass to fasten the buttons of her coat.

"I am most terribly sorry that you feel that way."

The clock upon the mantel chimed eight. A look of horror passed over Marchelline's face.

"The Comte was to collect me from my home at seven – and I wandered off in a daze to come here. How shall I ever explain myself to him? He will be furious with me. No, no, now I am certain – I must never return. Forgive me, and pray beg my forgiveness to Paul for this rudeness. I must go. Goodbye."

In a panic I caught her arm. "Please!" I implored. The look of terror on her face as she spun around made me recoil with self-disgust. That I should ever frighten her … Her eyes shot down to my chest, at the blood that continued to seep there, and she gave a cry of fear as she ran from the room and out into the night.

CHAPTER FIVE

I could not sleep that night. Marchelline's expression of fear burned in my brain with searing intensity. How could this have happened? The book had brought her to me – just as had been promised – but it was dread that filled her heart when she saw me, not love. What had I done wrong?

Paul had tried to ease my distress with his assurances that Marchelline had always been deeply superstitious and that one had to expect these occasional displays of melodrama from theatrical types, but it was no use. I could not explain to him why she had left any more than I could explain why it had crushed me so.

Now, alone in my room, I returned to the wretched book that had so far only succeeded in driving my love away from me. I dried my eyes, replaced my spectacles, and, in despairing exasperation, tried to discover what I might have missed before in that maze of tiny writing. I turned to the page of symbols.

In my haste to achieve my ends I had not given much study to this long list of arcane glyphs and their meanings, which were written alongside in the tiniest of hands. I had been foolish enough – arrogant enough – to think that calling her to me would be all it would take. I had thought that if only she was near me, she would see the good in me, the love in my heart, and then she would love me too.

But her love for that undeserving and haughty other blinded her. Gildian Greene had spoken of other effects that the book could cause. Perhaps here might be an answer. There, the very next symbol that caught my eye made my heart race. It was a stylised image of fire. I swallowed as I read its meaning: "To make thy subject burn with love for thee." Anxiously I flicked the pages until I arrived at the one before mine. What had my predecessor done?

Alongside the first name, Mari-Thérèse Charpantier, there was the symbol of calling followed by the sign of the flame. Next to this there were still other glyphs – an image of an eye, two hands in prayer, and last, the symbol of calling in mirror opposite form – this last had been struck through more than once.

Unschooled, I feared what I might unwittingly do. I had to find Monsieur Greene, whoever, wherever he was. There had to be a way to fix things. I prowled to my study and pulled down all the postal directories I still had, both old and recent. The recent editions showed nothing, no entries in Paris for any Solomon Henri. It was only when I got to the much older copies – ones that must have belonged to father – that I had some luck. There, "Solomon Henri, 15 Allée Vivaldi ..." I wrote down the address, threw on my coat, scarf and hat, and rushed out to find him.

I was happy to walk all the long way there in the quiet of the night, with few others in the streets to see me. I had hoped that the exertion of my brisk, restless march would alleviate my anguish, but it seemed that nothing could. Only Monsieur Greene could do that. At last I turned into the Allée Vivaldi, peering in the low gaslight to perceive any numbers on the buildings that might aid me. The street appeared to have enjoyed a brief moment of luxury and prosperity that had long since passed. Here was a short row of terraced townhouses, not dissimilar in size to my own, but all in varying states of disrepair, and some it, seemed, abandoned altogether. In the midst of them sat number fifteen. The sight of it stirred a forgotten, drunken memory, and I had no doubt that this was indeed the place where Monsieur Greene had taken me.

I crept up the front steps to find a door that was heavily padlocked. Heedless of the hour, I rang the bell and knocked loudly on the dull black painted panels. I pressed my ear to the wood and listened – nothing. Leaves were piled upon the doormat and crunched on the step under my feet. I moved quietly towards the windows and noticed now the elegantly shaped but formidable black iron bars that secured them. Without thinking, I intruded my fingers between the bars and tapped upon the window. For a second I thought I heard some faint sound echoing my own tapping. But as I tapped and listened again, the silence of the early hours was rattled by the noise of a baker's cart driving by, a twig caught in its wheel clattering harshly. The suspicious glance of the driver made me feel like a thief and I moved away from the window and down the low steps into the street. It was only then that a realisation struck me.

The night that Greene had brought me here, we had sat in the front parlour of the house. It was there that I had heard the sound of the tree scratching the window behind me. I stopped in my tracks and spun around to look upon the house once more. Enclosed on both sides by identical houses, the only windows were those in the front, facing the street: but there were no trees in this part of the street, nor any sign that there had ever been any.

More confused than ever, I wandered away, trying to fathom some way out of this mess. In the stillness of the pre-dawn, there were some stirrings of life, as workers of the small hours were beginning their long day. But all I wanted was privacy. I found myself on the Rue de Picpus and something about the lonely serenity of the cemetery there drew me in. I had to be on my own to think. The gate was closed but not locked, so I silently let myself in. It could be no blasphemy to look for sanctuary in this consecrated place. The dead were not the only ones who sought peace here.

I walked quietly among the silent monuments. Would any of this business with Marchelline matter when I went to my own grave? I would surely go there alone, so why could I not accept that Marchelline could simply not be mine in this life? Out of all the people in the world, living and dead, why should she matter so desperately to me? Passing grave after grave of noblemen and women, it struck me that all our vanities and struggles to achieve our petty ends and our attempts to win – to achieve some success to elevate ourselves above our fellows – seemed so absurd. Here, all were equal in eternity. All ranks were levelled in the grave. As I walked on, the first birds of morning began their quiet songs in the trees around me.

I turned a corner and found myself in the open, walled square whose gravelled surfaces covered the burial pits that had swallowed up the massed, headless victims of the Revolution in their many hundreds. Noblemen and commoners, priests, nuns and sinners, men and women alike all slept here beneath my feet, tangled in each other's eternal, indiscriminate embrace.

A crunching step on the gravel shattered my reverie. My eyes shot up from the ground to see a female form, spectral in the early morning light, diagonally opposite me on the other side of the square. A long mauve cloak covered a white gown beneath. A hood concealed the face.

I took an involuntary step to my left, towards the wall. The figure mirrored me, even before I knew what I did. I stepped back, and the figure stepped back in synchrony with me. The crunch of gravel beneath her feet told me that this was no spirit. I steeled myself and moved forwards, towards the vertical stone monument in the centre of the square, drawn by the reassurance of the cross that crowned it. As I crept forward, I studied the figure that moved towards me, its feet in step with my own. Only satin slippers adorned those tiny feet. Only a thin nightgown did she wear against the chill of

45

the morning. I knew instinctively that it was Marchelline and I prayed that whatever calm possessed her now might not shatter once more into terror at seeing me.

At last I stopped, resting my hand on the hard stone edge of the monument – seeing her hand do the same. Her skin was a dreadful purple grey with cold. I leaned down a little, trying now to see the face beneath the hood. Her lips were a bloodless white, her face chalky. Her beautiful eyes were open but somehow unseeing. I heard her breaths coming in shallow irregular gasps, in time with my own. I dared not move or speak, lest I break the spell and distress her once more.

"I might have known," a clipped voice barked roughly in the silence, his anger ringing around the high walls. As I started in fright, Marchelline emerged violently from her trance into the most dreadful state of fear and confusion. Behind her, the Comte marched fiercely forward, a terrible sneer upon his red face. "Running away with him are you?" he shouted into Marchelline's wild, uncomprehending eyes. "Or does it merely amuse you to profane such a sacred place with your foul fornications?"

"What is happening?" Marchelline cried. "Where am I?"

"Please," the Comte hissed at her, "You may think you have deceived me, but pray do not treat me like a fool now that I have caught you out. I suspected something was going on yesterday. Have the decency to at least admit it – for you can hardly deny it now that I have discovered you here together in such an indecent state."

"Please, my lord," I implored, fearing what he might do, "you are quite mistaken; it is chance that brings us both here, nothing more. The lady has done no wrong."

"You!" Marchelline shrieked, coming to her senses as her eyes adjusted to the dim light. She shrank from me.

"So you admit that you know him,' the Comte accused.

"Yes, yes, but not by choice – he is doing something,

acting upon me in some way I cannot understand. But my love, this has nothing to do with me, you must believe that! I do not know how I got here, or even where I am!"

"Do not insult me," the Comte growled, menacing Marchelline so that she cowered and backed away from him. "I saw you rise and put on your slippers and your cloak, I followed you walking, fancy as you like, all the way here from Montmartre!"

My blood risen at his brutish bullying, I could not restrain my anger. I lunged forward and pushed him away from her.

"Oh, you will regret that Monsieur," he laughed at me savagely, striking me a fierce blow on the jaw that sent the spectacles flying from my face. Thrown off balance, I clutched at him lest I should fall and grappling, we struggled, our sliding and kicking feet sending gravel flying. Again he struck me, and again upon the face and in the stomach. Blindly I struck back, somehow hitting him in the throat so that he fell, pulling me down with him against the monument.

"Émile!" Marchelline cried out in horror as she saw the Comte's face strike hard against the corner of the monument and she began to hyperventilate at the sight of the blood that quickly spilled from the gash in his cheek. Coughing and wheezing, the Comte touched his face and saw the blood on his hands. On his knees, he crawled away from me, dripping and trailing crimson gouts onto the gravel beneath him. She rushed toward him, in spite of her horror of the blood, but he pushed her roughly away in his rage.

Marchelline backed away, now taking in the larger scene before her with some inner revelation that seemed to greatly increase her terror. "No, no! What have you done?" Marchelline wailed in rising panic and distress, "This is a cemetery! You are fighting over a grave, spilling blood over those angry murdered people who would give anything to have flesh and blood of their own again – no, no, no, this is nothing but a taunt to the dead to rise again. Oh Holy Mother forgive us ... " Wild with terror, Marchelline fled into the gloom.

Catching my breath, pain throbbing in my face and belly, a tumult of agony coursing through my heart, I wished that the ground would swallow me up.

I heard the Comte spit, struggling to rise from the gravel, shouting after her. "You stupid superstitious whore! ... You want her, Monsieur? Have her. Take her! I am finished with her. You might like to play in the gutter, with the dirty sluts who wallow there – but you will find that it leaves a stink on you that might turn your stomach in the end." He spat out some more blood.

I lay there on the sharp gravel, catching my breath as the Comte staggered away, clutching a handkerchief tightly to his bleeding face. High atop the wall, a raven strutted and croaked his mocking cry.

I rested on my sofa that afternoon, nursing my wounds and feeling miserable beyond endurance. When Maxim screeched towards the front steps I thought that my heart would burst from my chest. Félix, who was clearing away the lunch that I had not eaten, nodded to me. I had warned him about the Comte and instructed that should he ever come to the door he must not be admitted.

Félix glided out of the room and a moment later, I heard my aunt Mathilde-Hélène barging past him, drowning out his most polite protestations with a barrage of shouted pleasantries. The Comte would perhaps have been easier to stop.

She burst into the room, swathed in dark grey-blue silk and black ostrich feathers, her tall, slender frame as always the picture of fashionable elegance.

"Well, it is all true, I see," she observed as she landed on a chair, her voluminous skirts spreading out around her and her parasol gripped like a walking cane in her daintily gloved hand.

I winced. "What have you heard, Aunt?"

"My beloved nephew and the Comte de Mortaine, brawling in the Père Lachaise Cemetery, over a chorus girl of all things!" She pursed her lips but could not curtail the smile of amusement that curled the corners of her mouth. "Well I'll give you this much, Nicolas, dear – you never were one to do things by halves."

"Not quite true: it was Picpus Cemetery, and the lady is a chanteuse of some note, not a chorus girl."

"But it was the Comte de Mortaine? Did I at least get that part right?"

"I'm afraid it was."

"Well, there are those that might say it is no more than he deserves – the nieces and daughters of one or two ladies of my acquaintance, for instance."

"Well, that is some consolation I suppose. What else are people saying?"

"I believe current speculation has it that the young lady in question found out about the Comte's habitual philandering and sought revenge in your arms."

"Also untrue."

"The Comte of course, is busy blackening your name to whomever will listen, trying to play the victim, but to little avail. He is far too well known as a roué to garner any sympathy on that count."

Mathilde-Hélène rose from her chair and came to perch on the edge of my sofa, scrutinising my face with pained and tender eyes.

"Oh my dear," she consoled softly, clasping my hand. "You are very unhappy. So she is not your lover – but perhaps you wish that she was … ?"

I could only turn my face away, feeling the heat of tears rushing to my eyes and struggling to blink them away.

"There, there, my dear. You are just like your father was when he was young: so desperately romantic and painfully tender-hearted. Well, shall I tell you what else I have heard?"

I nodded.

"If it makes you feel any better, the lady is now free. The Comte has severed all connection with her. He would never have married her, in any case. The family would simply never have permitted such a match, despite whatever he may have told the poor girl."

"Thank you, Aunt, but I fear it is too late in any case. She simply does not want me."

"Well that is her loss. I, for one, am aware of several extremely charming young ladies who do appreciate your charms and who would love nothing more than to further an acquaintance with you."

I smiled. "You are very kind to say so."

"But being like your father, you only want the one that you cannot have – the prize that is hardest won *seems* the sweetest. Well, there is little I can say to that, except that I do hope you grow out of that way of thinking. Time doesn't seem quite so cheap a thing to fritter away when you get to my age – nor does love."

Suddenly a thought entered my mind.

"Aunty – I know that there are few people more in tune with society gossip than you are –"

She shot me a reproving glance. " – You know I do not care for that term, Nicolas." She smacked my hand playfully, then stood and strolled over to Maxim's cage as she spoke. "No, I am a collector of social intelligence. Gossip implies trivial information. But the information I collect is seldom trivial – no, no, quite the opposite."

Maxim sidled along his perch flirtatiously, chirruping warmly and twisting his head, so that Mathilde-Hélène might scratch it for him. "Hullo, hullo" he intoned quietly, then started on his repertoire of words and noises to impress her.

"There are those who merely repeat what they hear," she observed, scratching Maxim's neck so that he pressed himself against the bars to be closer to her. "But I collate, I file, I cross-reference and I deduce. It is a study to which I have devoted my life. It is all quite scientific, I assure you, and when put together it forms an utterly fascinating picture of what is *really* going on."

"Well might I ask you to look into your archives for anything you might remember of a gentleman named Monsieur Solomon Henri, and a Mademoiselle Marie-Thérèse Charpantier. Monsieur Henri may also be known by the name of Gildian Greene. Does that ring any bells?"

"Parisian?"

"He has a house here, but I believe he spends much time elsewhere – perhaps he has a country home as well."

"And the girl?"

"I know nothing at all of her, save her name. But the man I *would* like to find – I need to find him, or to find out anything I can about him, his past, where he might be … "

"Solomon Henri … hm – leave it with me, Nicolas. I shall get back to you. I believe I may have heard that name, but not for many years, and not in Paris. It is a most distant and tiny fragment of memory. It may take some excavating. I am assuming he is somehow tied up with this business of the beautiful singer, so I shan't ask you about it." She turned back to me and smiled slyly. " … For now …"

"Well I suppose I should leave you to your pining." She bustled back towards me, and clasping my shoulders, leaned down and kissed my forehead. "Oh my dear, I do hate to see you so upset. Be sad if you must, but do not indulge your melancholy nature too much. Make it serve you – turn it into music. Do not be possessed by it, nor by her: life is for the living. And you have too much talent not to make something of it." She headed for the door. "Your cousins send you their best regards – I hope we shall all see you very soon in Giverny. Take care, my dear."

I lay on the sofa for some hours, watching the fire dance, and trying to let its heat warm me. But it could not. In his cage, Maxim chattered and whistled happily to himself.

51

My thoughts made little more sense. My cage was of a different kind, but it felt jut as real. What was I to do? I had at least, if accidentally, freed Marchelline from a man whom everyone agreed was nothing but a callous philanderer. But she would not thank me for it. She loved him – that brute, that surly, superior thug. And I, who had only ever wished to love and cherish her: I was now somehow her enemy.

I knew that the book had caused this, but I tried to convince myself that it was only because I had not yet inscribed the right symbols. I was struggling to learn how to master the book – was it not to be expected that I might stumble before I flew? I wrestled with a million justifications and arguments, but in the end it all came down to this: I was desperate with my own misery and the thought of the unhappiness that I had caused to Marchelline. The book said that its effects, once caused, could not be undone. All that remained was to try again. I simply could not leave that possibility untried.

Kneeling once more in the circle of flames, I unbuttoned my shirt and removed the little dressing I had applied to the seeping red weal. The racing pulse drumming furiously in my ears caused the wound to bleed more freely. I shuddered as a warm red drop ran down my chest and over the emerging bruises on my ribs and stomach. Picking up the raven's quill, I filled it from the running source and crouched low, my brow sweating as I inscribed the sign of the flame after Marchelline's name.

CHAPTER SIX

The next morning I arose with difficulty, painfully aware of my bruised ribs. I moved stiffly to the mirror, wondering if I looked as bad as I felt. All the animation had gone from my face. Now there was only this awful mask of sorrow, coloured by a bluish-red mark upon my swollen jaw, and a lesser abrasion above my right eye. What an unspeakable mess I had made of things.

With sore effort I pulled off my nightshirt that I might see the state of my ribs. The flash of blood running down my chest startled me. I gave an involuntary cry as I realised that close by the first arrow-shaped weal there had now appeared a second wound, angry-looking and raw.

"No, no," I whispered angrily as I rubbed and scraped at the mark with my nightshirt, hoping against hope that, like the blood, the mark itself might be wiped away. Alas, it was not so. Now I saw it clearly: a shape formed from red, raised scar-like ridges of skin that continued to seep tiny droplets of red – it was the sign of the flame. I cursed my own weakness that had impelled me to use the book again.

I stared into the eyes of my reflection and tried to calm myself. Yes, I had done it – I had used the book – I could not pretend otherwise. These were the consequences. What a terrible fool I had been to listen to Gildian Greene. And how cruel he had been to take advantage of my weakness with this poisonous lure that he must have known I would be utterly unable to resist. He had promised me that it would transform

53

my life. He never said it would be for the worse.

"Get a hold of yourself," I urged the sad man in the mirror as he blinked away the tears that came to his sorry red eyes, embarrassed and ashamed of myself.

I shuffled to the cupboard and found some gauze dressings and bandages, and an old jar of some medicinal salve. Up until now I had ignored the wound, too preoccupied with other matters to attend to it. Perhaps when properly dressed such wounds might heal and disappear. Could I show them to a physician? How would I ever explain it? At least if they were covered, I would not have to think of them. I dressed the little wounds and tied a bandage around my chest to hold the gauze in place over them. That, at least, made me feel a little better.

I wondered if I should perhaps talk to a priest about what I had done. I could not be the first man foolish enough to dabble in black magic without really understanding what he did. There must be some way to reverse the spell, the harm? Perhaps a priest might know how to safely destroy the book lest I, or anyone else, be tempted to use it again.

As I dressed, I thought of my summer home in Giverny and of the tranquil beauty of the countryside there. I might go there early this year – remove myself from the city and all of its associations; leave the wretched book behind me and find peace in solitude and composition.

Maxim gave a screech and I dropped the bottle of cologne from my hand, sending it smashing to the floor. The doorbell rang and I strained to hear above Maxim's excited chattering as Félix spoke with someone. There were footsteps. I suddenly felt inexplicably cold. Without waiting for Félix to come knocking for me, I burst from my bedroom and rushed downstairs to the drawing room.

There she stood facing the fireplace – Marchelline. She turned to me and I gasped aloud at the wonder of what I saw. It was her eyes. No longer wide and pained with fear, they now glittered brightly at the sight of me, with a look that I wanted to believe was love. Was I mad to imagine that I saw it there?

She rushed forward as if to embrace me, then stopped herself with great effort. "Forgive me, Monsieur, forgive me, forgive me, for all that I have said, and the hurt that I must have caused you. I – I do not know exactly why I am here, but I simply had to see you. I just wanted to … to know that you were all right. I have been so worried – frantic to know that you were not harmed."

Almost unconsciously she edged closer, warm concern colouring her face as she took in my bruised jaw and brow, my reddened eyes, the stiffness of my gait. She reached out gingerly, to touch my jaw, then held back. "Oh, Monsieur, I am so sorry for what happened yesterday. The Comte's temper is quite dreadful. I know that only too well." She raised her hand to her own left cheek and touched it lightly. As she turned her head I perceived some slight reddish purple mark there and I felt my blood boil.

"He did that to you?"

She nodded. "I tried to tell him that there was nothing between us but he would not believe me." Her gaze fell to the floor, she went to speak but hesitated. Her voice grew very quiet. "Now … now I begin to wonder, if perhaps … he might not have been right all along."

She drew closer to me still, and reached her hand up to my neck, caressing it with an exquisite gentleness that stole the breath from my lungs.

"I … I feel so strange. What is it that keeps drawing us together, Monsieur?"

"Nicolas," I whispered into the sweet face the looked up searchingly into mine.

"Nicolas … I have been so confused and afraid, since that evening I came here – when I was so unkind to you. I have battled with a constant powerful impulse to return, to be near you. I did not know why. It was so strong it frightened me – I do not know you after all. Yesterday I was filled with despair, the Comte had spurned me: I thought my happiness destroyed. But then, late last night, even as I wept, the pain in my heart began suddenly to melt into warmth and joy and longing ... your music lived again in my mind and somehow I felt my torn soul healed by it. It was then that I realised – It is you ... It is you that compels me, you who fills my heart. But how could that be – we are strangers?"

"I have longed for you since first we met, so many long months ago. I have thought of no-one else, wanted nothing but to be with you; to hold you in my arms and to love you."

I drew her to me and kissed those deep red lips of which I had dreamed a thousand times. With what sublime and tender ardour her lips met mine. With what supernatural passion our desire ignited. Breathlessly, she clung to me, her arms tight around my neck, her body pressed closer and closer to me. Marchelline gasped into my ear, her burning cheek scorching mine, "If I don't have you now, I fear I will die."

I carried her to my bedroom, the urgency of my hunger for her unlike anything I had ever known. She tore off my clothes, as I tore her from hers and we made love with such wild and furious abandon that at times, I was almost afraid of the animal passions that held us in their frenzy. And in the half-light of that curtained room I had to close my eyes, for in that strange delirium of rapture – that dizzying, unreal sensation of a dream becoming flesh – my fevered, guilty imagination conjured once more some flickering shadowy form watching from the fire's light as it danced upon the walls.

Marchelline moaned and wailed with pleasure, clutching and pulling me always closer, tighter, deeper. I thought at that moment that the bargain I had struck with the book had been worth any price, for now Marchelline was truly mine. Now, as she writhed and trembled and convulsed beneath me, crying out my name in ecstasy, she was mine.

I proposed to Marchelline the next morning and she accepted without a moment's hesitation. She was everything I had imagined: warm, vivacious, intelligent, amusing and delightful beyond all measure. It filled me with joy just to be near her – and she wished always to be close to me. She had taken leave of her role in the café-concert at Les Ambassadeurs while the scandal surrounding me, herself and the Comte died down. Even her ladies' maid, formerly paid for by the Comte, had abandoned her mistress. I had Marchelline all to myself.

Those first three weeks, while we waiting for our marriage license, were the happiest that I had ever known. Ensconced in my apartment, we spent every waking moment together, much of the time making love. I had never known anyone so full of life – and who could find such amusement and gaiety in any situation. Her laughter and love rang through the house, and I realised then all that had been missing from my lonely life before. I cherished her.

The only times I shunned her company were when I had to change the dressings on my wounds. As much as I prayed that the wounds would stop bleeding and heal, as the days passed, they showed no signs of change. The bleeding, while never significant enough to cause me any concern for my wellbeing, nevertheless continued its slow and subtle seeping unabated. I seized any moments in which Marchelline was otherwise occupied to replace the bloody dressings and burn the soiled ones in the fire. She and Maxim had quickly become the best of friends and he kept her diverted whenever I needed a few minutes of privacy.

Several times, Marchelline asked me about my bandages, but I always found some way to distract her and evade more probing questions with some vague, dismissive remark.

Very often she would ask me to play again my "Song to the Unrequitor," and the other piece that I had improvised for her on that day she had first come to my home with Paul.

"Did you really write them for me?" she asked, passing her arms around my neck and pressing her cheek against mine as I played.

"Yes, my dearest, only for you. All to win you."

"Well now I am a requitor of your love, you shall have to write me another song as well – a happier one. Now I have my own captive composer!"

"I shall write you a hundred songs. Nothing would give me more pleasure."

"Nothing?"

"Well, I'm sure you could think of something. You are exceedingly imaginative that way."

"But I should like so much to sing your music – anything you write – I will perform it at the club, until all of Paris knows your music and sees what a genius you are."

"The club ... " I stiffened, "do you think it will be all right when you return? You don't think the Comte would, well, make trouble for you there? I know it was one of his regular haunts – as you said, that was where you met him."

Marchelline released me from her embrace and walked to the vase of long-stemmed lilies that sat on the narrow, marble-topped table across the room. She busied herself rearranging them, her back to me. "Why should he? He said he never wanted to see me again." There was strange coldness in her voice that disquieted me.

Maxim's screech sent Marchelline rushing to the window. She clapped her hands in gay excitement and went running to the front door before the bell had even rung.

"Paul!" I heard her exclaim.

"You!" he cried, in mock outrage. "So the rumours are true!"

Marchelline laughed and they walked back into the room, arm in arm. A wide smile lit up Paul's face. "I couldn't be happier, Nicolas. Two of my favourite people, together! I never would have picked you two as a match, but I'm very happy that you've found happiness with each other." He collapsed onto the sofa with a broad grin.

"We are very happy about it too," I said quietly as Marchelline returned to stand behind me, her hands upon my shoulders. "And we are to be married next week – I wanted to

58

ask you Paul if you would be there, as my best man?"

"Well, I suppose I could bear the scandal – my shoulders are broad. Of course, I'll be there – you couldn't keep me away! But you're not the only ones who are nauseatingly happy, I'll have you know – nor the only ones who've been keeping something under wraps. I had wanted to tell you – well I've wanted to tell you for weeks now – I've been keeping company with someone myself of late."

"Oh Paul, that's wonderful – who is he?" Marchelline effused, running over to sit next to Paul.

"His name is Étienne Doucette and he is the most talented portraitist and the sweetest, funniest and most obscenely desirable man I have ever met. He spends most of the year in Marseille, and he has asked me to go and live with him there. As far as his family and neighbours are concerned, I am to be his new studio assistant. I shall play the piano to keep his sitters entertained."

"Well that is marvelous, I am delighted for you – but we shall miss you terribly!"

"What of our collaboration, Paul? Shall we postpone it until you next return to Paris?" I asked.

"Well we can work on some music until I leave and afterwards, there is always the post. And you must come and stay with us. Are the two of you free now? Have you any plans? We might make it a musical afternoon …"

That night as I began to prepare for bed, standing before the mirror of the washstand, Marchelline came up behind me and passed her arms around my chest. Normally I had contrived to change into my nightshirt while she was out of the room, but now it seemed I had not that choice.

As her hands rubbed my chest, they stopped, detecting the ever-present bandage below. I tensed, fearing her questions.

"Nicolas," she began, "must you still wear this bandage? Oughtn't your wound to be healed by now?"

Fidgety, I moved away from her embrace and busied myself tidying some books on a shelf. "As I explained to you my dearest, Maxim gave me a nasty bite there, and then in the scuffle in the cemetery, the wound caught another blow which seemed to greatly aggravate things and caused more bleeding. I think it best to keep it covered, to avoid any risk of infection."

"You have seen a doctor about it, haven't you?"

"Well – yes – he told me to keep it covered, and gave me this salve to aid the healing. I shouldn't worry, it does not give me any pain. There is no sepsis."

"But is it healing?"

"It's just taking a little while."

"Will you let me see it? I am worried about you, that is all." She followed me, trying to unfasten my shirt. I caught her hands and kissed them.

"No, no, darling, I know how blood upsets you. Please don't worry yourself."

"Blood?" She blanched. "It is bleeding still, after all this time?"

"It is fine, honestly."

"Why do I feel that you are lying to me?"

"Really, you are making far too much of this. It is nothing: it will soon be healed. Perhaps I am a little run down – I have been spending all my energy in keeping up with you, after all," I teased, through a thin smile.

"I will not have lies or deception," she warned, a shadow crossing her face that made me uneasy. "I will not be made a fool of."

"No, of course not – never … "

She looked at me a long time and then climbed into bed, saying nothing.

Any tension between us was quickly forgotten as our wedding day fast approached. Not wishing any fuss, we had arranged the simplest of civil ceremonies, attended only by Paul and Étienne, and Poupette, a friend of Marchelline's who was a dancer in the show at Les Ambassadeurs.

As we drove to the civil register, I clasped Marchelline's hand, wondering at her beauty anew. She was radiant in a gown of cream silk, with pretty satin bows at her shoulders above short, frothily puffed sleeves. A little cream hat was perched upon her head surmounted with white dove's wings that only emphasized her angelic loveliness.

Every day I had grown to love her more – more than I ever dreamed possible. After a life of solitary musical pursuits and melancholy dreaming, the joy that I had found in her arms, in her company, in the warm embrace of her heart, had been nothing less than a revelation to me. To have my love returned by this most divine of women was a prize worth any cost.

"From the first time I met you," I murmured, "I somehow knew that this day would come. I have never wished to take any other as my wife. You are a dream made flesh. You have brought colour to the greyness of my life. You have brought joy where before was only emptiness. You have filled my life with happiness and I love you with my entire being: my body, my heart and soul."

Marchelline kissed me and wiped a tear from my face with her white glove. I drew out my handkerchief and dabbed it under her eyes to dry her own tears.

"Whatever miracle brought us together – perhaps it was Fate, perhaps it was God," she replied. I swallowed. "Whatever mysterious force brought you to me, I shall be eternally grateful. I love you Nicolas, and nothing makes me happier than the thought of spending the rest of my life with you."

The carriage came to a halt.

"Then let it begin," I said, climbing down that I might aid her in alighting. The day was beautifully warm and the sun shone down on Paris in all its glory. Marchelline smiled at me as she placed her hand in mine, holding out her skirts as she stepped down and onto the pavement. As I watched her face, she froze, and the smile died on her lips. She was staring at something over my shoulder. I spun around to see the Comte de Mortaine leaning casually against a wall near the entrance to the civil register. His face was impassive as he stared at Marchelline. A red scar glowed livid upon his cheek.

"We will not let him spoil our day," I whispered to my bride.

She nodded and forced a smile as we walked past the staring Comte and inside the great stone building. But as we passed him, I was certain I felt her tremble. I told myself that it was nerves that made her so unusually subdued throughout the ceremony and later, as we celebrated our marriage over dinner with our friends.

In the carriage on the drive home she was silent, her face towards the window.

"Marchelline? Are you all right?"

" … I am fine. It has just been an emotional day. "

I turned her face toward me and I saw that she was crying.

"Tears?" I asked, "on our wedding night?"

She shook her head and tried in vain to smile. "I just wish that my mother had been alive to see this day, that is all."

I knew that she was lying, but I was too afraid to ask her why.

CHAPTER SEVEN

I had wanted to take Marchelline to Nice for our honeymoon, but she had insisted that we postpone our trip and stay in Paris. There were still a couple of weeks before Paul was to leave for Marseille and she was eager that we should complete the songs we had begun so she might perform them publicly.

It was true, our collaboration was proving a fruitful one, and the music that Paul and I were developing showed very great promise. But I could not escape the feeling that somehow this was not Marchelline's only motivation in wishing to stay in town.

In the days after our wedding – as the news of the happy event had spread through the grapevine of gossips in the cafes and bars – cards, flowers and gifts had begun to arrive at our home. All of these Marchelline had received with exuberant delight, unwrapping parcels like an excited child at Christmas time, arranging notes and cards proudly upon the mantel: all except one. When the florist's delivery boy knocked one morning with a huge bouquet of blood irises, Marchelline's cheeks flushed red and she rose to collect them with some hesitation.

Paul looked up from his corrections of the manuscript we were working on as we sat side by side at the piano.

"My word, what glorious irises!"

Beside him on the piano stool, I was boxed in and could not easily remove myself without disrupting him and his work. I watched Marchelline examine the flowers. She stood with her back to me, removing a little envelope that she then palmed.

"Yes, they are quite beautiful," I agreed cheerfully. "Who are they from?"

Marchelline's ears went pink as she tore open the envelope and read the little card. She drew a rapid breath. "Colette, Poupette's sister – how very kind of her, I must go and write a thank you note." Marchelline put her head down and left the room.

"Ah, Nicolas, I have it – here, what if the line was 'I am a shadow in your light' – let's try it again … "

We dined that night with Paul and Étienne at The Sparrow's Feast, a noisy little bistro in Montmartre that Marchelline had been eager to visit to hear some of the new American music they featured there.

"It's wonderful to see Paul so happy, Étienne, you are truly to be congratulated." I said, raising a glass of wine to our friends.

"Well, I think I'm the lucky one," Étienne smiled, discretely patting Paul's knee under the table.

"We just seem to be so well matched – we have so much in common – we want the same things out of life," Paul concurred in wonder. "I had quite given up hope of finding anyone."

"Yes the only thing we disagree on is how many children we shall have," Étienne joked. He looked from myself to Marchelline with admiring eyes. "Can you imagine what beautiful children these two shall have, Paul?"

"Oh yes indeed," Paul agreed. "Are you planning a big family, Nicolas?"

"Why, yes, as an only child myself, I've always thought a large family would be splendid – but it isn't all up to me, is it darling?" I nudged Marchelline.

"What?" she asked, emerging from some daydream.

"I was saying a large family would be lovely, but that it isn't all up to me." I smiled at her. She screwed up her face and shook her head.

"Children? I've never wanted children – I can't stand them."

Taken aback by the vehemence of her response, I could only stammer, "Oh … well … that complicates matters."

"Might I suggest a compromise?" Paul interjected, "Dogs?"

We laughed, but Marchelline was not laughing. She had been withdrawn all evening and now seemed little short of upset. I had tried repeatedly to draw her into the conversation. I held her hand, but I could not hold her attention. It seemed that she was somewhere else. It was only when the little orchestra struck up with a very lively and raucous tune that she seemed to return to us, and that spark of radiant vitality reignited in her eyes.

"Oh, I love this music!" she exclaimed, clapping her hands together. She grabbed my hand, "Let's dance, darling! Yes, yes let's! Come on!"

Paul laughed uproariously at the suggestion. Marchelline shot him a look of confusion.

"Nicolas? Dance?" he scoffed.

"What?" Marchelline's eyebrows rose.

"I'm most awfully sorry, darling, but I don't – well, I can't dance. I'm afraid I really have two left feet. It's most embarrassing."

"No!" Her face fell in utter dismay.

"It's true, my dear. I've seen it with my own eyes and it wasn't pretty. Nearly broke a young lady's foot once, didn't you, Nicolas?" Paul smirked.

Étienne extended his hand to Marchelline, an inviting smile on his lips, "Come, I shall dance with you – I love to dance."

Marchelline looked at me, uncertain and disappointed.

"Go on, enjoy yourself," I urged her.

65

Off they went onto the dance floor, moving so easily, so gracefully together in time to the racing beat of the music. I stared into my glass.

"You're very different, you and she," Paul mused.

"I suppose we are – I hadn't quite realised … " I trailed off.

"Haven't been doing a great deal of talking, I imagine," Paul smiled.

"Well, no," I laughed, but the smile died on my lips.

"Marchelline is passionate, impulsive: gay and vivacious most of the time, yes – but she has her dark moods, her flights of melodrama – she is a creature of extremes, of spontaneity, she lives in the moment. Whereas you – well, you are steadier, more restrained, more of an introvert. This is why I was surprised when the two of you got together. Oh please, don't misunderstand me – I'm not saying it can't work – they say opposites attract after all, and clearly they have here, but you need to be aware of the differences, that is all."

"Yes, yes, I am becoming quite aware of them … "

"Love is one thing, but what is it without true acceptance … ?"

I watched Marchelline as she danced, and the wild abandon of her movements both aroused and unsettled me. She was so exquisite, so lovely and desirable, but what was I to her? She twirled and swayed in Étienne's arms, his arm tight around her slender waist, their gleaming faces close together. The book had made her love me, but was it enough to keep her in love with me? Was I enough to keep her from loving any other?

On she danced and drank. When Étienne threw up his hands and staggered, perspiring, back to his chair, she followed him to our table, trying to drag him back.

"Come and sit with me, darling?" I asked, reaching for her hand.

But her hand moved instead for her glass and she drained it.

"No." She shook her head petulantly, swaying a little. "It's getting quite late, shall we go home soon?" "No." Her lips smiled, but her eyes showed pain. She took up my glass of wine and drank it down, before grabbing Paul's hand and dragging him out to the dance floor. He could only shrug his shoulders as Étienne and I looked on.

I had been worried that if I stayed out too long, the blood that continued to seep from my weals might soak through the bandage and onto my clothes. It would not normally be so very much, but the heat of the place, the wine and my worries had made my pulse rise. In the end, I had had to go into the bathroom and use my handkerchief as a fresh dressing, but still I was uneasy. When I returned to the table, I saw Paul back in his seat, perspiring and exhausted, while Marchelline danced on with a stranger, one of the coloured musicians from the orchestra.

It was the early hours of the morning before Marchelline could be persuaded to leave. By this time she was very drunk. She had barely spoken to me all night. Losing herself in drink and in dancing until she was perspiring and dizzy and barely aware of where she was seemed to be some desperate attempt to escape – but from what, I feared to imagine.

In the carriage on the way home she said nothing, but clung to me, her hands restlessly caressing my neck, my chest, my thighs. Her breath was hot and smelt of wine as she kissed my cheek, my throat and my mouth with fierce ardour.

"Marchelline, darling," I demurred, exhausted and ill at ease.

"Don't talk, please don't talk. You only confuse my feelings." She silenced me with her mouth upon my own. She straddled me, pressing herself against me so that I responded, despite my misgivings.

"I want you so badly it is killing me," she moaned into my ear. She pulled my hand up under her skirts, moaning softly into my mouth so that I wanted to take her there and then.

The carriage stopped and I could only fling the money at the driver as Marchelline dragged me inside, tearing at my clothes.

In moments she had me on the floor, before the fireplace in our room, riding me wildly, almost violently. Her shadow rose and fell upon the wall and ceiling, distorting into monstrous shapes so that I had to look away. I did not notice at first, that she had hooked her fingers around the bandage at my chest, consumed as I was in the heat of her, and the fire that burned so close to us. It was only when she came, her fingers clutching and pulling as her body shook and convulsed, that the bandage came off.

I looked up at her glistening, flushed face, her red lips open and breathless, her eyes closed. She swayed a moment, then looked down at me. Her unfocussed eyes fell upon my chest. I felt blood running from the wounds and down around my ribs. She made a breathy noise and whimpered before she collapsed onto me in a dead faint.

I put Marchelline to bed, but I could not sleep. I walked the streets as dawn broke, feeling something in the air, intangible, but undeniable – some foreboding like invisible wings, beating close by me but always out of sight. As I neared the little park at the end of the street a raucous noise of birds caught my attention. Unconsciously, I wandered toward it. In a branch above my head, two little sparrows were crying and flitting about in great agitation trying to drive away a great black raven. I supposed their nest must be very close by. Unperturbed by the frenzy of the sparrows, the raven merely stalked along on the branch, his pointed beak thrusting forward aggressively with every stride and his cold white eye betraying no emotion as he lurched ever nearer to the tiny eggs the sparrows held so dear.

"Did I do anything stupid last night, Nicolas? I simply

cannot remember," Marchelline groaned as she emerged later that morning into the drawing room at the sound of Paul and I talking and quietly singing the music we would normally have been playing upon the piano.

"No, darling, of course you didn't." I smiled and she came and sat upon my knee, resting her weary head on my shoulder.

"You always know just what to say, darling. I love you so." She squeezed me tightly and planted a tender kiss on my cheek.

Félix entered with a tray of hot chocolate and pastries.

"Oh, Félix, you are an angel," Marchelline purred in gratitude. "Could I trouble you to bring me a headache powder as well?"

"Certainly Madame. And I have your mail, Sir. Would you prefer it here or shall I leave it in the study?"

"Here is fine, thank you."

Marchelline moved to sit near her breakfast things while Félix returned with the letters on a tray. Instead of coming directly to me, he went first to Marchelline.

"There is one for you today, Madame."

Her eyes flashed up nervously at Félix and she took the letter, the breath catching in her throat as she looked at the handwriting. She put down her cup, hesitating, then took up the pastry and slowly bit into it without enthusiasm, a faraway look on her face.

"You know, I think 'Song to the Unrequitor' is ready, Nicolas, and I believe we can easily finish the other two this week as well. So if La Rossignol is agreeable, I don't see why we can't debut at least one of the songs before I leave for Marseille next week."

"Yes, a splendid idea. What do you say darling?"

"What?" She emerged from her torpor and strained to concentrate as Paul repeated his suggestion. "Well, yes, that would be splendid, and I'm sure Pierre would be delighted to have some new songs in the show," she replied distractedly. "I might go out today." She coughed and stood up, slipping the letter into the pocket of her dressing gown. "I shall have a new dress made for my return to the stage and call in on Pierre at Les Ambassadeurs and arrange things."

"If you would like me to accompany you," I offered, "I can take you tomorrow morning, I shall be free then."

"No, no," she forced a smile. "You and Paul finish your music. My head is so sore, I will be happier away from the noise of the piano today. Some fresh air will help to clear my mind."

Late that afternoon, after Paul had left, I went to the bedroom. As the day had grown warm, the fires had not been relit since the morning. I poked around in the ashes with the fire-iron, finding, amongst the soot, blackened scraps of paper that disintegrated at the slightest touch. It seemed just as I had feared. She had burned the letter she had received. Crouching there, on my knees, on the hearthrug where only last night she had made love to me so passionately, I glimpsed another scrap that was darkened by the heat but not wholly burned. It had fallen down at the side of the grate. I could not reach in with my fingers but had to flick it out towards me with the fire-iron, onto the hearth. The words it bore were legible enough to send a chill through my heart: " — beg you to come back to me." I picked up the brittle scrap and crushed it in my hand, blinking away tears. It had to be from the Comte.

But the book had made her love me. I knew that she did. I saw it in her face every time she looked at me. I felt it in the fervor of her embrace and the tenderness of her touch. She was my wife and all that I had ever wished for. We were happy together – she could not ... she *could not* want to go back to him. Just because he had entreated her did not mean that she would ... But why should she burn his letter if it meant nothing to her: to spare my feelings, or to conceal her own? Why did she seem so troubled if we were as happy as I liked to think?

I thought then of the book for the first time in weeks. It said its work could not be undone. But as the late hours of afternoon darkened into evening I wondered where she was or if she was ever coming back. In my mind I called to her and felt the weal on my chest burn and bleed anew as the blood throbbed in my head. I wished her to continue loving me as she had done and looked down with a gasp as blood soaked through my dressing and onto my shirt.

I heard her come in just as I finished changing my clothes. The bedroom door opened and she shuffled into the room and collapsed upon the bed, her face drawn with anguish.

"Darling?" I moved to the bed and sat beside her, my heart pounding. "Has something happened?" I wanted to take her hand, but fear restrained me.

She stared into my face, half-accusing, half-imploring, as her beautiful eyes welled with tears. She could only sigh, and shake her head.

"If you have guessed, won't you say?" she cried.

I swallowed hard. "The letter you received this morning … and the flowers the other day that upset you so?"

"Yes, yes they were from him – Émile. I wanted to tell you, but I did not want to hurt you."

"But … tell me you have not seen him?"

She nodded, closing her eyes.

"You have not made love with him?" I asked, my voice breaking even as my heart was.

" … No, we just talked."

"But you love me! How – why?"

"Yes," she wept. "I do love you, desperately, uncontrollably. I could not stop loving you even if I wanted to, but …" She sat up and clutched my arm, searching my eyes. "Falling in love with you struck me like a bolt from the heavens – it was something I never expected. I was deeply in love in Émile then and had thought we would marry. When he threw me aside, in that moment of crisis, somehow it was you

71

who filled my thoughts, you that I ran to, not even knowing why I did so. And the love that we have has been like some miracle, but … when the flowers came I worried, and today when I saw him, I knew … I have never stopped loving Emile. You made me forget him for a while, but his card and letter … he begs my forgiveness. He is a changed man. He wants me back on any terms."

I shook free of her, jumping to my feet and pacing involuntarily about the floor, barely able to breathe.

"How can you say this? How can it be true? If you love me – you cannot still be in love with him? Don't confuse pity for l —"

" — I am confused, unbearably, but not about how I feel. I love you both. I never thought such a thing possible – I cannot understand how it has happened – but neither can I deny the feelings that are tearing my heart to pieces."

She fell onto the pillow and sobbed. I rushed to her, holding her tightly, afraid to let her slip out of my reach.

"Then if you love me, do not see him again, Marchelline, I beg you! I know I can make you happy if you will only give me that chance – I do not want to lose you. I cannot."

"I could never leave you," she murmured, her voice thick with tears. "Even being away from you this afternoon, for the first time, I felt all the while that relentless pull to be near you. I am being honest with you Nicolas, because I do love you and because I feel that I am going mad. What I feel inside, it is pulling me apart."

"You forgot him once, you might again – will you try? As you love me, I pray you, please, please try?"

She nodded, her reddened eyes downcast and her face marked with tears. I held her in my arms as night fell around us, and drew us both down into an uneasy sleep.

CHAPTER EIGHT

In the days leading up to Marchelline's return to Les Ambassadeurs I did all that I could to keep her amused, happy, distracted. We practiced her songs, we made love, we taught Maxim to greet her and say her name whenever he saw her. I even let her try to teach me to dance – without much success. But her behind her smiles and laughter, I feared that sadness was always in her eyes.

I had asked Félix to intercept all the mail and to remove any letters addressed to Marchelline. And if the Comte telephoned, he was not to be allowed to speak to her. I had offered to contact Pierre about cancelling her performance if she wished it, but she had insisted that she owed it to Paul and me to present our songs to the public.

I tried to lavish upon my beloved all the devotion and affection that burned in my heart. As we had been too occupied with recent events to see to employing a new maid for Marchelline, it was I who drew her bath, filled it with rose petals and perfumed oil. I scrubbed her back for her and I washed her glorious long hair. She seemed at peace then, relaxing in the warm water, her soft skin pink and glistening in the lamp light.

"Come," she invited, holding out her hand. "Join me, I want to hold you here in my arms."

How I would have loved to immerse myself in the water with her. I would have given anything for that. But my wounds … If the dressing got wet she would see the blood –

and how could I explain? I made some excuse: the water might spill, the tub was too small. She merely nodded and sank down lower in the water, so that only her nose and eyes showed. The steam rising from the water beaded on her forehead and ran down her face like tears.

The night of the show was a balmy and clear one. As the audience assembled, merry with drink and the thrill of a glorious evening, it was I who took a seat at a table close by the stage. It was I who waited for my love to appear. I was afraid to look behind me into the assembled masses, in case *he* might be there. It was some little consolation when Paul and Étienne joined me, ordering a bottle of champagne to toast the fruition of our collaboration and Marchelline's return to the stage. We steadied our nerves with drinking. Paul and Étienne were all a jitter with anticipation, but my unease was of a different character.

Finally, after numerous introductions and the interminable performances of two other artists, the moment arrived.

"And now, Messieurs and Mesdames, it is my delight to welcome back to Les Ambassadeurs that prettiest songbird of Paris, *La Rossignol*, singing a new song, written especially for her by Messieurs De Bresson and Petit. Won't you please show your appreciation for the glorious Madame Marchelline De Bresson with a 'Song to the Unrequitor' ... "

Applause erupted as Marchelline stepped out onto the stage, radiant in a gown of cerulean blue, with deep blue feathers in her hair and trimming the fan that she moved with such sublime grace. A gentle breeze fluttered Marchelline's feathers and ruffles as she swept to the front of the stage. I should have been listening to the orchestration of my music, but all my attention was captured and held by Marchelline as she struck a pose and began to sing.

If you could see my heart

If you could feel the love it bears
If you only knew –
Would you
Would love me then?

Now heard afresh, the song and its ravishing singer transported me back to that night of my utmost longing and despair for her, and my heart stung again to see her thus, on the stage, the object of massed desire and admiration, once more out of my reach. Marchelline's eyes found me and she sang to me, her beautiful voice aching with emotion, her slender arms reaching out as my words rang in the air.

If you knew I was yours
If you only saw me as I am
If you could hear my song
Would you
Would you love me then?

The oboe insinuated the apprehensive melody of the bridge and Marchelline raised her arms towards the lights, her face melancholy.

I am a shadow in your light
Hidden in darkness, and you so blind
You are all I see, a shining star in my night.

I saw a flicker in her eyes, and her glance fixed upon another far behind me. I did not have to look to know who was there. The pain in her eyes was no performance.

If you could feel me dying
Without your love to give me life
My heart lies in your hand
Crushed by the weight of your wedding band

Marchelline covered her face with her fan, her hands balled up into tight fists, and she turned away from the audience for a moment, before turning back for the final refrain. Now she could look at neither of us, but only at the white lanterns that hung like full moons over our heads, her eyes glittering with tears in the light.

Would you
Would you love me then?
Oh would you
Would you love me then?
If time turned its pages and I tried again
Would you
Would you love me then?

A roar of applause and wild cheers went up. I stood and threw my bouquet of red roses at Marchelline's feet. At the same moment another bouquet flew over my shoulder and Marchelline caught it in her hands: a golden ribbon tied a bunch of blood irises.

Suppressing a sob, she curtsied, sweeping up my bouquet and then running from the stage. I jumped to my feet and spun around, feeling Paul and Étienne's arms holding me back me as I lunged toward the stony face of the Comte de Mortaine that loomed toward me. Gasps and shrieks tore the air at the suggestion of violence in this pretty place of refined amusement. I jerked against my restraint, unable to move, my lip curling as I growled at the Comte, "Leave us alone – she's my *wife*, damn you!"

"I warned you that you would regret crossing me, Monsieur," the Comte hissed under his voice into my ear. "How much sweeter it will be to win her now – and I *shall* win her. She always said we were kindred souls, so very alike. No piece of paper can change that."

Anguished and exhausted, Marchelline took a sleeping

draught as soon as we got home. She did not wish to speak to me and had spent the entire carriage ride home looking out of the window, tears rolling down her cheeks. She shook with the torment that was wracking her heart and I cursed myself that I had caused her such agony. Blundering blindly with the Book of Calling, I had fired cupid's arrow into a heart already full of love for another. And now that heart was bleeding and torn. Should I really be surprised? How could I blame her for what I had caused? I could not bear to see her thus, anymore than I could bear the thought of losing her.

When I was certain she was fast asleep, I crept into the bedroom and quietly unlocked the bureau. There was that smell again that made my nostrils flare. I hoped that it would not reach her – lest that smell that she found so abhorrent colour her dreams with its morbid stain. Taking up the book and the raven's quill, I padded away to the study.

I had recalled seeing a symbol in the book that excited certain possibilities now in my mind. If I did nothing, I had everything to lose. I could see no other remedy than to try to fix by magic the problem that magic had caused.

The evening's gentle breeze had now coarsened into a much harsher wind. As I knelt within the red chalk circle, the four candle flames flickering and dancing in the darkness cast jittery, infernal shadows onto the high walls. The low moan of the wind seemed to ask me again, "Who is to be called?"

I tore off my bandage and filled the quill with my blood, tears stinging my eyes as I inscribed that name that I hated so violently, "Émile Philippe Chasseur, Comte de Mortaine." The windows rattled, as the wind seemed to whistle and roar those despised syllables. Indistinct with tears, my vision distorted the shadows into a monstrous height and a vaguely human form, and I flinched and rubbed at eyes, blinking the illusion away. Then a quieter murmur of the wind groaned, "How is he to be called?" I scratched at my chest with the quill until it was filled again, and now inscribed the sign of the upturned, supplicating hand: "That thy subject

77

shalle relinquish unto thee all that is his."

I awoke in panic at the confusion of sounds: banging, Maxim's excited calls, and Marchelline's shriek of horror. I opened my eyes to see her shrinking from me, edging to the side of the bed, her swollen eyes wide with revulsion and her face deathly grey in the early morning light.

"What? What is happening? What's the matter?" I mumbled, in bewildered alarm.

"Blood," she hissed, pointing at my chest, "blood. I'm afraid!"

"It is nothing," I tried to reassure her as I hurried into my dressing gown to discover what all the noise was about. I raced to the front door to see Félix cautiously opening it. Disturbed in the act of dressing for the day, his hair was unkempt and his collar unfastened.

Over Félix's shoulder I saw that face that I dreaded and I heard myself voice a queer exhalation of distress. The Comte stood on the doorstep against the mauve light of the morning, his cold, imperious countenance now transformed into an expressionless, blank, staring mask.

"Monsieur de Bresson," he said to Félix in a monotone, "I must see him."

I heard Marchelline emerge into the hallway behind me. She gasped at the sight of her lover.

"Monsieur does not receive callers at this hour," Félix stated sternly.

"No." I stopped him and steeling myself I marched towards the door. "It's all right Félix, you may leave us."

I stood at the threshold, now face to face with my enemy. I could hear Marchelline's rapid breathing some little way behind me. I stared into the Comte's eyes, now eerily devoid of their usual fire and cruelty.

"I had to come here," he began in a quiet, regular tone, "to tell you that I do not want Marchelline anymore, I no longer love her. I relinquish all claim upon her heart. She is yours. Yours."

I heard Marchelline cry. "Émile? What has happened?"

But somehow the Comte neither heard nor saw her. He only looked at me. All the hate was gone from his eyes. In its place, I saw calm submission. I felt a thrill of something like power ... victory.

"Thank you," I said to him. "Yes, you have done right. Her happiness must come first and the bonds of marriage are sacred."

The Comte nodded. "There is more. I have more to give you. You must have it all, I see that now."

I frowned in confusion. "I have all that I want."

The Comte produced a handkerchief from his pocket and held it out to me. "Please, take this, you are bleeding."

I hesitated. "Thank you."

Suddenly Marchelline rushed forward, bursting past me, trying to grab the Comte by the shoulders, straining to peer into his face. Never meeting her gaze, he merely shook her off, waving his hand before his eyes as though to brush away some imaginary insect.

"Émile?" she sobbed. "What is wrong with you? This is – not like you."

Oblivious to her entreaties, the Comte took the gold watch from his pocket and unfastened its fob chain from his waistcoat. Turning back to me he smiled mildly and pressed the watch and chain into my hands. "You must take these, for they are yours."

"No," I protested.

The Comte only smiled. "Please," he insisted earnestly. Turning on his heel he went back down the front stairs and walked away.

Marchelline followed him a few paces then stopped, shaking her head as she demanded to herself, "Am I dreaming? Have I gone mad?" She turned to me with a look of suspicion and fear that struck me with a dreadful pang. Her red eyes were once more wet with tears. "What is going on here?"

Not knowing what to say, I blustered, "Perhaps he loves you enough to let you go – because he knows that he can never make you happy. He does not want you – *but I do, more than anything* – forget him," I urged, moving onto the doorstep, holding out my hands toward her.

Her eyes fell upon the wet bloodstain at my chest and I saw her nostrils flare and her eyelids blink rapidly. All at once she screwed up her face and ran inside, pushing me out of her way.

If all had not gone exactly to plan, then at least I had gained one thing of vital importance: that the Comte no longer wanted to take her away from me. If she still loved me – as I knew she had to – there was at least hope that she would again be mine. She could forget him – we might be happy once more.

I returned inside and searched for Marchelline, finding at last that she had locked herself in the bathroom. I pressed my ear to the door and heard her quiet sobs.

"I know you are unhappy now, my love," I whispered at the keyhole, as though it were her own sweet ear. "But perhaps this is a sign of what is not meant to be. Think not upon what you have lost, but of all that you have, here, with me. I love you from the depths of my heart – if you only knew – I would do anything, pay any price for your love and to keep you always as my dearest beloved."

At first she would say nothing, but after some little time, she moved closer to the door and would answer me with some small, tearful sound, or a word. At length she spoke to me, her voice like a hurt child's – the very sound of it stinging my heart with guilt and pain.

"I have always been frightened at the sight and smell of blood. It is bound up tightly with some instinct or intuition about death – my own death," she sniffed. "You tell me that the way you bleed is harmless, but you cannot explain it. It frightens me – makes me afraid … for you – and the way you hide your wounds makes me feel that some dark secret always hangs between us. I love you, but how can I trust you? I know you are lying to me."

I was grateful that the door concealed my wincing from her, and also hid the blood that still flowed from the newest wound on my chest as the anxiety I felt cause my pulse still to race. I had sought for some time to find a plausible explanation to explain away my weals. There was nothing for it now but to try. I pressed myself against the door, feeling her presence on the other side.

"Yes, you are right," I lied. "I should have told you all before now, but I was afraid it might repel you. There is a hereditary condition in my family: a weakness of the superficial blood vessels that causes this bleeding when one reaches a certain age. The slightest scratch or abrasion can begin it. There is no cure. But neither is it dangerous – only unsightly. I feared the sight of my wounds would disgust you. And I feared that if you knew the truth, you would not want to marry me, nor bear my children, lest they also be afflicted. But if there are to be no children, as you seem to wish, then perhaps the thought of my condition might not be so hateful to you."

I heard the key turn in the lock and at last she opened the door a crack. The fear had gone from her eyes, but pain still shone from them as her tears continued to fall. She looked at me imploringly, willing me to take her anguish away. But just as I reached out my hand toward her face, there came again that same insistent knocking upon the front door.

I ran and threw open the door to see the Comte returned, that same placid look so strange to see upon his face. His arms were piled with books, papers, and antique ornaments that he pressed into my unwilling hands.

"Here, these are yours," he stated calmly, "the deeds and titles to my estates, this rare Bible, treasures from the royal court: they are yours."

Oblivious to my protests, he placed the items upon my

threshold and returned to the carriage that waited for him in the street, to fetch more of the belongings with which he had crammed it. I felt Marchelline creep up behind me. She clutched my arm as she peered over my shoulder. A whimper escaped her at what she saw. The Comte retrieved priceless paintings and enameled jewel boxes from the carriage and laid them before me on the doorstep. A passerby stopped to stare at the strange scene, then others did the same. Neighbours stared down from windows and some emerged into their doorways at the spectacle.

I felt Marchelline's little hand tighten its clasp on my arm as she struggled against some urge that soon overcame her. She rushed out, grabbing at the Comte's arm, trying to stop him, to speak with him: but he would not, could not, see her.

The gathered crowd began to whisper and eyebrows were raised. My heart sank. I closed my eyes tightly, wishing that it would all disappear. Marchelline at last gave up her appeals to the Comte and ran back up the steps. "Nicolas," she implored, "I know you have every reason to hate Émile, but you must see that he is very ill! I fear that he has lost his mind. We cannot leave him thus! I must look after for him and make sure that he is all right – I owe him that much."

From his perch on the streetlamp, the raven with the missing tail feather looked down silently, then turned his back and flew away. As the Comte drove off, shortly to return again, I drew back into the darkness of the house, leaving Marchelline scrambling to collect the Comte's things and to make them safe, out of reach of the crowd and away from the rain that was beginning to fall lightly upon the street. I shuffled into the drawing room, past Maxim's excited swaying and bobbing, and found myself sitting alone at the piano, slumped in despair.

The Comte may have relinquished his desire for Marchelline, but all I had really succeeded in doing was making her worry about him and care for him all the more.

CHAPTER NINE

I passed the rest of that endless day hiding in the study. What was going on outside my front door was far too painful to watch. The Comte's appearances on my doorstep continued though the day – and Marchelline had enlisted Félix to help her bring the piles of expensive heirlooms and treasures into the drawing room for safe-keeping where they now sat piled: putting my own belongings to shame with their fineness.

It only paused when neighbours, exasperated at the obstruction the Comte was causing in the street, summoned the police. Crowds of onlookers had continued to come and go as word of the notorious nobleman's very public descent into madness had spread through the city.

The police had wanted to take the Comte away, satisfied at the undeniable evidence that he had indeed lost all semblance of reason. It was only Marchelline's insistence that she be allowed to take charge of him, until his family or other friends might be able to have him seen by an alienist, that caused the constables to reluctantly withdraw.

Marchelline and I were supposed to go the station to wave goodbye to Paul and Étienne, but clearly that was impossible now. From behind the locked door of my study I heard Marchelline in the hall, frantically telephoning to the Comte's friends, trying to locate his sister, her careworn voice recounting over and over the Comte's terrible symptoms – all of which I had caused. It was not too long before I heard some more commotion and another female voice in the hall, whom

Marchelline addressed as Frédérique-Elyse, the Comte's sister. Just as quickly they were gone, taking the protesting Comte with them.

What a silence fell then, at once a respite and a torment. I was grateful indeed to see Félix when he knocked with my letters on a tray and a glass of brandy. Happier yet was I to see the handwriting of my beloved Aunt Mathilde-Hélène – finding some comfort in that warm familiarity.

My dear Nicolas,

I am very cross on returning from my stay with my dear friends, Monsieur and Madame Aubert, to learn that you are now a married man, and had breathed not a word of the matter to your doting aunt! But how I rejoice that you have found someone to love – I wish you all the blessings and joy in the world, and I hope that I may soon meet your bride when you both come to Giverny.

As to that other matter you asked me about, I have some information for you, but in light of your happy news, I wonder if it is still of any interest to you? In case it is not, I shall be brief – well, as brief as ever I can be!

It finally returned to me, in what connection I had heard that name you mentioned: Monsieur Solomon Henri. I recalled hearing some story about him from a fellow collector of social intelligence, Madame Berthe Sisley, whose husband, Inspector Sisley, as a young police constable had sometimes had occasion to visit the little village of Sainte-Geneviève-lès-Gasny in a professional capacity. This is perhaps some thirty years ago now and Madame Sisley's recollections were vague when I asked her, but here is the essence of what she said.

In Sainte-Geneviève-lès-Gasny at that time there lived a very respectable family named Charpantier, who ran the bakery there. Their youngest daughter Marie-Thérèse was a lovely young girl of unusually devout faith, who had, from the earliest age, felt herself called to the life of a nun.

It happened that the family were selling their wares at a country fair, when a handsome and apparently respectable young gentleman, Monsieur Solomon Henri, visiting from the city, saw Mademoiselle Charpantier and fell instantly in love with her. But his overtures to her family, however polite and well-intentioned, were rejected out of hand. As Monsieur Henri was of the Jewish faith and Mademoiselle Charpantier had no interest in marriage to anyone but Our Lord and Saviour, there was simply nothing more to be said. Monsieur Henri went away – but two months later he returned, even more desperate to press his suit. Again it was refused – this time more vehemently.

The date was set for Mademoiselle Charpantier to enter the convent as a postulant, but as fervently as she had always desired this, she awoke one morning with the strange feeling that some force was drawing her away from her calling, against her dearest wishes. She feared the hand of the devil was pulling her away from God. As a stranger and a heathen, suspicions fell upon Monsieur Henri – and Mademoiselle Charpantier now loathed and feared him with violent intensity.

She ensconced herself in the church, under the protection of the village's rather formidable priest, Father Jean-Baptiste Pétain, and together they prayed through the night for deliverance from this nebulous evil that they both perceived to be extending its claws towards the girl.

And indeed, some great change did occur – but not the one they had prayed for. In the morning, Mademoiselle Charpantier announced that her heart was suddenly filled with love for Monsieur Henri and that she meant to go away with him, as his wife or even his mistress: she cared not but she must be his.

Neither her parents nor Father Pétain could stop her and as hard as they tried, she escaped their guardianship and ran away with Monsieur Henri. Father Pétain pursued them, convinced that his young and devout parishioner had been forcibly bewitched or mesmerised. When the priest died in mysterious circumstances a few months later, the mystery deepened. And even though the spontaneous and catastrophic haemorrhage that killed him was observed by several witnesses, and Monsieur Henri was proven to be nowhere nearby at the time, questions remained about what had really happened. After the priest's death, the girl's brother took up the quest to find her, but without success.

Some few years later, news got back to Sainte-Geneviève-lès-Gasny that Marie-Thérèse, now Madame Henri, had been killed in an accident. Monsieur Henri married again very soon after. Suspicions remain alive in the village though, that Marie-Thérèse did not die. Her brother found her supposed grave quite empty. Rumour has it that she and Monsieur Henri had staged her death and changed her name to throw her family off their trail once and for all.

So there you have it, my dear. I could probably make further enquiries if you wished it, but I doubt that much more is remembered today.

Please let me know when we can expect the pleasure of seeing you and your dear bride – whom I am most eager to meet. Your cousins are very excited and send you, as ever, their warmest regards and most felicitous congratulations.

I remain,
Your loving Aunt.

I threw down the letter and raced to my desk, hastily unlocking it and turning the pages of the Book of Calling until I reached again the page of Solomon Henri. There was the name of Marie-Thérèse Charpantier, with its attendant symbols. Beneath it was the name of Jean-Baptiste Pétain, struck through with a thick and deliberate line. A terrible thought began to formulate in my mind.

When Marchelline returned, late that evening, I was emerging from my study. She rushed into my arms, her face gaunt and despairing. I held her close, afraid to speak and afraid of what she might have to say.

"The doctor came at last," she said sadly. "He fears Émile's case is quite hopeless. He has given him a strong sedative. I do not think he knows what else to do, save locking Émile away in some wretched bedlam to rot. Only time will tell, it seems. Frédérique-Elyse is with him and the Comte's brother is also on his way. Oh, Nicolas – I simply don't know what to make of any of this. I feel as though I were living in some terrible nightmare. I … " she trailed off, utterly exhausted.

"Something occurred to me today – you may think it foolish, perhaps it is. But you have always had a strong sense of intuition: you told me so yourself, and I have seen it with my own eyes. Is it possible that these strong feelings you have had for Émile so recently were not love at all, but rather concern for this crisis that you somehow sensed was just about to come?"

Her weary eyes stared away in thought, her brow furrowed in confusion. "I – I don't know. I can't think … " She shook her head in exasperation.

"Do you still love him now?"

"I care very much what happens to him – it pains me to see him suffer, but … oh, I'm so very tired. I just can't think anymore, please don't ask me …"

I took up her hand and kissed it, afraid to look in her eyes. "Do you still love *me*?"

Feverishly, she clasped my face between her hands, her gaze burning into mine. "Yes, yes, now and forever – I burned for you today, even there at his bedside and as worried as I was about him, I felt your absence desperately all the while. My love for you is not a choice. I recognize that now. Perhaps I have been mad too. I hardly know myself anymore. I feel my heart has been pulled in different directions and the torment of it has left me utterly spent."

"Come." I put my hand on her shoulder. "Let me put you to bed and I shall have Félix bring you a warm drink. You need rest my love."

Marchelline nodded and obediently turned around to precede me down the hall to the staircase. I saw a smudge of red chalk on her back, a partial print from where my hand had been. Silently, I wiped my hand upon my trousers and then brushed the mark from her dress.

I felt a terrible pain and the sound of my own cry woke me from my sleep. I clutched at my chest in the semi-darkness, feeling hot wet liquid spreading over me. Marchelline sat bolt upright at the same moment, gasping with fright, then both of us heard it – outside, a cry that seemed to echo my own.

"What? What is happening?" Marchelline slurred, still drowsy from the sleeping draught she had taken.

I tried to shrink from her, to hide the blood that I knew was running freely from some new and terrible wound. Then the sound came again and Marchelline lunged at me, clutching my arm in her terror. It was a cry on the edge of humanity, distorted by pain into a howl of incoherent, half-animal savagery. It echoed in the street in the stillness of the dawn. I grabbed for my dressing gown, pulling away as Marchelline dragged on my arm, her breaths ragged with fear.

"Don't go, Nicolas!"

The cry came again, now a lowing, haunted moan that seemed to be coming ever closer. I broke free and rushed from the room, down the stairs, hearing Maxim chattering and screeching wildly in his cage. Afraid to open the front door, I ran to the drawing room and lifted the curtain. A cold, white, unblinking eye stared back at me and a long, pointed beak jabbed fiercely at the glass so that I reeled back, sending the curtain swinging wildly back over the sight of the raven that clung to my windowsill.

From outside, the noise came again, now a thick, wheezing bellow of pain. It was not from the windowsill but from the street that it came. Feeling Marchelline shivering nervously behind me I strode to the door and flung it open. The noise came again – very close now, some low bullish groan of supreme effort and agony.

I ran out, down the steps, seeing lights being lit in neighbouring houses, curtains twitching. I heard Marchelline's footsteps close behind me. There he stood in the middle of the road, the Comte de Mortaine, dressed, like a mirror of myself, in his nightdress and dressing gown, his feet bare. It looked like him, but somehow horribly changed. His face was a deathly purple-grey and his movements were slow and irregular, jerking, stumbling. But most horrible of all was the distortion at his throat – it bulged, swollen, red and engorged like the throat of a frog puffed out. His stomach, formerly lithe and taut, now bulged in the same unnatural way, like some hideous bag of heavy fluid

"Émile!" Marchelline shrieked in horror at the sight. "In God's name, what has happened to you?" I held my arms out to hold her back.

The Comte did not seem to hear her, only staring at me and trying to make some noise, even as it sounded like his airway was half closed off. "Here," he wheezed, stepping forward haltingly, his wavering arms held out in a gesture of offering. He was no more than two or three feet away now and edging closer. I held my breath, hearing doors opening in the houses around me. His hands clutched awkwardly towards his chest and belly as if he no longer knew where they were. A thin line of blood ran from his mouth as he gurgled, "It is yours."

His clawing finger touched lightly at his chest and instantly, like a beast being gutted, his body seemed to split open from the bulging protrusion at his neck and down. Blood squirted and burst from him like a tide of wet, crimson heat exploding out towards us, showering us, spraying into our eyes and washing over our feet. Marchelline's screams pierced my ears as I watched through bloody eyes the Comte toppling backwards. His head bounced on the road as he landed with a thud. He was dead before he touched the ground. I spun around, clutching for Marchelline, her screams ringing like madness in my brain, her hysterical, hyperventilating shrieks stabbing into my soul over and over.

In the dawn light her wild eyes glowed white against her face that was spattered and dripping red. The sight of me, similarly blood-stained, was too much for her and she screamed again as she fought free from me, backing away, shaking violently as I reached out for her, her eyes rolling back in her head, until she collapsed on the ground at my feet. I fell to my knees and cradled her protectively in my arms, breathless with the fear that some greater terror may be poised to strike.

Steam rose from the gaping maw of the Comte's body. All I could smell was blood. For a long moment the world seemed completely still and silent, save for the ringing of Marchelline's screams in my mind, and my own gasping breaths.

CHAPTER TEN

The carriage rolled steadily along the tree-lined, country road. The long journey and the warmth of day had made me sleepy and the soft sounds of leaves rustling in the breeze provided a soothing counterpoint to the regular rhythm of the wheels and the horses' clopping hooves. In the trees that lined the road, birds sang prettily.

I felt at peace for the first time in weeks. My rival was dead. We had left the police in Paris behind us, satisfied that the Comte de Mortaine had committed suicide, even if the exact details of how he had done so still eluded them. Enough witnesses had thought they had seen a knife or razor in his hand to make that seem a reasonable assumption, despite no weapon having yet been found. Self-ingestion of poison or acid was the more widely accepted theory. As the Comte's madness was beyond doubting, the precise method of his self-murder was considered to be something of a moot point and of no great importance to the police.

I reached for Marchelline's hand and felt her jump. My deepest regret in the whole matter was how badly it had affected her. The doctor attending the gruesome scene had had to sedate her heavily for he considered her state of shock so severe as to be quite dangerous. Nightmares had left her screaming since that day. She could not sleep without drugs and she ate but little.

Her phobia of blood had intensified a thousandfold, and the merest suggestion of it, even in a slightly undercooked

91

cut of meat, was enough to cause her the most acute distress. Now I had to be ever more careful that she never saw my wounds. I tried to change the dressings even more frequently, lest any smell or trace of blood be apparent to her.

With the increased rate of my blood loss, I had become increasingly vigilant. The new wound that had appeared on the morning of the Comte's death had been concealed quickly enough by his blood as it covered me. It was only later, after the police and doctor had come and asked all their questions, that I had had the opportunity to take off my reddened nightclothes and wash myself.

To the three weals that already adorned my chest with their raised and subtly weeping pink shapes was added a new and larger wound. The shape of the upturned palm now bore a broad line striking horizontally through it and extending well beyond its limits to a size of about three and a half inches. The original symbol was all but obliterated by the thickness of the line and this latest bled with greater volume and frequency than its forbears. Such was the price the book demanded for the service it had rendered me.

I tried to pretend to myself that the book had killed him, but all it had done was to magnify my own murderous will. I knew that I should have been disgusted with myself and horrified that I had caused a man's death, but, in truth, as much as the spectacle had sickened me, I still felt a thrill at the power I had found. For once, I had prevailed.

Now Marchelline was mine alone, just as I had wished from the beginning. It seemed that the clouds had finally passed and as we rolled quietly towards that country house where I had always been so happy, I felt sure that now we might begin our life together anew.

With the great obstacle of the Comte overcome, the power of the book had begun to spark new ideas in my mind. I was learning to master the book: what else might I try with it? My original thoughts about its uses had been limited to winning the woman I loved. But what was to stop me now from realizing other dreams? My music was waiting to find an audience. If killing a man by magic were possible – what was not?

Maxim, clinging, almost upside down, to the bars of his cage as it sat on the seat opposing us, made some squawk at a bird he saw perched on a fence as we passed it by. Marchelline awoke with a start from her drugged sleep, gasping and looking around in fear, taking a moment to realise where she was.

Maxim swung down to his perch and danced from side to side in his usual excitement to interact with her, squawking, "Hullo Marchelline, hullo Marchelline."

Marchelline looked at me with a tight smile and leaned back into her seat.

"Nearly there," I reassured.

She only nodded uncertainly and clung to my side, resting her head on my shoulder like a frightened child. I patted her hand, certain that sunshine and country air would help to restore her formerly vivacious spirits.

As we rounded the bend in the long driveway and the house at last came into view, Marchelline seemed to come to life a little. Wildflowers scattered the sides of the track with brilliant flashes of red, purple and yellow, but these were as nothing to the gorgeous abundance of colour and life that filled the gardens that surrounded the house. Hubert, the old gardener, rose from his arthritic knees, lifted his battered hat and bowed to us as we passed: quietly proud of the splendour of the tableaux he had created. Behind the dazzling array of flowers, the sprawling yellow house glowed golden in the warm sun: its white shutters and windows open to let in the balmy breeze, and its old wooden door ajar, waiting for us.

Marchelline tore her gaze from the window of the carriage and looked at me, her eyes glistening with tears. "But it's so beautiful!"

"I have always been at my happiest here." I stroked her sweet, sad face. "And that is what I wish for you: that we may find new happiness here together, and peace."

As the carriage stopped and we got out and stretched our legs, Félix appeared, having travelled down on the train the day before. Marchelline ran over the lawn to the pond, staring at the duck and drake that noisily chased and circled around each other among the reeds and water lilies. As Félix saw to our things and collected Maxim, I took Marchelline's hand and drew her inside. She took off her hat, turning around and gazing about her in wonder at the light and airy open spaces of the house that seemed to radiate with the sunshine that flooded in from the many tall windows.

"I have spent all my life in the city," she began. "If only I had known that another world existed out here. Why, it's like Heaven!" She ran to me and embraced me tenderly. I led her through to the morning room – always my favourite part of the house, as it was there that I kept the piano upon which I had first learned to play.

I breathed in deeply of the room's familiar scent, as the wind ruffled the sheer white curtains and carried with it the fresh scents of the flowers that were blooming so abundantly outside. Familiar paintings smiled down on me from the powder blue walls, welcoming me like old friends. I felt Marchelline freeze and stiffen, and heard her gasping tightly through her nostrils. Looking back at her, I saw that the colour had drained from her face as she stared at something, her mouth falling open and her head tilting back.

There, on the piano, in my mother's beloved blue and white china vase, the housekeeper, Madame Grudet, had thoughtfully arranged a great bouquet of flowers: blood irises interspersed with bright crimson poppies. As we stared, the flowers shivered in the breeze and an overblown poppy dripped its red petals down onto the black piano. Outside the window a bird began to sing. Marchelline pulled back violently, dragging at my arm as she sought to escape the room.

A walk around the gardens seemed to calm my beloved, while a crestfallen Madame Grudet reluctantly disposed of the flowers. But as night fell, Marchelline grew more and more nervous. Accustomed to city life, the quieter sounds of the country disturbed her. The blackness outside the windows filled her with fear. The calls of insects and frogs made her jump. Somehow the hooting of owls in the wood behind the house, and the nocturnal song of the nightingale, seemed to frighten her most of all.

She hung on my arm so insistently that it began to oppress me. She tried to settle her nerves with too much brandy, but all it seemed to do was to inflame her emotions. Against my warning she then took her usual sleeping draught. Her eyes were glassy as she pawed at me.

"Please, come to bed, my love," she implored, tugging at me. "I only feel safe in your arms."

As much as I still loved and desired her, for the first time I felt some hesitation as she drew me into bed. Her cloying kisses and the suffocating tightness of her embrace seemed to infect me with the fears that she was trying so hard to put from her own mind. But I could never resist her – she whom I still desired with such fierce intensity.

As she had wished, she lost herself in her pleasures, throwing herself with the wildest abandon into our lovemaking. In the low lamplight, she seemed to hang over me, sweating, breathless: her long curling tendrils of her dark hair falling over my face and into my eyes. Her eyes were closed as she rocked and twisted and loomed toward my face unceasingly, now smothering my mouth with her own, now pressing her fisted hands upon my chest so hard that I feared the blood would seep through the bandages.

Now it was I who feared the shadows as I turned my face toward the lamp whose flame danced and wavered, distorting and reflecting in the tall glass shade. In the corner of my eye moving shadows seemed to threaten, my imagination conjuring flickering black figures there, and for a second I even thought I saw the same image reflected in the lamp's glass, but when I tried to look closer, Marchelline's hair fell once more into my eyes and her hands grabbed my wrists and pinned them beside my head. Her devouring mouth caught me, and her slender thighs tightened around my hips. At last she came, crying and gasping into my mouth. She collapsed upon me, breathing hard into my ear, her damp face sweating against mine. Within moments she was asleep, and I lay there for some minutes, feeling trapped and unbearably hot beneath her, until I managed to gently roll her off me.

I felt wetness at my chest and realised the bandage had soaked through. Looking down at Marchelline's near motionless form I winced to see my blood staining her milky white breast, just above the heart.

I lit a candle and wandered the dark, silent house. I was drawn to my old piano, and longed then, more than anything, to play it. Until Marchelline had entered my life, music had been my only constant companion. I had so lost myself in my longing for her that I had neglected this, my first love. But now Marchelline was mine, surely I could start to think of other things, return once more to that which had always been such a central part of who I was. We did not have to spend every second together as we had been. I had missed my music very much. I had missed the precious time alone that I had formerly spent in playing, practicing, and composing.

From the youngest age, I had always been told I had a gift for music. Great things had been expected of me – by no-one more than myself. Now that I was settled with my love and happier than I had ever been before, what was holding me back from realizing my own potential? And the book – the book …

I crept to my study, where Félix had left my little valise as I had asked him. Here, among books and manuscript papers, I had secreted the Book of Calling, wrapped in a dark cloth, with the raven's quill and the red chalk.

With new dreams and desires swirling through my mind, I light the lamp and scanned again the page of symbols and their meanings, feeling myself tremble with excitement at the plan that began to formulate in my mind.

Kneeling in the red circle, my heart surging with confidence and exhilaration, I filled the quill and leant over the book. Under the name of he whom I had killed, I now inscribed my own name, and beside it the symbol of an opening flower: "That his gifts may increase." I heard the faintest squeak as though something rubbed against the window and thought that I perceived some vague movement in the darkness outside.

I took up a candle and rushed thither, but nothing could I see there save the black silhouettes of the slender trees and nebulous bushes waving softly in the breeze. It struck me then, that I perceived no windy voice as I performed the ritual of the book this time. Perhaps my fevered thoughts had at last returned to some normalcy. Perhaps those tricks of the mind and the eye were the result of a creative imagination not given its usual exercise through music. The light of my candle caught a mark on the window, as of a small spindly hand dragged down the glass. No doubt it was a frog from the pond. I started at a scuttling noise behind me, and span around, holding my candle aloft.

I took a deep breath and laughed at myself and how nervous and full of dark fancies I had become. I had forgotten the sounds of the house, with its resident field mice and frogs and curious insects. Now it all flooded back with a warm sense of familiarity and contentment. I was safe here. And at last I had begun to master the book, rather than allowing it to master me.

Music was my passion, and returning to it would begin to put right the imbalances of recent weeks. An overactive imagination put to work would find no more menace in shadows.

I awoke very early the next morning with the most glorious music filling my mind. It had swirled through my dreams, along with a story, characters, scenes. I hurried to creep from the bedroom without disturbing Marchelline, and redressed my bleeding wounds with all possible haste: little caring that one more had been added while I slept. What was one more weal, if it brought me this wonderful gift?

I rushed to the piano and hastened to note down the theme in my mind, filling page after page of manuscript with the rough outlines of an overture, arias, duets and songs for chorus, themes for this character and that one – a whole opera taking shape in my mind with the most astonishing clarity and ease.

"I've never heard so many birds – they would not let me sleep. Did they awaken you too?" Marchelline yawned and leant over my shoulder, passing her arms around my neck and kissing my cheek. Her slender hands touched the sheets I was writing on, moving them even as I rushed to finish a phrase that was playing through my mind.

"Please, give me a moment, darling."

She withdrew her arms and shuffled away in silence to look out of the window. "It must be nice to feel so inspired and alive," she said with what might have been bitterness in her voice. I was only half-listening. I put down my pen and took a deep breath.

"I dreamed the most wonderful music," I explained. "I have the strangest feeling, a queer presentiment that this may be the work that will establish my name as a composer just as I have always dreamed."

"Songs? That I may sing?" Marchelline asked, moving towards the piano, a momentary hope illuminating her pretty, brown eyes.

"It is an opera," I explained excitedly, "It is called 'The Siren's Tear.'" I looked at her, expecting her countenance to mirror my own excitement. Her face fell.

"But I am not an opera singer – is there anything in

your opera that I might sing? Anything we might work on together?"

"Well, I don't know – I had not thought of it that way … but I shall write other songs just for you, my darling, as I promised I would, as many as you like, after this is written. Writing an opera has always been one of my greatest ambitions – and one I always lacked the confidence even to attempt before today. But see! How easily it flows! I never dreamed it could happen like this!"

"So I suppose you will not be able to take me on that drive today as you promised."

Remembering another sequence from my dream I began to write once more. "What? Ah, well, no, I'm very sorry – but I shall another day, tomorrow perhaps. One must strike while the iron is hot when the muse visits, no? Perhaps there is something else you can do to amuse yourself today."

"I just want to be with you. Mayn't I just sit here beside you while you work? Perhaps I could be of some help." She came and perched on the edge of my piano stool, bumping my elbow so that I blotted the manuscript.

"Darling!"

"I am sorry … I can see I am not wanted here."

I took her hand as she rose from the stool. She looked back at me with tears in her eyes.

"All I want is to be near you. I need you so. I cannot bear to be alone. In the silence all I can see is blood – all I hear are his cries. You are all I have – you are all … "

"Well we must find some diversion for you. What might you do if you had a day to yourself in Paris? Would you perhaps read, or write a journal, correspondence to attend to, needlework?" I asked, hoping that she have some interest to occupy her while I was busy.

'I would go out to meet friends, to look at shops, to visit the galleries or listen to music. But what can I do here?"

"Well, you might take the air – put some roses back into those beautiful cheeks. There is a garden to explore – I have

99

sketchbooks and paints you might play with if it would amuse you? I know you are an artiste of song – perhaps you have other talents with which to express your beautiful soul."

"My art is in interacting with people, I cannot sing if no-one is listening. Who will listen to me here – these wretched birds? Can't you understand? I hate being alone!" She fell to her knees, a tear spilling down her cheek, her hands clutching at my neck. "Make love to me?" she whispered into my ear. "When I am alone I see it all again." Her hand fell between her breasts. "I see that ... *chasm* and I fear it will swallow me somehow. Please?" she implored through her tears, clasping at my hips, caressing my thighs, rubbing her tear-stained face in my lap as she tried to pull up my nightshirt. "Only your love can make me forget. I need you so badly."

I caught her face in my hands and kissed her lightly, pulling back as she tried to entangle me deeper. "Darling, darling, pray don't take on so. You are safe here. Why not go for a walk outside, let sunshine and the beauty of nature inspire you and chase away your fears. Maxim will sit on your shoulder and keep you company – he loves to go outside. He needs companionship too while I am occupied. Tomorrow my aunt and cousins are coming over to entertain you – and soon you shall be inundated with invitations to meet their friends in the area too, and visits from our neighbours. Today, I shall be here, close by, but I must work while the inspiration is with me: I simply must – you understand. While the music is still so vivid in my mind – it may never come again. This is so very important to me. I want to be a success: someone that you can be proud of."

I wiped her eyes. She nodded and walked silently from the room.

I worked feverishly all that day and long into the night, the music and lyrics flowing from me with such speed, such delight, that at times I even laughed with the joy and ease of it. Orchestrations, scenery, costumes: I seemed to see and hear the whole finished opera as though it were being staged, fully formed, in my mind.

I was vaguely aware that Madame Grudet brought food in on a tray at some point, then returned to take it away again, untouched, some time later. I barely noticed when Marchelline returned and quietly sat before the fire, the clinking of her glass, and the repeated pouring of brandy into it, the only sounds she made.

At last I put down my pen and began to play the overture. At this Marchelline rose and moved close to the piano. I looked up at her, ebullient with the beauty of the music that had poured out of me and that now came to life beneath my fingers. Her eyelids were heavy and she appeared to sway a little as she listened, her mouth hanging open.

"'S'beautiful," she slurred. "Your opera – what is't about?"

"It is about a destitute young woman, Agnès, who longs for a man who does not even know that she exists. In her despair she tries to drown her sorrows in the absinthe bottle, then to drown herself in the Seine. But before she can, the green fairy appears to her and gives her a strange and beautiful green jewel. The fairy tells her the stone is the crystallised tear of a siren, distraught that Odysseus had heard her song yet resisted her allure. It was caught in a rock pool before the siren threw herself into the sea, and now it can give its owner the power to win over whomever they desire. Agnès takes the jewel and … but I'm getting ahead of myself. Here, this is Agnès' song as she stands by the river – forgive my attempts to sing it, you must imagine that I am some great soprano." At first I merely hummed the melody, but soon lost myself in singing the words.

… But no, invisible!
Now I shall sink to where
The wrecks of lost boats shall carry me
Down, without light without air,

101

To a land below –
Where all the forgotten fall
Where cold is all.
The river swells with tears
Of the forgotten,
And all I held so dear
Shall be forgotten.
Forgotten, forgotten:
To melt into the water and disappear ...

Thrilled at the sound of my music played aloud I looked up to gauge Marchelline's reaction, but she was no longer there.

CHAPTER ELEVEN

I was still at the piano when Marchelline entered the next morning. I had fallen asleep where I sat, my manuscript serving as an uncomfortable, makeshift pillow. My limbs and neck were stiff from sitting and working for so long. It was not long after dawn and the air was filled once more with the cacophony of birdsong.

"I had the most terrible nightmare," Marchelline said quietly. "That hordes of shrieking birds were tearing the flesh from my bones." She held up her hand before her face. "I saw my own hand, picked clean, just bones – you cannot imagine … " She frowned and moved stiffly to the window, drawing aside the curtain to look out. "I suppose it was their wretched cries that got into my brain. When I woke up you were not there. For a moment I thought you stood in the corner of the room, watching me, but it was only a shadow."

"Forgive me, my darling," I implored as I rose, stretching my aching neck and moving to put my arms around Marchelline's waist. She stood looking out of the window. At my touch, she shivered. "But it is the most remarkable thing, my love: I have done it. It is only a first draft yes, but essentially the bare bones of my opera are there, merely waiting for me to add and refine the material to flesh them out. I am quite exhausted but so satisfied and so hopeful that this work will help to establish my name as a composer. I know you understand that special pleasure that only music can bring."

She sniffed, then violently expelled the air from her lungs. Her stomach contracted under my arms and I feared she would be sick. I felt a hot trickle run down my stomach and looked down to see the bandages soaked through. In my distraction I had neglected to change them. "It's all right," I tried to reassure her. "Yes, there is blood, but no danger, I promise you. You are completely safe and so am I. It is nothing, nothing at all." I backed away from her, mortified at the red stain I had made on the back of her mauve silk dressing gown. "All will be well," I called as I rushed from the room. "Please do not let it upset you."

When I returned, Marchelline had retired to dress, as my aunt and cousins were expected later in the morning. We spoke little as she busied herself with her toilette and I arranged and tidied my piles of manuscript pages, then went to dress myself.

How beautiful she looked in her dress of blue and white striped silk, as she emerged to meet our guests. Only her eyes showed a little tiredness and her cheeks were not so full, nor so pink as they customarily were. But she seemed happy then, to be in company and to meet my aunt, her son Yves, and the twins, Martine and Clémence, who were not so very much younger than Marchelline and both in awe of her clothes, her beauty and her cosmopolitan air.

As the twins grilled Marchelline about Paris fashions and what it was like to sing at a famous nightclub, Yves took me aside. He appeared to be trying to grow a moustache, no doubt in an effort to appear older than his seventeen years.

"I say, old man, how do you fancy leaving the ladies to their silly talk and helping me on a little errand? I'm to pick up a new horse over in Sainte-Geneviève-lès-Gasny – what about coming there with me in the barouche? Then you can drive it back and I shall ride the new pony home: he's quite a splendid walker, and such wonderful dark eyes – not a bit of white. What do you say? I should be ever so grateful for some intelligent conversation." He gazed disdainfully in the direction of his mother and sisters.

"Must you go?" Marchelline cried when Yves announced our plans.

"I shan't be awfully long," I consoled, kissing my beloved on the cheek.

"What touching devotion," my aunt observed with a wry smile. "You can't bear to be apart for even a moment now, my dear: ah well, let us hope you still feel that way in a year or two."

Marchelline shot me a pained look as Yves dragged me behind him out the door.

I barely listened to Yves' incessant horse talk as we drove along, thinking only of what I had learned from my aunt's letter about our destination and what had happened there. After I had left Yves it was not difficult to locate the little bakery in the sleepy village. Its worn pale pink façade had seen better days and it was clearly no younger than thirty years. I wandered in, seeing a middle-aged man behind the counter, who was occupied in wiping down some empty shelves.

"Good day, Monsieur." I bowed my head to him, trying to look casual as I studied the loaves of bread on display, and the shelves with their various pastries.

"Good day to you." He smiled and put down his cloth, dusting his hands together. "How may I help you, Monsieur?"

"Is your name Charpantier, by any chance?"

"But of course, this is Charpantier's bakery, established by my father in 1848," he said proudly, puffing out his chest. "I am Thierry Charpantier. I am the baker here now."

"I hardly know how to begin, but can I ask you Monsieur, do you recall the name Solomon Henri?"

Monsieur Charpantier stiffened and colour suffused his broad, round face. The smile died on his lips and he peered at me searchingly. "How could I ever forget the name of the devil?" he asked quietly, knotting his brow as his gaze fell to the floor. "But what could you know of that fiend, or of me and my family, Monsieur? Who are you? Why do you remind me of such terrible things? What do you want here?"

I swallowed, preparing the story I had invented on the journey over. "My mother went missing when I was just a boy. No-one could tell me how or why. Her diary from that time mentioned a Monsieur Henri's name but no more. I had heard a whisper of a man by that name coming here, taking your sister away with him. I thought if I could trace him he might know something … "

He glared at me, his eyes narrowed in pain.

"My sister Marie-Thérèse was the most pure and innocent child," he muttered bitterly, "just seventeen when he bewitched her. Yes, bewitched – that is what he did, make no mistake." He prowled away from the counter and through a dusty green curtain. I feared I had upset him and that he would not come back, but a moment later he returned, clutching a faded photograph in a frame. "This is all we have to remember her by." He pushed the picture into my hands.

I suppressed a gasp at the beauty of the young woman in the image. Her hair was very fair, and her expression one of indescribable sweetness. Her slender hands were clasped together in prayer and a rosary was wrapped around them. It was something in the expression of her eyes that was so captivating – they seemed to sparkle with vitality and warmth, even through the time-worn picture.

"She did not want to leave us, or the church – her faith was everything to her. Being a nun was all she had ever wanted – to serve God and love Him. I know it was witchcraft or mesmerism of some kind that carried her away, and she knew it too, but even knowing it she could not resist it. She said she saw shadows around him that were not his own: shadows in the shape of men. She thought they were demons. Perhaps she was right." He held out his broad, calloused hands for the picture and took it back, clutching it to his chest. "What could we do, Monsieur, against such forces?"

106

I shook my head, biting my lip, and I shuddered.

"I'm not so traditional as my mother and father were – if she had wanted to marry outside the faith, it would not have mattered so very much to me. I would not have stopped her. But I tell you, Monsieur, she feared and hated that man, right up until that morning that she told us she was leaving with him. Her eyes had changed – lost their spark. Somehow he had turned her against herself, robbed her of her own free will – that is why I followed them. What kind of monster would make a woman his wife against her wishes? And I *know* he killed our poor priest who went after them. I saw the body and I tell you, nothing natural caused that." He pawed at his chest and shook his head at the horror of his recollections. "There was nothing natural about any of it. The thought of her, bewitched into living with a man she feared, did not love – even now, it turns my stomach to think of my poor little sister being used so ill – monstrous, monstrous … "

"Do you think she is still alive, and with him?"

"I saw her coffin dug up and opened, Monsieur – empty. Why else would they do that but to throw us off her scent? That was when I gave up hope. If he had made her love him so much that she would go along with such a cruel hoax, then the sister I knew *was* indeed dead. My parents were destroyed by the whole affair. Alas that their coffins were not empty when I stood at their gravesides so soon after."

"Did you ever hear anything more of him – where he might be?"

"Nothing." He paced back behind the counter, agitated. "If your mother went with him too, then I can only advise you to try and forget her. You are not some wizard who can defeat the power of the devil, I think." He looked me up and down with a bitter smile. "No, no more than I am. And I would not waste my time with the police either. They said no crime had been committed – can you imagine?" He sucked his teeth.

"There are a few other names I have come across in my research, Monsieur Charpantier. There may be no connection at all, but I thought I would ask you all the same: have you ever heard of a Jeanne Laffite or a Marthe Chabot?"

At the second name he flinched. "Yes, yes, Chabot, it does ring a bell. Forêt-la-Folie, I believe was where she came from. It was a scandal of course, which was why we heard of it down here. Well it was a long time ago, but I do remember now that you mention it. The young woman ran away from her husband I think, and did she leave a young child behind her too? It stuck in my mind because it made me think of my sister – this Madame Chabot was around the same age that Marie-Thérèse would have been at the time. It was only a few years after, not long after the time she was supposed to have died. It was said that this Chabot woman had run off to live with some man in a farmhouse in Farceaux. *She* was not your mother, was she?"

"No, she was not. Well it is very regrettable, but I suppose there needn't be anything so unusual in a woman's forsaking one man for another."

"No. And think on that Monsieur, when you wonder where your mother might have gone."

"And one last name, Monsieur, Esther Cécile – does that mean anything to you?"

"No, that name I never heard." He slumped now, wincing and exhausted by his painful recollections. He rubbed at his face with his floury hands, then took up his cloth once more and made some agitated movements towards the shelves with it.

"Perhaps I ought to take your advice and leave the whole matter in the past," I lied.

"What good did all my searching and digging do in the end?" he asked me. "I couldn't have helped her, even if I'd found her. The truth of it is just too painful to think about. That God would permit such a thing – and to one of his children who loved Him the most. It is enough to make one doubt. Likely your mother just ran away Monsieur, with another man, as Madame Chabot did, it is not so uncommon, as you say. That is what I would tell myself, for to allow the thought of these darker shadows to enter one's life … well, they will only grow to banish all the light." He looked up at me with red eyes staring sadly out of his white-dusted face.

Feeling bad for upsetting him so, I bought a great quantity of bread and pastries, and hastened back towards home.

I arrived home to hear my own piano music wafting from the open windows. Marchelline's pretty, trilling voice drifted towards me, intermingled with the songs of robins and swallows.

If you could feel me dying
Without your heart to give me life
My soul lies in your hand
Crushed by the weight of your wedding band
Would you
Would you love me then?

My aunt, Yves, and the twins were applauding as I entered the morning room. Maxim danced on his perch, bowing and twisting his head around when he saw me and chirping excitedly.

"Nicolas darling, you never told me your wife was so exceptionally gifted," Mathilde-Hélène gushed when she saw me, "and the music, my dear, is quite superb. And Madame de Bresson tells us that you have now written an opera, no less?"

"It is true, I have been very inspired."

"Well I should think so! Any man who did not find this ravishing and delightful creature an inspiration would have to be blind or a fool. And you must promise me that you are going to write more music to show off her magnificent voice too. Now this opera of yours, I know it will be marvellous, please tell me that you are not going to leave it unfinished or just consign it to a drawer."

109

"Well, no I should love to see it produced, if such a thing were ever possible."

"Excellent, well you know I am acquainted with Monsieur Combet of the Paris Opera? And also Monsieur Alati of the Opera National Lyrique. They are the men of consequence of this field. I shall write to both of them immediately, introducing you, commending your work to them and telling them to expect to hear from you in due course. This is a great opportunity – it is up to you to seize it."

Taking their cue from their mother, Yves and the twins rose and kissed us goodbye. Maxim's screeching would not be silenced until the twins had made much of him and said goodbye to him as well.

After we waved them off, Marchelline threw herself into my arms. "I missed you so much. All I wanted to do was follow you."

"Didn't you enjoy getting to know my aunt and the cousins? They really are the most warm-hearted and kind people, and I can see that are very taken with you."

"Yes, yes – but they are not you." She stared at me searchingly, some question formulating in her mind, her countenance troubled. "I want to be with you all the time – I need to be, in some way that I cannot explain and do not understand. It makes me feel so pathetic and weak: as though I had lost myself."

"Well," I flustered, "Is that not in the nature of love?"

"It frightens me," she murmured.

I held her close to me as we stood in the garden. "We have both been through much of late – you, most of all. I think it is quite natural that you should feel unsettled, and even frightened by all these changes." I took her hand and we began to walk together around the garden, across the lawn. "But there is nothing to fear here." We stopped beside the pond and Marchelline laid her head upon my shoulder, passing her arms around me. Before us, the drake still chased the duck, circling noisily, rippling the water in their dance. I

110

swallowed.

"I forgot to ask you, last night, what do you think of my opera – I mean the story of the girl and siren's tear?"

"It is quite brilliant, darling – an ingenious idea. I cannot imagine anyone who has not, at least once in their lives, longed to be able to make another love them and who hasn't desperately craved some means to make such a thing happen."

"Really?" I asked her, thrilled at her sentiment – for the first time my guilt assuaged by the notion that perhaps she too understood what had driven me to use the book upon her.

"Yes, in a story, I think it's marvelously appealing."

"In a story?"

"Of course, or in your opera. In reality though, I think it would be unspeakably cruel. To be forced to love – to be made the puppet of another's will. Well, it would be hideously cruel – a kind of murder of the soul."

CHAPTER TWELVE

I tossed and turned through the night, my dreams twisted and circling with obscure figures that sang incomprehensible words to infernal, ominous music – music that never seemed to end. The figures climbed and scrambled over an endless black fence of five high horizontal rails that stretched, spiraling, curving into infinity, imprisoning me in a gargantuan ring of sinister sound and restless, jittering shadows.

Into this strange, inhuman symphony, the familiar sound of a piano began to intrude, taking up the haunting tune, setting the frantic figures abuzz with more violent motion and making some sing higher, others lower, in strange harmonies such as no mortal voices ever produced.

"Nicolas ... " a pleading, frightened voice called to me from far away. "Nicolas!"

I opened my eyes into darkness, knowing that I no longer dreamt but still hearing that menacing, unearthly music in the air. A hand shook my shoulder.

"Nicolas! Stop it! Nicolas!" Marchelline's high voice cried through fearful tears.

I still did not know quite where I was and strained to see in the dark. Dim white shapes moved rapidly below my eyes. My hands – my own hands – were moving over the piano keyboard as I sat in the nocturnal darkness, the song from my dream filling the air with brooding, urgent unease.

It was not my own will that moved my fingers. My

112

fingers, hands and arms seemed no longer to belong to me, and raced over the keys, ever faster and more furiously than I could normally play, picking out harmonics that made the hairs on my neck prickle. I was so absorbed in the terrifying wonder of this automatic playing that I barley noticed Marchelline's increasing distress as she tugged at my arm.

"Stop! Stop it – please!" she cried, wrenching my arm with such force that all at once the spell simply broke and my hands fell limply to my sides. The notes in the air died away into silence and all was still save for Marchelline's agitated breathing at my ear.

"Nicolas?" she hissed.

"Yes?" Confused, I turned to face her, straining to see her in the gloom. She looked very afraid and pulled back from me. "I don't quite know – what is happening, Marchelline? What is the matter?"

"Your playing awoke me," she whispered, "and I came out and found you like this – in a trance! You could not hear me, and that music, that horrible music – I could not make you stop playing it! You would not awaken. You only played louder, faster, as though you were possessed."

"I was dreaming ... I dreamed of strange music," I struggled to explain, not understanding at all what had occurred.

"Pray, light the lamp," she whispered. "That music – it was like all the terrors of darkness found a voice – as if some nightmare escaped your mind and engulfed me."

"It was only a dream. All is well," I urged, even as some fierce instinct told me it was not. I felt my way in the dark to the mantel, groping for the Vesta case to light a match: filled all the while with some nebulous dread of what the light might reveal. With my back to Marchelline I lit the lamp, and as its glow suffused the space I heard her rush forward to the piano, a guttural cry escaping her.

At the same time I looked down and saw that my chest was bared and my bandages pulled down, blood smearing my

113

skin and marking the white cloth of my open nightshirt. My fingers, too, were bloody. Hurriedly I pulled up the dressings and tried to cover myself.

"What is this?" Marchelline groaned. "What ... what is wrong with you? There is evil at work in this ... It is unnatural – unholy."

I turned stiffly to see her backing away towards the door: her terrified eyes fixed upon the piano. The white ivory keys were smeared all over with blood, but stranger still was the stream of manuscript paper that lay in a tangled heap on top of the instrument. Marchelline fled back to the bedroom as I leaned in closer to look at the paper in the low light.

The lines of the stave were crowded with more than notes. Scratched and scrawled in blood, the notes of the unearthly melody formed the heads of innumerable tiny stick figures – faceless, featureless – that climbed and scrambled, danced and hung off the bars, just as they had clung to that stave-like fence in my dream. Some had escaped the confines of the bars and cavorted, fought and fornicated in the empty spaces on the pages. I could not count them, but there must have been hundreds. The music notation was in places barely discernable amid the hordes of swarming figures.

Where the notation ended, the raven quill had been set down on the page. My blood turned to ice.

I sat at the piano the following morning looking over the manuscript. Outside, the sun shone and a balmy breeze rustled the curtains. But as warm as the day was, I felt cold looking at this grotesque and bloody music. Beyond the inexplicable fact that I had produced this while unconscious, there was something in the character of the figures that disturbed me very much. I recognised them somehow. I had seen something so very like them before, in the demonic figures illustrating the illuminated letter in the Book of Calling.

Marchelline sat silently on the sofa, absently petting

THE BOOK OF CALLING

Maxim as he walked about on her knee and then climbed up her arm.

This music was completely unlike anything I had ever written. I studied the complex notation and attempted to play a section of it, struggling to get my fingers around its twisting figure and its weird, disquieting counterpoint. Maxim squawked some cry of unease and his feathers prickled. I noticed Marchelline shifting in her seat.

"Must you play that again?" she asked nervously.

"Well I only wanted to hear it once more, to try and determine if I dreamed it up myself, or if perhaps this is some piece I heard elsewhere and forgot about." I went on playing. "Does it remind you of anything, darling?"

Maxim climbed onto the back of the sofa, striding about in agitation, whistling and shaking his head.

"Yes, it makes me think of blood," she exclaimed hotly, rising to her feet and pacing about the room in time to the rising tempo of the music that once again seemed to take over my hands and play itself. "When I hear it I see your blood and Émile's. I can even smell it! Nicolas, there is some essence of darkness and evil distilled into that horrible music. I don't know how. Where it came from, I'm afraid to know, and you should be too. It scares me – Nicolas – stop it! Stop it, stop it! You are frightening me!"

She ran from the room, and I watched as my animated fingers froze upon the keys. From the hall I heard the front door bang and at once I ran after Marchelline and out into the garden. Her pale lemon day dress flowed out behind her as she ran over the front lawn, past the pond and around the side of the house to the arbor. It was there that I caught her, as she sheltered beneath the weeping mauve blossoms of the wisteria, trying to catch her breath.

Her beauty should have been an ornament to the splendour of the day and the garden at the height of its colour and glory, but even out here, her countenance was pale and haunted, her movements twitchy and nervous. I moved to her as she clung to the side of the arch, weeping. I wished only to comfort her. But she stiffened in my arms, drawing back her head and looking at me with an expression of suspicion and fear.

"Is this some cruel game to you? Are you trying to frighten me? Does it amuse you somehow?" she asked, her voice thick and broken.

"What? No! Not for all the world would I wish that." I drew her to me and enfolded her gently in my arms.

"Then how do you explain that music? Last night? Hearing it again just now filled me with the same unbearable dread that some catastrophe was about to engulf me. It is the very same feeling I had when I first came to your house that day – with your music in my mind. Why? Why should I feel that way? Why does every fibre of my instinct tell me to fear you – to fear for my life – and to run when I love you so … so unbearably?"

"Then your instinct must be wrong! Quite wrong!"

"What if we are most attracted to that which is most dangerous to us? What if, as I first feared, you are my death – and that is the very reason why I am compelled to love you so?"

"Darling, darling, you mustn't say such things. You don't know how it hurts me. How can you think that?" My voice caught in my throat, my eyes moistening as I held her face in my hands.

"I don't think it." She shook free of me and turned to look through the arbor to the wood beyond the back garden. "I know it in my heart, just as I know that I will always and only love you. But even loving you as much as I do – you frighten me. Perhaps that is Émile's curse on us … " Marchelline began to walk , then to run, through the arbor and away from me.

Breathlessly I followed her down the sloping lawn and into the trees: my heart pained to feel her once more slipping away from me. At last I caught up to her. She was leaning against a tree, her head buried in her hands as she silently wept. All I wanted to do was hold her, but the fear of upsetting her more held me back.

"Darling," I ventured, quietly. "All will be well … There is nothing to fear, I promise you. You have nothing to fear from me – you never have. Things that have happened have badly strained your nerves, that is all. All I ever wanted was for us to love each other: pray do not let your imagination, your guilt, you pain over Émile's death spoil what we have – what we could have. We love each other: we have much to be happy about and thankful for. We must try to forget that past and make our life together a happy one."

She turned to me then, her lovely eyes glittering as they searched mine for reassurance and some way to escape her fears. I kissed her, clasping her to me, never wanting to let go of her again. She clung to me, clutched at my hair, my face, my shoulders, smothering my face with kisses, pulling me down with her, to lie upon the bed of wild flowers, grasses and leaves at our feet. Birdsong coloured the air as we lay so close together there, our bodies pressed together, a thousand kisses returning the colour to her beautiful cheeks and reddening her lips.

In the trees around and above us, the whistling and singing grew louder, and I recalled that song that she had sung so bewitchingly and the love that had ignited in my breast when first I had seen her on the stage. I began to unbutton her dress, and she to pull up my shirt. I rolled over her, kissing her shoulders, her collarbone and décolletage as I exposed them to the warm air. She sighed softly, but the sweet sound was drowned out by a bird shrieking on a branch just overhead. What joy it was to touch her, to love her, to feel her pleasure rise as she entwined her legs around my own.

To feel so close to my love once more, as her tender hands caressed me, as her warm lips inflamed mine, brought delight to my heart as much as it did to my senses. I slowly pulled up her skirts and she clasped me tighter, ardently kissing my face and whispering eagerly into my ear. But I

117

could not hear her words. For by the second, it seemed that the air around us grew thicker with shrieks and cries. From every direction we could her the frantic flapping of wings as birds assembled and descended in a deafening multitude into the tall tress above and all around us. Marchelline's skin turned to goose flesh.

No pleasant song did the birds sing but a raucous tumult of screeching, so that the air grew thick and sharp with the sensory assault of their fearful cries, even as those hundreds of gathering shapes in the branches seemed to darken and chill the ground around us with their twitching shadows.

Marchelline looked around in fright, covering her ears against the mounting fury in the air. And still the sound grew louder as yet more birds congregated above us in a swarm of wild alarm. Desire, that had burned so ravishingly in those beautiful eyes, was extinguished once more by fear.

Clutching at her disarranged dress, she scrambled to her feet and ran away from me. And in the tumult of disharmonious notes that rent the air, and in the rhythm of Marchelline's running feet, my imagination heard again that nightmarish music from the spindly branches above my head that swarmed with tiny, restless, shrieking shadows.

I returned to the morning room to find Marchelline crouched over the hearth.

"Are you all right darling? What – what are you doing!" I lunged forward as I saw a bundled up bunch of papers in the grate catching fire beneath the match she held to them. My manuscript burst into flames, and I smelt once more my own blood burning into grey smoke.

"There was evil in that music – there is evil in …"

"In what?"

She bit her tongue and shook her head shakily, fetching a bottle of cognac and a glass from the cabinet. She wrapped herself in a rug and curled up in a tight little ball at the far end of the sofa, and drank, saying nothing; staring into the flames as they burned and died away until all that remained of the paper were fragile charred fragments that fluttered like tiny black wings in the smoke.

Not knowing what else to do, I retreated to my study, where I finished my letters to my aunt's Paris opera contacts. These I sealed in their packages, along with my synopses of The Siren's Tear, and the extracts I had copied out, and rang for Félix to post them for me. When he answered my bell, he came with his silver tray – a letter from Paul awaiting me.

> *My dear Nicolas and Marchelline,*
> *Just a quick note to say, I am happier than I have ever been in my life – hoping you are the same, my dear friends.*
> *What is news with the two of you? I do miss hearing about all the goings on in Paris down here. Still, E keeps me entertained and very busy. I hope that you will visit us as soon as you can – it's paradise! E sends warmest regards.*
> *Much love,*
> *Paul.*

In anger at myself, I screwed up the letter and threw it on the floor.

I read and reread the Book of Calling, trying to fathom some way to fix what I had done. But now I wondered how much worse I might make things if I ventured further with the book. Marchelline loved me but feared me too – the wretched unhappiness I was causing was written all over her dear face and it killed me to see it and to know that I had put it there. I wondered if it was ever to be my fate to feel so alone; unlovable, and unable to love without bringing pain and ruin to she whom I held dearest in all the world.

I changed my dressings and burned the soiled ones in the fireplace.

I did not stir from my painful reverie when Félix entered to light the lamp. All I could think of was that I had to find a way out of this mess. I had to find Gildian Greene before I destroyed Marchelline's life. I would not only give my blood but my life itself for some way to bring Marchelline and myself together in happiness.

I heard soft footsteps in the hall and stiffened, yearning to be near Marchelline, but afraid of what further sorrow or fear I might bring to her. I heard her heavy breathing in the doorway as she opened the door.

"S'room smells like blood," she slurred drunkenly. "I can't get away from that smell. I can't ever get away." She shuffled into the room and fell down on her knees before me, her moist eyes glassy and faraway with drink. I did not know what to say.

She held my hands in her own wet hands and leaned on my knees, peering up into my face unsteadily. "Love me," she urged, "I need your love so badly, and I'm so drunk I don't care about the fear – if I live or die. I don't care. Love me … "

I took her hands and held them to my lips, smelling the cognac on her breath, peering into those unfocussed, sad eyes. "What have I done to you?"

"My desire," she began uncertainly, "I wanted you and won you. That is my punishment."

"What? What do you mean my love? Punishment for what?"

She blinked and looked confused. "What happens to the girl in your opera?"

"What?"

"The girl who gets the siren's tear an' can have whoever sh'wants. In the end, what happens t'her?" She pulled herself up and curled around me on the chaise longue, so that I cradled her in my arms. She stroked my face.

"Ah, she takes the jewel back to the sea, to return it to the siren, and she falls into the waves and drowns," I explained, distractedly.

"Mm," Marchelline replied, not really listening, as she drew closer to my face, curling her fingers into my hair. "Perhaps we are all t'be punished for getting what we want. I just want you. I want you, I want you. But why can't you be … diff'ren'?" she murmured sadly, pulling my face to her own, engulfing me with her hot, wet, fumy kisses.

It was without joy, but in fearful, clinging need and desperation that we made love then: she bewitched to love me, and I consumed by guilt and fear as much as I was still consumed by my love for her.

Chapter Thirteen

I rose while it was still dark, eager to escape the house before Marchelline awoke.

Everything I did now seemed to horrify and frighten her. I hoped that in my absence, her nerves might settle. If Greene were to be found, perhaps he could advise me what to do. All I had to go on was "a farmhouse in Farceaux." I had to follow that tenuous lead, for even to know the truth about how Greene had used the book might help me to understand what I was doing wrong and how I might begin to fix things.

My two chestnut carriage horses trotted along before me at a steady clip. The morning was quiet and still, and only the sight of the occasional farm worker or hare distracted me from the worries that circled unceasingly in my mind. For so long I had turned away from the harm I had done with the book. But I had killed a man in the most terrible way. I had caused Marchelline such immense pain and distress. Even now, the spell of the book forced her to love me, even as she feared me.

For a moment I wondered: if the spell were broken, would she love me still? If the Comte had never existed to steal her heart, would I ever have stood a chance with her? We were more different than I had ever imagined. I had thought that it would not matter, but it seemed that it did. I had made her love me, but her love was not unconditional, and it strained against her inability to accept me as I was.

I had acted out of love – but I could not undo what had

been done. Not unless Greene could tell me how, if it were possible at all. Even then, would I do it? Could I do it without tearing my own heart out?

At last, as the morning wore on and the bright sun rose in the sky, I reached the outskirts of the village. I slowed down as I saw an old man with an aged farm dog, herding a skinny cow along the road. He was old enough to have been here twenty-five years ago – but was he too old to remember?

"Good day, Monsieur," I called out as I pulled the horses to a halt.

The old man touched his battered cap and eyed my chaise with a narrow look that might have been envy or suspicion.

"'Day."

"Forgive me for disturbing you, but I wondered if you might be able to help me? I have been told that my mother moved here some twenty-five years ago. I have not seen her since I was a small child and I would very much like to find her if I could. Her name is Marthe Chabot."

The old man blinked several times and frowned, staring down into the milky eyes of his dog for a moment, as if silently conferring with him.

"Can't say I remember," he said, without looking up.

"Please Monsieur, I know she was here, with a man by the name of Solomon Henri I believe." I fished in my pocket and drew out some coins, holding them out toward him. He peered at me from under the brim of his cap, biting his lip to reveal a haphazard arrangement of crooked teeth. He slowly raised a weathered hand to me and took the coins.

"I wouldn't go mentionin' them names too freely," he said gravely. "There were somethin' not right about that man. It weren't decent what they were doin' – a man living with two women as 'is wives. A sin and a shame is what it were. They never talked to nobody round here. Never went to church or nothin'. What kind of wicked folk carry on like that? More than wicked they was. We never even knew they was

123

gone until old Jacques went up there one day, snoopin' like, and found the place deserted. That's when 'e saw the blood, and them symbols, signs of witchcraft - evil. It ain't been touched since. Us farmers are a superstitious lot, I s'pose you'd say. But you don't need to be rich or clever to know where danger is. The place has probably fallen down by now. Well, I hope it 'as. I don't know what you'd find there but maybe a nest of foxes, or rats."

"Please Monsieur, where is this place? I must see it for myself."

The old man sniffed and rubbed at his nose, his hand absently scratching in his collar to touch the crucifix he wore. "Go up the Rue de l'Abbé Divay a mile or two." He pointed the way. "At the crossroads take the left track. Follow that for a few miles until you see a narrow track on the left - I can't say as it's not grown over with brambles and bushes so you might miss it - you might not even be able to get through. That's the place though. The house is sheltered by the hill at the back, and well, a great mess of trees and brambles that hide it altogether at the side and the front. But I wouldn't be too sorry if you couldn't find it, Monsieur. That might be for the better, I reckon. 'Day to ya."

On he trudged, hitting the grazing cow with his stick and whistling to his weary dog to wake up and follow him. I drove on.

As the regular old hedgerows became wilder and more unkempt I knew I was getting closer. Here the tangled hedge grew high, twining around and beginning to engulf some great gnarled trees. I watched the edge of the track, searching for any signs of where another track might once have branched off into a drive. Then I saw it - a little patch where the mess of the hedgerow was not quite so high. On the ground I perceived a little hollowing, although now covered with weeds and snarled with intertwined trees and brush. I pulled the chaise off the narrow road as best I could and tethered the horses. It seemed unlikely that there would be much traffic for them to block at any rate. I tried to pick my way through the tangled mess. In the end I realised that there was no way through but over, so I clambered up the precarious knot of wood and thorns, jutting twigs and ivy, doing my best not to tear my clothes or my flesh.

I jumped down into a mess of rotten leaves and stagnant mud, then followed the vestiges of the path around a curve that lead to a yard full of abandoned and rusting farm implements, in front of a very old, half-timbered farmhouse that leant alarmingly to one side. Close by, a barn was in the slow process of falling to pieces, its doors lying on the ground and half of its roof caved in. The carcass of a hare lay twisted and desiccated at my feet.

I stepped up to the farmhouse door that hung slightly ajar and crooked on its hinges. I gave it the lightest push and it fell in, sending some catastrophic explosion of flapping, feathers, foul dust and stink into my face. A horde of pigeons flew past me in fright, cooing and whistling their cries of alarm as I reeled back from their onslaught. I coughed and waved my hand to clear the air before me, peering into the swirling dust inside the farmhouse. I stepped onto a floor deeply crusted and wildly uneven with decades of birds' droppings and the carcasses of pigeons and rodents.

A stove sat in the corner, pots and pans hung on the wall, plates still stood on the shelf – and in all of these, every available nook had been recruited for a nesting box. Everything was covered thickly in dust and spattered with the feces of birds. The acrid smell burnt my nose and eyes so that I covered my face with my handkerchief.

Opening a second, inner door to a sort of parlour sent mice scurrying and squeaking for their bolt holes. The bones of a fox rested in a pile of dusty hair and filth. The floor was marked with dark stains here. Some instinct made me think the marks might have been blood. There was something about them that troubled me – a kind of smearing, as though someone had made some effort to scrub them away. In the blackened hearth, amid dusty feathers, and bones of mice, there was a half-burned rag, likewise darkly stained and rigid.

I opened a narrow door to my right and found a small bedroom. The old double bed was lousy with squealing mice and their young and their filth. A cupboard door hung open revealing several women's dresses still on their hangers. There appeared to be two sets here, one for a woman of petite size, the other made for a taller, more curvaceous frame. At my touch one of the dresses fell, and set the others to swinging and swaying. I hurried from the room, jumping to avoid stepping on more dark stains on the floor.

Back in the parlour I noticed a ladder in the corner leading to some kind of loft. I climbed it and had to duck and hold my breath as yet more pigeons flew at my face when I intruded my head into the room. The roof was cracked and the chinks of light illuminated the wooden surfaces a hot, yellowish-red. I covered my face against the smell as the startled pigeons settled down, some walking the floor with rapidly bobbing heads, while others perched nervously on ledges or cracks.

But what I saw on the floor made me freeze. Still visible beneath the thick encrustations and scattered feathers was a large red circle drawn onto the wooden boards. Closer inspection determined that wax had dripped into piles at the cardinal points of the ring. And here again, dark spots and drops of that same hue I had seen downstairs. I could almost smell that the book had been here. Within the circle I noticed then too, other marks in red chalk: strange kabalistic symbols of which I had no knowledge and which I had never seen in the book. I took my notebook from my pocket and hurriedly scratched down the symbols. The birds begun to coo in unison, and the noise soon grew so loud that I had to remove myself.

At the bottom of the ladder once more, I looked around me, frustrated that I could see nothing that would give me any lead as to Greene's whereabouts or any further insights into the book. I jumped at the suggestion of some dark movement in the corner of my eye, my nerves taut. But it was nothing save a bird's feather, drifting down from a gap in the ceiling above. There was something very peculiar though about the spot where it had landed.

Close to the wall I saw a crusted raised line upon the floor. Thick dust coated it, but it looked like salt, nibbled away here and there by tiny mouths but still just as someone had deliberately left it. The wall behind this line was likewise unusual: a shape about the size of a door had been bricked up and very roughly plastered over. From a distance it was little noticeable, but standing this close it was very plain to see. The job was so rough that when I touched the wall a great chunk of plaster fell away, revealing bricklaying of the most rudimentary sort.

I gave tentative push and felt the bricks shift with a grinding and crumbling sound that had clearly sent chunks of mortar falling into a cavity behind. I pushed again, harder this time and recoiled as bricks collapsed inward; into some unseen void and a great cloud of dust flew out at me and made me cough. I tried to blink the wretched coarse stuff out of my eyes and wiped my face as the irritation of it had started my eyes to watering. Involuntarily, I spat out the foul taste of the dust, then wiped my glasses and peered into the void.

Steps led down to some kind of cellar or basement. Light from the parlour I stood in filtered dimly into this lower room through the swirling cloud of dust and particulate debris. The dust began to settle and my eyes, adjusting to the low light, perceived that this was a brick cellar, into which no other light shone. I supposed it had only known darkness these past decades.

I stepped with great caution through the jagged and narrow gap I had made in the doorway. The steps beyond were treacherous with loose bricks and rubble and I stumbled to find my footing, fearful of falling into the darkness. Steadying myself, I surveyed my surroundings. There was nothing here at all. The room was utterly bare. Why in the world would anyone take the trouble to seal up such a space that might easily be of use? I shivered at the cold of the cellar as I descended, swallowing against the bitter taste of the stale air. My footsteps resounded on the old stone floor as I walked around peering into the gloom for a sign of … anything. As I reached the far end of the room, I felt some very slight irregularity under my feet. The cooing of the pigeons above rang in the echoing chamber and I shivered without knowing why.

I felt the floor again with my shoe, then crouched down to test it with my hand. The old flagstones were very smooth and so cold they felt damp. These four stones looked like all the rest, but I was certain they were lying a fraction of an inch higher than the others. It was barely perceptible to the eye, but under my hand the singularity of the thing became clearer. There was movement in the stones as though the ground underneath was slightly uneven. It was but the work of a moment to intrude the blade of my pocket knife between the stones and lever one of them up.

I pulled it out and slid it aside with a heavy scrape. The other three followed. A glint in the dirt drew my hand toward it. Brushing it clean I found a snaking shape that lay half buried there. It was a chain of silver and, as I pulled it out, the crucifix that hung from it arose from its strange grave. The soil, now disturbed, yielded easily to the digging blade of my knife and in only a moment the blade struck something hard below: something hard and hollow.

Furiously I dug, now scraping with my hands to unearth what was hidden. The object was made of wood and was wound around many times with some kind of cord. At last managing to insert my fingers under the painfully tight cord, I pulled and felt the weighty object move; and with its movement I heard objects slide within it. I dragged it out onto the floor.

It was a box of some heavy wood, once painted a very dark green. It was perhaps over sixty centimeters long and just over thirty wide. A narrow red cord was tied around the box some nine times. The entire length of the cord was marked with a series of knots that seemed to form some kind of deliberate pattern: three and seven, then one, one and two. At one end of the lid was affixed a piece of paper, which curved around the side of the box. At both points the paper was fixed to the wood with a large lump of red wax, into which some symbols, not unlike the ones I had observed upstairs, had been roughly scratched. The paper bore the ghosts of other symbols, but was so perished and discoloured I could not distinguish them.

My knife sliced easily through the knotted cord and the rotting paper. I pulled off the lid and squinted into the dark box, not believing what I saw as I knelt low over it. I fumbled to light a match from my Vesta case. Among a great quantity of ash and soot, rested the fragments of many charred bones: recognizable at once were the curved surfaces of two burnt and damaged human skulls and part of a jawbone. These sat huddled together. Nearby I recognized the head of a thigh bone, the disk-like protrusion of a hip, the curve of a rib, and many other fragments too broken to identify: all sat, half-submerged in a deep layer of ash. I gave an exhalation of horror and my breath blew up a tiny puff of ash into the air that made me recoil and drop the match.

The sound of the cooing birds suddenly grew much louder and echoed out of time. The hairs on the back of neck prickled as I felt an icy wind blast into the chamber from behind me with such force that it sent a great cloud of the ash bursting up into the air. I reeled back, crashing onto my side to avoid breathing in the ash as the wind increased, whistling and swirling around the room until it seemed that ash entirely filled the air. I tried to scramble back, feeling the sharp grit of wind-borne bone chips and fragments blasting my face and ash coating my tongue.

Squinting into this cloud that seemed to light up the room with a strange yellow grey glow, I shook my head and

129

tried to cover my mouth from the hideous tornado that had begun to spin violently around me, my ears deafened by the howling of it, as it whistled and groaned in horrible disharmony: underscored by the ever louder cacophony of the birds whose cries seemed to vibrate through my body. Amid this dissonant assault on my senses I strained to hear what sounded like voices faintly calling out but masked by the birds and the tumult of the wind. I shuddered and shrank into the floor at the name I thought they cried: "Solomon." Louder they grew, even as the storm in the room grew wilder: the voices were distorted, surging and failing with overtones and echoes, but recognizably female and so raw with pain and longing that to hear them filled my pounding heart with horror and pity. "Solomon … Solomon …"

My spectacles were thick with dust and blinded me. Behind me I heard footsteps, and around me, from the dark corners of the chamber, from the high ceiling, from the walls, came sounds more real than echoes, that froze me against the stones in terror. In panic, I tore off my glasses. Through the violently spinning fog and the ash storm, through my own eyes that were half-closed and fast filling with the dust of these cremated bodies, I began to see them: glimpses of indistinct shadowy forms that moved on the outskirts of the cloud, almost imperceptible through the opaque air – but every few moments, between the surges of the violent gale, I caught sight of them, obscure shadows clinging to the walls, scurrying upside down across the ceiling, lurking in corners, flying through the air. I could not breathe. I prayed that I would not black out. I felt that my heart was about to burst from my chest with the unbearable force of its hammering.

Then I saw them: two shadowy forms crawling low on the ground, nebulous and featureless, creeping their way towards the box before me. Spindly arms and clawing hands grasped into the box and scrambled to clutch the two fragmentary skulls, now lifting them out and holding them up. One of the shadows pressed its blank black face against the

130

skull, as if to kiss it. The other flew at me, enveloping me in utter darkness so that I screamed and shrieked, gasping in lungfulls of ash that choked me. The broken skull loomed at my face, its terrible empty sockets searching my own: the blackened, half-shattered upper jaw leering its broken and burnt smile into my face. A high plaintive voice thundered through me, the bones of my face vibrating with its power: "Solomon." At the sound, the skull began to disintegrate, cracking and caving in, only centimeters before my eyes.

I screamed and suddenly found my feet scrambling, my hands grabbing for any hold that I might flee from that mad horror. I stumbled blindly towards the stairs, tripping and crawling in a frenzy to escape, falling and slipping over broken bricks, blinded by ash and panic, until at last I crashed through the broken doorway. I fell among the collapsing bricks, but did not stop, clambering on my hands and knees like some mindless animal over that stained wooden floor, finding my feet and running now through the doorway, into the kitchen, where birds exploded into flight around me, bursting out with me into the open air.

I ran past the ramshackle barn and on and on, along the path that I feared would never end. I saw the wall of brambles and hedges that obstructed my way and I leapt at it, hauling myself over it with frenzied abandon, heedless of the sharp prickles and barbs that tore at my flesh. The horses reared and whinnied at the sight of me in my terror, jittering and stamping the ground as I rushed to untie them. I grabbed at the reins and yelled at them to run before I had even fully gained my seat.

At a gallop I flew from that village, my heart still hammering, my mind wild with disbelief and the fear that I had lost my reason. I coughed and spat, almost retching, but could not escape the taste of burnt flesh and bone that polluted my mouth with its ashy grit. Even as the horses raced further and further away from that place, I could not stop looking over my shoulder, terrified that whatever I had unearthed might still be following me. It was some time before I could breathe normally once more. Even then I was alert to every sound, every movement in the landscape around me. It was then that I realised, as I regained myself: the day was as calm and still as it had been earlier. There had been no wind, no gale out here – even in the debris-strewn yard of that abominable farmhouse as I ran from it, all had been quiet and still.

By the time I returned home, the day was growing overcast and dark. Exhausted and still deeply shaken I lurched into the house, thinking only of the decanter of brandy that waited in the morning room. From the doorway I saw Marchelline, slumped in a chair, her back to me as she stared into the empty fireplace. A glass and a near empty bottle rested beside her on the table.

At the sight of me, Maxim, on his perch, gave a wild shriek and flapped his wings. Marchelline's head spun around, her eyes widening as she rose with a start and an exclamation of horror, knocking over the table and sending the glass smashing onto the ground. She seemed to waver, blinking her eyes as though trying not to pass out, the colour draining from her face. "Émile!" she cried, shaking her head. She slumped forward, supporting herself on the chair. "Émile?" she implored through sudden tears, now reaching out, but with her feet frozen to the ground.

"No, no, it is I, Nicolas – do not be afraid!"

I rushed to her and she shrank away, half falling over and crawling behind her chair. It was then that I caught a reflection in the mirror that tore a cry of fright from my own throat. Here was a specter of ashen hue: its face, its garments, its hair, all a deathly powder grey – save for the horror-stricken, red-rimmed eyes that blazed out, and the blood that spread out and down in a dark crimson stain over its chest. Smaller red drops and lines spattered its face, its hands and its legs, from countless scratches and cuts it had incurred.

"Stay away from me," Marchelline whimpered, "in the name of God."

"I – I was in an accident," I lied, desperately fumbling for any explanation. "A miller's cart overturned and lost his load of flour, the horses bolted and I was thrown – into bushes, nettles, I – I am all right, truly."

Marchelline began to wail in the most heart-rending manner. "You smell of death," she slurred through her tears. "And every word you say to me is a lie! Why am I here? Why did you marry me only to deceive me and keep me cooped up here like a bird in a cage? Why can't I stop loving you?"

"No! No, my love."

"Your aunt was here." She gestured towards the tea tray that rested on another table, two sets of used cups and plates telling the story. "She said there is no bleeding illness in your family! It is all lies! What is wrong with you? And what else are you keeping from me?" She sobbed again and collapsed onto the floor, her face buried into the crook of her arm. I edged toward her, smelling the alcohol in her sobbing breaths. "Stay away!" she screamed, not raising her head, "I don't trust you – I am afraid of you! I would run away, but I – I cannot, and I despise myself for it."

Her body shook with sobs, and her misery tore the heart from my chest.

CHAPTER FOURTEEN

I ran outside to the water pump and held my head under the icy water that flowed out as I cranked the handle, wishing that it could cleanse my mind of what I had seen. I stripped off my jacket and waistcoat and even my shirt, tearing off the blood soaked bandaging, desperate to scrub away the unnatural filth that seemed to fill my every pore. The water ran a disgusting pink grey into the drain and the water's chill stung at my senses. My scrubbing hands seemed to find a thousand cuts and scratches and the grit of the ash abraded them so that I feared I might be rubbing the poisonous matter into my open wounds.

"Sir?" I heard Félix's concerned voice behind me. "Are you all right?"

"Yes, thank you Félix," I gasped, afraid to turn around lest he see my chest. "Only Madame De Bresson is very … indisposed: would you ask Madame Grudet to fix her a sleeping draught and help her to bed."

"Of course, Sir," he replied, with something approaching disapproval colouring his voice for the first time since I had known him.

"Thank you Félix, that will be all for now."

I heard him hesitate behind me before he went back inside.

I half-sat, half-collapsed onto the gravel, clutching the wet cement base of the water pump as I shivered with more than cold. What had I done? What had Solomon Henri done?

The ash that still stuck under my fingernails and stung my eyes assured me that what I had seen had been no dream. The acrid smell of charred bone still clung to the inside of my nose and mouth. He must have killed those poor women, his "wives," and buried them there – but why? How could he commit such an atrocity? Had he grown bored with them? Had it all gone wrong, as things with Marchelline were going wrong? Or was it just cruel sport to him to use women so and them dispose of them. In the wrong hands the book might do the most terrible evil. Were mine also the wrong hands?

As rain began to fall, I clutched my balled-up clothes to my chest and ran inside, listening to make sure the way was clear before I crept hastily to my study. I lit the fire and threw my clothes and bandages onto it. My trousers too I pulled off and burned. I could never wear any of them again. Blood dripped down my chest as I trembled before the smoking flames. I grabbed at some clean dressings from my store and redressed my wounds. The long smoking jacket that hung on the back of the door served as a makeshift dressing gown as I sat on the chaise longue before the fire and lit a cigarette, my thoughts racing. I had opened one of Father's prized bottles of port from my cabinet and sat staring into the glass between sips.

Only Gildian Greene knew the truth. Only he could tell me what had happened – what was happening still. I despised myself for the dreadful mess I had made of things. All I had ever wanted was to love Marchelline, to make her happy, but I seemed only capable of upsetting her. All the vivacity and gaiety that had made me love her had been stolen away by my own actions. Why should loving her have to come at such a cost? It was I who had been bewitched, compelled by *her* long before any book had entered our lives. She had bewitched me unwittingly, but bewitched me she had, all the same. Was it so wrong that I had tried to mirror the effect in order to win this divine creature who had claimed my heart so completely? Why did it seem that I was being punished for it? Why was it so hard for her to love me?

I could not accept that there was no way to put things right – to make her happy once more – to let her love for me be a source of joy rather than pain. The alternative was unthinkable: that she should be bound to me, irreversibly, loving me compulsively but living in fear of me and in misery. To condemn her to such an existence – I would give anything to avoid that. I recalled the words of the book: *He who shalle be called can never be released save by the giving of this book, and thereby, thine own fate, into his hands.*

But if I released her, she might not love me at all. She might hate me. She would know then what I had done to win her, what I had done to her lover – and what vengeance might she seek through the book's magic? Impulsive and hot-blooded as she was, my very life might be the price that she would demand in reparation. I could not cross out her name from the book, but could I ... a thought seized hold of me and I rushed to unlock the bureau, twitching and looking over my shoulder as the fire crackled behind me.

I could not destroy the book itself but perhaps ... I opened the book to my own page, hoping that perhaps I might be the first to think of a way to undo the harm and begin again. I seized my page by the top corner and pulled at it, hoping to tear it free. At that very instant the most intense tearing pain incised deep into my throat and my body bent double as blood sprayed from my mouth and gurgled down my windpipe. I saw blood spatter the book and I turned away, staggering, retching, trying to gasp as blood ran down my chin, and sprayed in heavy gouts over the floor as I choked and coughed, unable to breath. In a panic, I pressed the bell, fearful that any instant might be my last if I could not breathe without drowning in my own blood.

Those few seconds until Félix came seemed an agonising eternity. I tried not to black out, knowing that if I did, all would be lost. Félix's eyes revealed his terror, but his steady demeanour never wavered.

136

"Try to sit down, Sir," he urged calmly, guiding me into a chair. "Lean forward if you can, Sir. Spit it out, there, yes, you will be fine, Sir." Seeing my open drawer full of gauze and dressings, Félix grabbed a handful of absorbent material and pressed it into my bloody hand, passing his arm around my shoulder. I felt him tremble. Blood pooled on the wooden floor between my feet, gushing still from my throat in spurts and dribbles that made me cough and sputter so that the fire sizzled with the spray of it. I watched the gauze turn red in my hand, trying to tell myself that the flow was lessening, that it might stop before I expired.

"It's easing, Sir, there. Try to breathe, just a few moments more and it will be over. I shall send for the doctor straight away. All will be well."

With only a little dribble more and a cough or two, it stopped. My throat burned as if scorched by acid. I could barely speak.

"Don't try to talk, Sir. Take a sip of this if you can, it will settle your nerves."

At last I could breathe. The relief of it was immense. I wanted to cry. I looked around the room, at the trail of blood that polluted the floor, the sprays of the vile stuff that stained the walls and furniture. I swallowed painfully, fighting a rising wave of nausea. I knew I must not vomit, lest I start the haemorrhage again.

So the book would not let me escape its hold. Recalling now its other blood-spattered pages, I wondered at my own naivety. I had not tried anything untried before. I could not outsmart the Book of Calling. I had to play by its rules. And there seemed no choice now but to play on. My only other hope was in finding Gildian Greene, if that were even possible.

"There, Sir. You're all right. If you please, I shall send for the doctor."

I stayed Félix's arm as he left my side, shaking my head fiercely, afraid to even try to speak. "But, Sir, you've had a serious haemorrhage – I don't want to speculate where I have

137

no business to, but the consumption, Sir, it might be a sign — "

"No," I rasped in a hoarse whisper, my mind racing to invent some story to appease him. I struggled to speak, "Piece of glass in drink – didn't realise till half swallowed – spat it out – will be fine – a near miss."

Félix nodded uncertainly. "Would you like me to fetch Madame de Bresson, Sir?"

I shook my head emphatically. "Only frighten her," I whispered.

"Then can I get you anything else, Sir, before I clean up the mess?"

"Some clothes, if you would."

Félix nodded and bustled from the room. All this blood might fill my raven quill a thousand times. What could I do with such power? How could I make it serve me better, to fix things and make Marchelline happier? I stared at the spattered floor and my imagination conjured an image in a thick drop of blood that was roughly encircled by dribbled and spattered drops.

After Félix had finished his work and satisfied himself that I was not about to die, I lay on the chaise a long time. He had covered me with a blanket, and left me with some more port and some bread and cheese on a tray in case I felt able to take any food. But I could not eat. All I could do was to think of my beloved. My heart was filled with love for her, as ever it had been. Why could she not see that? I was not so unlovable a man, was I, that life with me could be so utterly intolerable?

She feared she could not trust me. It was true I had lied about the wounds, and I had not told her about the book – but how could I do otherwise? My feelings for her were true. I loved her as truly as any man ever loved. If only she knew what was in my heart …

I drew a small red circle around myself upon the floor, and lit the candles at the cardinal points. Under the chaise, at my left lay a few drops of blood that Félix had missed. I filled the raven's quill and next to Marchelline's name I inscribed the symbol of an eye: *That the subject shalle see thee as thou really art.*

It was the early hours of the morning before I crept to our bedroom, uncertain whether to enter or to leave Marchelline to sleep alone. The new wound had emerged quickly, as I watched my chest in the mirror. How curious it had been to see such a thing happen. And how curious that such a terrible thing should now be a commonplace to me.

I entered the bedroom quietly and got into bed, trying not to disturb my beloved's sleep. In only a moment or two she rolled over, still asleep, and enfolded me with her arm. I relished the tender warmth of her embrace after the horrors the previous day had brought me. My heart expanded with love for her and hopes that the sun might shine brighter upon our future, if only she could see me as I was, in all my love for her. I prayed to God that she might.

Marchelline's chin nuzzled into my neck: the sweet smell of her hair and the silken feel of it a delight that I never tired of. Here, in bed, we had always been at our closest. Without words to complicate things, the loving intimacy we shared had always been our most constant connection.

Marchelline's hand caressed my shoulder and my chest. With desperate longing to be close to her again, I turned to her, holding her in my arms, her face and form merely shapes in the darkness. She moved against me and I touched her face, reveling in the curve of her cheek, the heat of her breath against my hand. She pressed those divine breasts against me and I kissed her. She moaned quietly, holding me tighter, kneading at my buttocks, feeling that I was hard for her and pulling me closer.

I pulled up her nightdress and lowered myself down between her slender thighs, kissing her, tasting her so that she cried out, pulling at my shoulders in her eagerness to have me.

"Love me," she moaned, "I must have you, I must. I

need you. I need you so badly. Please? Please my love?"

I wanted so much to please her, to fill her heart with joy, to make her remember the love and desire that brought us together. I moved over her, kissing her soft belly, caressing her breasts with my hands, my mouth, so that she writhed and sighed for me, reaching down to stroke me, pulling at me, even as she pulled my neck down towards her mouth, biting and sucking at me with fevered passion. I entered her then and she moaned in pleasure, clutching and clawing at me as I moved with her, wrapping her legs around my back.

"I love you, I love you," she gasped into my ear, her fingers curling tightly into my hair, pulling my mouth into hers as if to devour me.

"Oh Marchelline, my love," I whispered with a voice still hoarse, struggling for air, lost in the ecstasy of her.

She rolled me over, straddling me, riding me, her body taut and vibrating with delirious pleasure. Her breaths were jagged, her eyes closed. My eyes adjusted, my pupils dilating to take in the wonder of her beauty. Her long curling hair fell around her shoulders and breasts, moving gently as she rose and fell.

"I love you so much," I whispered, wishing that this moment would never end.

She opened her eyes and looked down at me. Her face, at one moment smiling in raptures of delight, was in the next instant transformed into a grimace of horror. She screamed and scrambled off me, even as I tried to hold onto her. She fell off the bed, crashing, clambering to escape from whatever it was that terrified her so.

"Marchelline! My love? What is the matter?"

"Light!" she shrieked, "Holy Mary, Mother of God, pray for us –"

She fled, running toward the morning room. I followed her, pulling on a dressing gown as I ran. I found her crouched by the dying embers of the fire, a glowing taper in her shaking hand as she struggled to light a candle. Her whole body shook with the tiny breaths that passed so quickly from her flaring nostrils. Her jaw was clenched. She looked like a frightened animal. At last the candle took flame. She would not look at me.

"My darling," I edged closer. She shrank a little from me, turning away. The candle silhouetted her. "What happened? What — "

" — I saw - a ghost," she whispered, placing the candle in its holder upon the mantel, hugging herself tightly. She was quite naked. I took up the rug from the sofa and put it around her. She flinched at my touch

"A ... ghost?" The most terrible sinking feeling struck me in the pit of my stomach.

"When I opened my eyes," she began, her voice shaking. "I saw a black shadow emerging from your chest. Here. It loomed up at me - right into my face - I cannot describe it: it was blackness - faceless death itself. It is Émile; I know it! He cannot rest. He was insane when he died and he cannot understand what has happened. He seeks me still. He will not let me be." Her eyes scanned the room, uneasily searching the corners.

"A shadow?" I swallowed, feeling my mouth dry up and trying not to let my teeth chatter. What might have followed me home?

She looked over her shoulder at me and gave a violent start, covering her eyes with her fists and curling into a ball. "Hail Mary, Full of Grace, The Lord is with thee. Blessed art thou among women, and blessed is the fruit of thy womb, Jesus. Holy Mary, Mother of God, pray for us sinners now, and at the hour of death."

"Marchelline?" I hissed, my body tensing into a rigid knot. "What do you see?" My skin prickled into gooseflesh at her fear.

"A shadow," her tremulous voice was barley audible over her juddering breaths. "Standing behind your left shoulder: a shadow in the shape of a man, faceless, black.

141

Light the lights, Nicolas! Light them all at once or I shall go mad." She began to whimper and sob, praying through her tears, over and over as I rushed to light the lamps. I caught sight of myself in the mirror, but I saw nothing save my own reflection.

She would not open her eyes until I promised her that the darkness had been banished. I kindled the fire and we sat together before it in the reassuring glow of its warmth. But Marchelline would not sit too close to me. She would not close her eyes again that night, nor could she pass more than a few minutes without looking over her shoulder or flashing me a searching, suspicious glance. She could only look at the flames, for in the moving shadows they cast about the room, she perceived form and menace.

After a long silence, Marchelline looked up at me with grave concern in her eyes. "Perhaps it is you that he wants."

"What? Why - why would you say that?"

"You *wished* him dead - didn't you? I don't know why I never realised it before now, but of course you must have, I see that now. You were *glad* that he died."

"Well, I - I can't deny that I wished him to leave us alone but dead? No, I —"

"It is as though the scales had fallen from my eyes," she went on, staring sadly into the flames, a tear dropping onto her cheek. "You wanted to steal me away from him - you always wanted that. That premonition I had, of danger, on that first day that I kept running into you - I was right, but I would not let myself believe it. You were pursuing me even then, weren't you? And you wanted Émile out of the way. The fact that I loved him meant nothing to you - you saw that only as an obstacle to your own happiness."

"No! It - it was fate that brought us together. Émile was unworthy of you - untrue to you - everybody knew it but you."

"You are lying again." An eerie calm fell over her. "You still have not told me the truth about why your chest bleeds so.

142

What really happened to you today? Where did you go? Why is your voice so hoarse, your colour so pale? There is something going on that you are hiding from me – I am more certain of it now than ever before. Can you honestly tell me that you had nothing at all to do with Émile's death?" She fixed me with a stare that seemed to burn into my very soul.

I fell to my knees before her, holding her hands in mine, imploring her with my eyes, but she only looked away. "But how? How could I have done? He was very unwell – as the doctor himself said. Marchelline, my darling, what *could* I be hiding from you – except my fears that I am not good enough, nor lovable enough to make you as happy as you deserve to be? My greatest and most secret fear is that you will stop loving me – that you think me some evil man who wishes to harm you. There is no-one else – there never could be for me. Yes, there is much that neither of us knows about the other – and we have a lifetime ahead of us to discover it. Is there not much about you I do not know, and perhaps things you hide from me for reasons of your own? Can you deny *that*? But if you can see into my heart you must also see how completely I love you. Everything I have done has been born of that love and you cannot – must not – doubt it. Should anything else matter? I would give anything, try anything, to please you – I wish I knew what more I could do. Don't you love me? Is our love not enough?"

Her face twisted in torment and she touched my face gently. "Yes, I do love you, fiercely, uncontrollably, but I am not happy. I can feel how much you love me, I know there is much good in you – but I also feel some great, dark shadow in your heart that terrifies me. I do not trust you. That is the heart of the matter. I know there is no-one else – it is nothing like that – nothing I could explain, but the same feeling of danger I have had from the start. There is darkness in you … evil all around you. What I saw tonight is what I have felt all along. And I know that you cannot – will not – explain it to me. I feel trapped by my love for you in a situation that fills me with

143

some dire foreboding. On the surface everything seems so perfect – but what lies beneath the bandages?"

CHAPTER FIFTEEN

It was only when dawn broke that Marchelline stopped fighting against sleep and dragged herself off to bed. We had passed the intervening hours in uncomfortable silence, which I had tried to fill by refining and copying out the score of The Siren's Tear. She barely seemed to notice me, lost in some serious train of thought that she never seemed able to resolve and would not discuss. Her glass was emptied many times, and just as frequently refilled.

Seeing myself reflected now in her eyes, I began to wonder what kind of man I truly was. If she saw the truth of me and was so deeply disturbed by it – perhaps I *was* cruel and hateful. Perhaps I could not make her happy. Perhaps I really did not deserve her. But I would not know how to let her go, even if I wanted to.

I suppose it was around eight in the morning when I heard some noise in the drive and saw the familiar barouche of aunt Mathilde-Hélène pulling up. Nervous of waking Marchelline, and of what she might say in front of my aunt, I went out into the garden to meet the barouche.

"Oh Nicolas darling, you look most unwell – whatever is the matter, my dear?"

"I am very tired, Aunty," I sighed, taking her arm as I led her around the gardens. She stopped and took me by the shoulders, her kindly face filled with concern.

"I know the difference between the blissful lethargy of happy honeymooners and the nervous exhaustion of one who is sorely troubled. Something is wrong between the two of you, isn't it? I felt it yesterday when I was here with your wife. She seemed very upset by something I said – I hope I have not caused some disharmony, however accidentally."

"No, no you have done nothing wrong. It is I. Whatever I do, I cannot seem to make her happy – and it is all I want to do. I fear I am simply not good enough for her – why could I not realise it before?"

"I can see that she loves you, devotedly, but she does appear … well, distressed in some way. Is she still very upset about this business with the Comte?"

"Well she did see him die in rather dreadful circumstances. "

"Yes, yes, of course. That must have been a most terrible shock – for both of you. Of course she is still mourning, and perhaps still in shock."

"I had thought to bring her here to escape those memories but it seems they are not so easily fled. She thought she saw the Comte's ghost last night. I have not slept since then. She has only just retired herself."

"Oh my dear," Mathilde-Hélène consoled, patting my hand with her lilac glove. "Madame de Bresson spoke very longingly of her life in Paris: her friends, her favourite haunts, the nightlife, the dancing. Perhaps she would be happier to return there, with gaiety and bustling life around her to distract her from these worries."

"Perhaps. If she wished it I would gladly take her back there. I do not know what to do. Everything I try seems to end in disaster."

"Time is the greatest healer," she reassured as we walked by the pond and around into the cool shade of the arbor. "But perhaps not too much time alone to reflect on what has passed. If you think she would enjoy company, the twins would love to see her again – they are quite besotted with her. They are already copying her hairstyle, and asking for dresses like hers. They are very eager to show her off to all of their friends."

We sat down on the little bench beneath the canopy of mauve wisteria blossoms.

"Oh and by the way, did you happen to visit Charpantier's bakery the other day on your errand with Yves? I did wonder why he returned so long before you did. Are you still following that mysterious trail?"

I coloured, nodding.

"And you still will not satisfy your aunt's curiosity by telling me about the matter?"

I smiled at her and shook my head. "I cannot, at present, I'm very sorry."

"But it has something to do with your beautiful wife, I fancy."

"In a way, yes, it does. It is not an insignificant matter, nor one I can discuss without being indiscreet, I fear."

"I can see by your face that it is not. How can I help?"

"All I have to go on now is one more name; Esther Cécille. Does that name mean anything to you?"

"Cécille? No, I never heard of an Esther Cécille. I only know of one Esther – a friend of one of my acquaintances, Madame Dulac. She has once or twice mentioned a friend of hers who joins her at cards sometimes at her house at Moisson. This lady's husband is frequently away, a Madame Esther Verine, or Marine, something like that … oh my memory is not what it was, how intolerable! I have never met the lady myself."

"Could it be Greene?"

"Well, it's possible. Yes, yes, it very well might be. You mentioned a Greene to me before – a Gildian Greene did you not? Won't you give me some crumb, Nicolas – who is this man to you and to your wife?"

"Marchelline lost contact with her father when she was very young," I lied in a confidential whisper. "She remembered a Monsieur Greene who gave her mother money sometimes – an old friend of her father's. Well it's a long shot, but I thought if I could track down her father, it might please her. I know she has often wondered what became of him … Please don't mention any of this to her – it might not lead anywhere. It is just a wild hope."

My aunt nodded thoughtfully. "Well, I shall write down Madame Dulac's address for you if you would like to enquire after her friend. Madame Dulac is a most effusive lady and quite susceptible to a handsome face, so I have no doubt she would tell you all you want to know – and probably much more besides. Oh and the other matter – I thought you would be eager to know, I have some very encouraging news for you. I have had word that my opera connections in Paris are utterly beguiled by those extracts of your opera that you sent them. You should expect to hear from them very soon – so prepare your best material. I know they will love you – and each is very keen to make you his own 'discovery,' I venture. Well, I must go, I only called in tell you the good news, and to invite your wife to come and visit the twins – when she feels up to it of course."

It was not so very late in the morning as I rode into the outskirts of Épône. I had left a note for Marchelline, confidant that she would in all likelihood sleep through most of the day. In truth I was glad to get away. The things she had seen in my heart, and the shadows she had seen around me had disturbed her greatly. I was disturbed too, as much by what had happened in that terrible farmhouse as what had happened when I returned home. I could only hope that Marchelline could see the good, alongside whatever foolish or cruel things I might have done to win her. I prayed that the love I had for her would shine through all of that. If she could not see that, I did not know what else to do. All the hope I had now was in finding Gildian Greene that he might have some answers to the questions that now plagued me without relief.

And this shadow she had seen – the shadows I had seen … the unquiet dead that lingered still: what did they want?

How was I to appease them and free myself from their darkness? At least out here in the warm daylight, such things could not touch me.

I looked again at the directions Madame Dulac had written out for me before I had made my escape from her ceaseless talk. Madame Esther Greene might be my only hope. Madame Dulac had only met her friend's husband only once or twice but the description seemed to fit, and when I asked his name, I knew that I was at last on the trail of my man. "A most unusual name," she said, reaching out to put her hand on my arm, "Gildian Greene: what romance it evokes ... "

I wiped the perspiration from my brow as the horse trotted on below the high azure sky. We rounded a bend in the road and there it was, just as Madame Dulac had described it: a very fine and imposing house with an enormous pitched roof surmounted by two chimneys. Three gable dormer windows gazed out from the roof like unblinking eyes. The house sat back from the road on an expansive lawn, whose well-tended garden beds formed a geometric pattern alive with dazzling blossoms. A more picturesque and inviting home would be hard to imagine.

I paused, now wondering what I might say to Monsieur Greene and how he might receive me. I kicked the horse on, up the sloping lawn towards the welcoming maison whose window frames and door glowed a dazzling white.

Knocking on the door I thought then of Marie-Thérèse Charpantier, whose sweet, pale features shone with such mystery in my mind. If she were not dead, would I find her here, her name changed like her husband's to protect their privacy? If that were the case, how could either of them welcome my intrusion or my questions?

A round-faced little maid answered the door, tucking a stray strand of dark hair behind her ear.

"Good morning, would Monsieur Greene be at home today?" I began, offering my card.

The maid shook her head. "No, Monsieur, the Master is

away."

"Madame Greene then? Is she at home?"

"One moment, if you please." She ushered me into a beautifully appointed front parlour, awash with golden light and radiant with an inviting air of warmth. Delightfully well-executed, still-life paintings depicting the most glorious flowers decorated the walls, and seemed to draw into the room all the vernal vitality that was so evident in the gardens outside.

Habitually, I checked that no blood was showing on my chest as I waited.

"Good morning, Monsieur de Bresson," a pleasant voice greeted me. I looked up to see a well-dressed lady of forty-odd years. Her smile was broad and her eyes full of kindness. But this was not the face of Marie-Thérèse Charpantier. Her complexion was olive and her hair a deep chestnut brown, threaded with a little grey. I rose and offered my hand.

"I am so sorry that my husband is not at home today," she effused, laugh lines softening her features. "Can I be of any assistance to you Monsieur?" She gestured for me to resume my seat as she took hers. A large, grey, longhaired cat wandered into the room and jumped onto the sofa beside her, walking around in circles with its bushy tail in the air as she petted it absently.

"Well, Madame, I hardly know where to begin, "I flustered. I took a deep breath. "Your husband suffers from … wounds on his chest that will not heal?" I ventured, studying my hostess' face. She frowned slightly and shifted in her seat.

" … Yes," she answered, some little note of caution in her voice.

"I met Monsieur Greene recently in Paris – it seems that we suffer from the same condition. I was hoping to renew our friendship that I might seek further of his advice."

At this, her face fell alarmingly, the mask of hospitality falling away to reveal some terrible sadness and worry. "My husband is in Paris today, seeing his doctor, Monsieur. I am afraid he suffered an attack last night." She tried to smile, as if to reassure herself as much as me. I felt my stomach tighten.

"An attack?"

"During the night, I heard him screaming in his room – the most dreadful commotion, as if he were fighting off some violent assault. The door was locked; I feared intruders, or – well, I did not know what to think. At last he came to the door, breathless, wild-eyed, bloody from where he had clawed off his own bandages. But there was no-one else in the room. He said he had had a nightmare, but I am concerned it may have been some sort of fit. He was very much distressed and did not wish to speak of it – he does not like to worry me. I pray it is only a temporary setback. It is most upsetting because we had thought his condition was improving these last months – we had thought his illness might at last be in some remission ..." She patted the cat's insistently demanding head, lost in thought as he purred at her.

"I see," I lied, more confused than ever. "So your husband's condition, it is a serious one then?"

Madame Greene looked up at me, her eyes moistening. She gave a slow, small nod.

"I hope you will forgive all these questions," I went on, "only I know no-one else who might answer them. Your husband is my only hope, and he had not time to discuss my condition more fully when last we met. I am in the dark and quite afraid, Madame. No-one else has been able to tell me anything. But this doctor, of your husband's – he has been of some assistance?"

She wiped at her eyes with her hand, composing herself. "Yes, Monsieur Greene has been consulting him for some years now, on and off. My husband says Dr Palissandro is the only one who understands. I take it he is a specialist in these rare tropical diseases. Perhaps he could help you too."

"I should like that very much. If you would be kind enough to give me his name and address, I would be exceedingly grateful."

151

"Of course." Madame Greene moved to a little table and wrote the details neatly on a small slip of paper.

"Have you and Monsieur Greene been married a very long time?" I asked, trying to sound conversational.

She smiled. "Oh yes, twenty-two years this August: twenty-two wonderful years. He really is the most kind and loving man."

"May I ask how you met?"

Her eyes crinkled in fond remembrance and she almost chuckled to herself. "I was sailing to America with my mother and father and my sister. I glimpsed Gildian a few times around the ship: this mysterious and haunted figure avoiding all company – but so handsome, so sad and intriguing. He was a young widower, you see, and very afraid to love again. He resisted me for a while, but … ah, I do like to have my way. In the end I won him over. We were engaged the day before the ship reached New York. What a party it was that night on the ship …"

"Did your husband suffer from his condition even back then?"

"Oh yes, the illness had first struck him some years earlier I believe. He had been travelling in the tropics – well, I'm sure his story is similar to your own, if you are afflicted by the same tropical parasites. He blamed himself for his first wife's death – fearing that somehow he had infected her too. But of course he had nothing to do with it – it was simply a terrible accident: a runaway carriage I understand. In his grief he thought himself disfigured, cursed even. But such things are of little consequence when you love someone. His illness has never mattered to me – other than that I hate to see him suffer and I worry about his health. Are you married, Monsieur de Bresson?"

"Yes, only a month or so ago." I forced a smile. Madame Greene studied my eyes and smiled at me with great kindness as she handed me the piece of paper.

"I'm sure your wife feels the same as I do. However it

might worry *you*, she sees you with the eyes of love, and love does not see such little blemishes as yours and my husband's. Who in this world is without a blemish of one kind or another?"

'Yes, yes, I hope you are right."

"You are very desperate to find some remedy, but do not make that dream your only hope of happiness. Even if no cure is possible, you might still have many years of good health before … well, do not waste the time you have chasing something you might not find. As I used to say to Gildian when we were first married – 'I would rather have ten happy years with you than a lifetime with anyone else.' In any case it was many years before the tumours started with Gildian."

"Tumours? Whatever do you mean, Madame?"

"Oh, Monsieur, forgive me – I assumed you would know? The same parasites that cause the wounds – well, over time, they begin to cause a dangerous illness: this is what my husband has been suffering from; what is making him so ill. I thought he would have told you. I can see that I have alarmed you. I am very sorry. You may have many decades of good health ahead before — "

" — I … I did not know … I — "

"Please do not despair, Monsieur de Bresson. As I said, this doctor seemed to be helping Gildian. He has been so much better these last few months. Last night's attack may have been nothing but a particularly vivid nightmare, as my husband said. It might be completely unconnected to his illness. That is my most fervent hope. Perhaps I am worrying over nothing. Go and see Dr Palissandro for yourself and see what he has to say. He is the only expert in this matter. I know so little – Gildian keeps the details from me to spare my nerves."

"Yes, yes I shall see him at once. Please Madame Greene, might I leave a note for your husband, leaving my address and so on? I do so desperately wish to speak to him of these matters – as one sufferer to another, you understand."

"By all means, please do." She stood and gestured me to

153

the little table, where notepaper was laid out, and a pen and ink waited close by, all upon a blotter of dark green leather, edged in gold. "I will leave you to your privacy." The cat rubbed against the hem of her skirts, then trotted after her as she walked away.

Dear Monsieur Greene, or Henri – I know not which is your real name.

I must see you urgently. Your wretched book has brought me nothing but misfortune and unhappiness, and now your wife informs me that whatever causes the wounds on my chest may also give me some fatal disease – I demand to know what you have done to me.

I need answers and only you can provide them. If I am doing something wrong with the book you must tell me how to put it right. I won the woman I love but it has been at the cost of her own happiness.

I know about the burnt skeletons in the farmhouse at Farceaux. I have seen the shadows shaped like men and been terrorized by things I do not understand. Please Monsieur, I am begging you to help me before my life and my wife's are forever destroyed by this book.

I do not know if your wife would believe the things I have to say, but do not doubt that I would even resort to such blackmail if you force my hand by ignoring this letter.

You put me into this position – you owe me at least some answers.

I await your reply,
Nicolas de Bresson.

Securing the letter with a stick of red sealing wax from a tray on the desk, I was impressing my signet ring into the molten wax as Madame Greene re-entered.

"I shall set it here on the mantel, so that Monsieur Greene sees it as soon as he returns," she stated, taking the letter with some reverence. She turned back from the mantel, intertwining her now empty hands. "I wish I knew when that would be. I am accustomed to my husband being away at times, but when his health is in question I do worry about him terribly."

I nodded and moved towards the door. My hostess followed me. I stopped and faced her.

"May I ask you a personal question, Madame?"

She looked puzzled but nodded sympathetically.

"You and Monsieur Greene – you said you have been happy together. Has your marriage truly been a happy one?"

"Oh yes, so very happy. We are devoted to one another. I could not imagine my life without him. I do not wish to. Don't allow your illness to get in the way of your happiness – it need not."

"Thank you Madame, you have been more than kind," I said, crossing the threshold.

"I wish you and your bride as much happiness as we have enjoyed, and may God bless you always."

CHAPTER SIXTEEN

By the time I was nearing home again I was dizzy with hunger and fatigue. I suddenly realised that I had not eaten since before my ordeal in the farmhouse, nor had I slept. I had been terrified too many times in the past day and I had lost a lot of blood in my hemorrhage. The terrible suggestions that Madame Greene had planted in my mind of a future that lay before me filled with disease, pain and an early death had made me sick to my stomach. I could barely think.

All the hope I had now was in the fact that she and her husband had found happiness through the book – and that perhaps this Dr Palissandro had some answers to the anguished questions that were ripping my nerves to shreds.

I was slumped in the saddle by the time the horse stopped itself outside the house. I slid off the horse, almost collapsing to the ground on my weak knees. I dragged myself inside and sank into the sofa of the morning room, grateful that a small fire burned and the lamps were lit as the evening began to close in and the heat of the day dissipated into a maudlin chill that seemed to numb my bones and my mind.

In a moment I was asleep, running through swirling clouds of ash, striving to find something I was only barely aware of. Through the grey and gritty haze I perceived the outline of a door, a brown shape in this realm of cloudy white. Squinting against the abrasive wind, I found the doorknob and turned it, opening the heavy wooden door into a room I recognized.

It was Gildian Greene's parlour in Paris. Lamps burned low in the room. Every surface was thick with dust and covers obscured much of the furniture, but I felt reassured that here I would find the answer I sought. I hastened to the far end of the room where the tall, sinuously carved bookcase towered up over my head. The silver key was already in my hand – I had somehow had it with me all along – and I unlocked the fine glass door that swung open with the slightest of creaks.

Here was the gap from whence Monsieur Greene had removed the Book of Calling and alongside this void another book sat – almost identical but its binding was of a deep, cool blue-green leather, inscribed with silver swirls instead of gold. I took it down and felt the most wonderful sense of anticipation. Somehow it seemed to smell like rain. Here on the first page I read the words I had been longing to find.

Know thee,
I am the Book of Release.
All thy sorrows are mine to resolve
All thy cares are as soon to be dissipated
As the rain.
Give me thy burthen
Written in tears
And as soon as dried they shalle be no more.

I turned a page and saw that a beautiful white feather quill rested there. The book's pages were clean and blank. With joy in my heart I felt tears well in my eyes that some remedy was at last within my grasp to right the awful wrongs I had done. I filled the quill, catching my tears as they rolled down my cheek and I began to write on the empty page, pouring out my sins and the harm I had done to the woman I loved.

And even as I looked at the faint words I had formed, they disappeared before my eyes and the crushing weight lifted from my heart. The book's pages glowed white, and the glow increased until all the room shone, luminous, pure and clean. And no more did I smell blood, but clean, fresh air, as after a rain shower.

I unbuttoned my shirt and looked down upon my chest, once more as smooth and unblemished as it had been before. My tears fell upon the unblemished flesh, running down my skin like a baptism into a new, unstained life. Joy filled my heart and hope returned to my mind. All at once I heard again the tapping at the window and the sound of a wind rising outside. I felt the chill of cool air upon my bare chest and turned to see the curtains blowing and slowly waving as the wind invaded the room. It was cold, and the chill on my chest made me shiver, but even so, I did not wish to cover myself up anymore.

I shivered and opened my eyes. My face was turned toward the window and, outside, the queer half-light made me wonder whether it was dusk or dawn. I was disoriented and unsure of how long I had slept. My chest did feel cold. I turned to face the fire and was startled to see Marchelline standing, swaying unsteadily before me: her face looked distorted and strange.

"So this is what you have been hiding all this while?" she said, her voice a hoarse whisper that I barely recognized. She made a gesture at my chest. Instinctively my hand went up to the level of my bandages but found instead only bare, wet skin. The raw raised weals felt obscenely exposed under my fingertips. I made a noise and gasped a great gulp of air.

"This is what you did not wish me to see," she whimpered, her face tormented in a dreadful frown of incomprehension. She looked at her fingertips, red with my blood and I heard her breaths quicken as she frantically wiped her hands on her nightgown. A pulse pounded in my head and I felt the blood run quicker from my wounds. She turned to look as the drops ran down and I saw her eyes watering as she fought to suppress the sickness and horror she felt. Her eyelids clenched shut and she tried to take a breath. "These symbols," she began, fighting to maintain her composure, "they are magic symbols, are they not? Marks of evil, of the devil, burned into your flesh?"

"Marchelline – please – no –you misunderstand! I – "

" – No, I do understand, God help me. I love you and – and I didn't want to know, but I had to know, I had to see you as you really are – even if only for a moment: to prove to myself that I am not going mad."

"I did it to myself," I lied, "I have cut myself because I hate myself and the unhappiness I cause you."

She shook her head. "No. It is the lies that make me so unhappy. The lies that have always stood between us and they are all bound up with this." She opened her eyes and peeked at the bleeding wounds, covering her mouth with her hand. "I know this is black magic," she murmured into her hand, "and somehow I am enmeshed in it – me and Émile and you: it is all bound up to this."

"No, no my darling. Please – "

"Save your words, my love. They can change nothing now. Your flesh has told me all that my fears had long suspected. I want to stop loving you, but I can't. I want to run away from this, but I can't. Even as I fear you and dread to think what this means – I simply can't leave you. And now we must keep lying to ourselves and each other, because feeling as I do, I know that hearing any more of the truth of this would destroy me.

"My instincts have always warned me of some danger connected to you. Now I know for certain that my instincts were right and where does it leave me? I loved Émile knowing his reputation and trying to convince myself that I would be the one to win his heart completely – even as my instincts told me that he was untrue. I still loved him. I still *love* him. Perhaps he too would have destroyed me in time. Even at my happiest with him, I feared that. But this is different. I feared for my heart with Émile, but I fear for my life with you. You are tied up with danger and death: Émile's death and mine.

Yet I still love you, God help me, and there is nothing I can do about it. So what difference does it make now, how or why or what you have done, or what you may yet do? My heart chains me to you – danger, fear, death and all ..."

Restlessly she began to move about the room, unsteadiness in her gait as she turned up each lamp, one after another. "So let us have light and let us drink, until our protesting thoughts are silenced, until our minds our numbed and only our hearts are still awake. And when we are drunk let us make love – for that is the only truth it seems that you and I can share now. I need you in some way that I have never needed anyone before. I love you compulsively and against all reason, and I hate myself for it. Why couldn't you just be honest with me from the beginning? Why did you have to catch me with your lies and deceptions? Why do have to spoil things by being – being ... you ... ?"

"Oh Marchelline, please, don't hate me, I have been foolish yes, but I love you more than anything. I have never meant you any harm – never."

"Now I have stolen a glance at what you have been so careful to hide, and now I have to live with that. Perhaps it is only fair that I tell you my secret too. Perhaps it will make you despise me and then – maybe you can tell me how we are to go on from here, because I do not know."

"Don't do this, my love – we needn't be this way – let us not –"

" – I told you I did not want children, but you never asked me why. Did you fear what I might say? Perhaps your own instinct warned you not to press me, for it is not a pretty story. I had a child when I was just thirteen. I never even realised I was with child until it came. I was so scared, ashamed, and the pain and the blood ... the blood terrified me. I thought I was dying. I think that was when my terror of blood began.

"I gave the baby away – I had to, for how could I look after her when I was struggling to look after myself? Mother was very ill, drinking, not often at home. She would have thrown me out. Afterwards, when I knew more, I got rid of three others before they could ever be born – a woman in the backstreets did it for a fee. The last time nearly killed me and left me barren. There was so much blood. And I knew then more keenly that my death was to be tied to blood. I was given the last rites. The priest's eyes were so cold. He knew what I had done and in his heart he condemned me for it. I thought then that if he condemned me, God must too and that I was being punished for the lives I had taken. But I survived."

For a long moment I could say nothing but stared at her in disbelief. I knew her childhood had been impoverished but I had never dreamed of … this. The thought of her, young and suffering such horrors filled me with pity, even as part of me flinched in disgust at her story. "Oh darling, I had no idea, I am so sorry —"

"Don't misunderstand me – I never sold myself. We were desperately poor but I always had my singing to earn a franc on the street-corners. But I had no father – I was wild, unsupervised and I longed for affection and love. Mother was always out or unconscious. There was no shortage of men eager to offer what I sought – even if only for an hour, sometimes with the promise of food or drink, or a friend of a friend who might put me on the stage."

"But you were … taken advantage of."

"Was I? None of them ever did anything against my will. I used them for whatever I could get, just as they used me. Perhaps you will think that makes me a whore."

"No, no." I leaned forward, hearing my voice rise horribly, my head in my hands, my heart aching. I heard Marchelline fill her glass once more and drink it down.

"But you cannot look at me now," she went on. "Am I soiled in your eyes? Stained with the hidden blood of those innocents? Stained by the dirty hands of all those men? Do my secrets horrify you? Are you afraid of me now? Do you hate the one you love now – even just a little? How can you go on?

161

How can I? How stained and soiled we both are beneath the surface – the surfaces we both fell in love with."

Overwhelmed, exhausted beyond endurance, I began to weep.

"You wonder why I fear ghosts so much?" she asked in a voice weary beyond imagining. "It is because there are so many I have been running from all my life – and now my poor Émile too. I had thought to escape them all with you, but perhaps it is you who will deliver me to *them*. Perhaps you are my punishment, and that is why I sought you out ...""

Exhausted, I fell asleep on the sofa and passed a restless night, half-awoken many times by the clinking of Marchelline's glass against the neck of the bottle. The hoarse, slurring lilt of her voice entered my dreams, and I stirred more than once to hear her singing quietly to Maxim, whom I glimpsed, perched and swaying on the arm of her chair, all the lamps ablaze around them through the night.

If you knew I was yours
If you only saw me as I am
If you could hear my song
Would you
Would you love me then?

I awoke in the early morning to find that Marchelline had at last gone to bed. Empty bottles littered the tables, and wine was puddled around an empty glass. My shirt was wet with blood, and blood stained the sofa rug, where I had lain upon it. Exhausted from the night's exertions, Maxim slept upon his perch, his head turned back and his beak tucked into his feathers.

I fetched some clean clothes and dressed my wounds and myself, before forcing myself to eat some of the breakfast that the increasingly disapproving Madame Grudet had provided. I had little appetite, but knew I must keep up my strength. I was sitting, tired and brooding in the arbor when Félix brought my letters on a tray.

Dear M. de Bresson,

It was with great excitement that I read the synopsis of your opera "The Siren's Tear" and with even greater delight that I read the extracts therefrom that you so kindly sent to me. I cannot remember the last time a new work dazzled me with such original and bewitching musicality and such a captivating story.

I should very much like to meet with you, and I am most eager to hear more of your opera, at your earliest convenience. It is not often that work of this quality arrives on my desk and I would like to assure you, that should you choose to allow us the honour of producing your work, the Paris Opera has all the resources required to do justice to a debut work of such importance as "The Siren's Tear."

I eagerly await your reply,
Claude-Marie Combet.

Another envelope contained an almost identical letter from Monsieur Alati
of the Opera National Lyrique. My life's greatest and most enduring goal was now within my grasp. I should have been overjoyed. But all I felt was grief and self-loathing.

I *had* to fix it – if there any way possible, or I could never live with myself.

CHAPTER SEVENTEEN

I knocked on a black door in an insalubrious Paris street, my balled-up fists white with anxiety.

At last the door opened a crack and an old face peered through it: large grey eyes, like an owl's, silently taking me in.

"I need to see Dr Palissandro," I began, "I do not have an appointment, but it is a matter of some urgency."

The owl-like face did not speak, but pursed its lips and uttered only a guttural knowing sound from the back of a wrinkled throat. The door opened and a long, sinuous hand beckoned me inside. The old man smiled: his nostrils flaring quickly as though he were smelling something in the air.

The gentleman looked very old – perhaps seventy, or more. He was very tall but bent and crooked of limb. His long face was deeply lined, and his huge eyes heavily lidded. Straight, grey-white hair streamed from his head, down past his shoulders. Over an old suit of some worn, dark brown stuff, he wore a curious robe or housecoat of dark blue that gave off a strange odour of chemicals. He closed the door and extended his long hand out towards me. It was then that I noticed the immoderate length of his fingernails and felt them scratch my palm as his hand clasped my own.

"I am Dr Johannes Palissandro, how may I be of service to you, Monsieur?"

"You know a Monsieur Gildian Greene, do you not? He is one of your patients?"

The doctor eyed me up and down, then turned away

164

and walked off down a dark corridor as he spoke in his slow and strangely accented voice.

"I suggest that you are troubled by something you have read, Monsieur de Bresson – a certain book. Am I correct?"

"Yes – but how do you know my name?"

"Monsieur Greene told me about you." He smiled over his shoulder, then lead me into a small dim room, crowded with books, stuffed animals and curiosities of every imaginable variety. Scientific equipment jostled for space on crowded shelves against piles of papers, boxes, strange paperweights made of glass, anatomical specimens and jars filled with dried herbs and powders.

A moth-eaten and ancient black cat glared at me with yellow-eyed suspicion and slunk from the armchair upon which the doctor directed me to sit. The cat jumped onto a high shelf and jangled the chimes of some obscure musical instrument, before settling to stare down upon me like a malevolent gargoyle.

"He did? But – "

"Yes, the oath you took. I understand your concerns. But it is all right – for I have taken such an oath myself. That makes us like brothers, bound by our blood to the book. I understand all. I have been able to help Monsieur Greene and I am certain I may help you also. Why don't you tell me all about it ..."

I poured out my story of the book and all I had done with it, while the doctor merely listening, nodding now and then as he gazed impassively into my face – all the while, his large eyes blinking slowly. The relief I felt to unburden myself of these most dreadful secrets was greater than I had imagined possible. My body had been clenched into a tight knot, but as I gave my confession and saw that he was not shocked by it, nor reproving of me, I began to feel that here might be some small hope at last.

"And now I learn from Madame Greene that I may contract some dreadful illness and die because of the book. I

165

am at my wit's end, Doctor! I fear I have destroyed not only my wife's life, but my own as well. What can I do? Is there any way to fix this, or is it already too late? Please, won't you tell me?"

He paused a moment, a kindly look on his face. "It is really nothing so very dreadful," he reassured in a soothing low tone, "and nothing that cannot be set right. Madame Greene was not correct in what she said. I can only assume that Monsieur Greene invented that, along with his other explanations concerning tropical diseases and what have you. Perhaps you have told similar stories to your own wife to ... protect your own privacy, and the book's." He smiled. "It is certainly true that Monsieur Green was very ill, but it is also true that with my help he has begun to make a full recovery. "

"But the attack he suffered the other night? What of that?"

"He has the most dreadful nightmares at times," the Doctor explained, an expression of grave sympathy on his face. "His first efforts with the book lead to some rather regrettable incidents that he finds hard to put from his mind. The Book of Calling is a very powerful tool," he explained, "and unhappily it does not come with clearer instructions for the uninitiated. Most of the adverse effects experienced are caused through incorrect usage of the book. The mistake that novice users make is in using the book too infrequently – and too timidly."

I suppose my suspicion and doubt showed on my face, for Dr Palissandro leaned forward and began to explain in a reassuring tone.

"Let me draw an analogy for you, Monsieur. Let us say you bought a very spirited horse to ride, to take you where you desired to go at your command. If you were frightened of this horse and only rode it once or twice, would you be surprised that it did not easily follow your commands, or that it cantered when you wanted it to walk, or even took you somewhere you did not wish to go, or threw you off?"

166

"Well, no, I don't suppose I would, but — "

"The book is no mere thing of paper and cloth, as you must realise. It has a life-force and an energy of its own – you feed that power with your own blood. To become its true master you must use the book much more frequently and with determination and authority. Did you know that some of the symbols can be combined to create more subtle effects? That is where your answer lies. The book has brought great happiness to Monsieur Greene and his wife, as I am sure you are aware: his life is content and he realised he no longer needed its help – as demonstrated by the fact that he chose to give the book away to you. There is no reason it cannot bring the same contentment to you – if you wish it, and if you are willing to try what I suggest. "

"But the wounds, the bleeding? If I use it more I — "

Dr Palissandro held up his long hand to arrest me and rose to his full height. He walked towards me, unbuttoning the top buttons of his shirt until he had exposed part of his chest as he towered over me.

"Do you see?" he asked, gesturing at his pale, sagging skin and the grey-white wiry hairs that threaded it. Faint silvery purple lines formed faded symbols on his skin, but there was no blood at all. The weals looked old and completely healed, if not altogether vanished.

"How?"

"If you follow my instructions, as Monsieur Greene has done. The fact that you have come to me so young, so early in your career with the book will go very much in your favour. You might avoid some of the pitfalls experienced by Monsieur Greene. I understand that he had many years of … misfortune and unhappiness before he found me."

"And the shadows? Can you tell me what they are? Am I in any danger from them? How can I get rid of them? My wife is terrified."

Dr Palissandro smiled and almost laughed. "A most common hallucination, Monsieur, simply another effect of

167

improper usage of the book. Your wife has been affected by them too because she is also connected to the book. The illusion of shadows or ghosts is your own mind manifesting its fears and uncertainties. The book manifests will, thought – these shadows are nothing but your own fears, the shadows in your own psyche confronting you. These hallucinations and your wife's unhappiness are things we can easily remedy."

"I cannot tell you my relief to hear that. I will do whatever you advise, Doctor, only I must do something to help my wife, she is so desperately unhappy. I cannot bear to see her suffer this way – I am so worried about her."

"Very well," he began, walking about the tiny room, somehow avoiding all the many obstacles and precarious piles of objects that seemed poised to topple at any moment. He opened a drawer and produced a piece of parchment and a bottle of black ink and a pen that seemed infused with the smell of whatever herbs perfumed the room with their queer odour. These he placed before me on a little side table.

"Now, look into your heart, Monsieur de Bresson. In all honesty – and you must be honest now – write down upon the paper what is that you desire most in this world – omitting nothing. Everything you wish for, and from whom, if you know. It matters not how magnanimous or how selfish your wishes, how kind or cruel, but you must write them all here, now. You must admit your own desires to yourself and own them, lest they own you. It is all possible – anything you desire, anything at all. And if you are to truly master the book you must give free reign to all of your desires: you *must*."

It was an hour or two later that I finally emerged from Dr Palissandro's darkened rooms into the daylight, with a long list of symbols in various combinations tucked securely into my pocket. As I had written out my list of wishes, some I had barely even acknowledged to myself before, he stood at my shoulder urging me on, encouraging me with his quiet utterances of: "Yes, very good;" or "Yes, the book can give you

168

this so easily;" or , "Why should you not have all that you desire? It is possible, you deserve it;" "Go further;" "Try for more;" "All this is yours if you will only claim it, boldly."

It seemed as though a great weight had been lifted from my shoulders, and I saw in the warm spring day that all was indeed possible. My life, that had seemed so damaged and dark, might bloom anew now and only grow and be filled with greater wonders if I seized this chance that fate had put before me.

With unaccustomed confidence I made my way to the offices of Monsieur Combet at the grand opera house and for the first time I thought it conceivable that I could stand here as a composer – the equal of those who had come before me. They were not gods, nor some rarified breed of creatures, greater than myself – they were men like me, filled with the same yearnings that I had: the longing to create and to express all the creativity that filled their spirits into music that would stir the souls of others. In that great chain of creation, I could form another link, if only I seized the chance and allowed myself to follow my heart.

I climbed the great staircase knowing it would happen – almost as though it had happened already. Even as I shook Monsieur Combet's hand I knew that I would be shaking it again on a night not so far distant, when my opera would fill this magnificent house with music and people. Even as I played for him sections of the score, I knew that I would soon hear them again, played by his orchestra, sung by his finest singers. I could have it all – whatever I wanted – but most of all, I could make Marchelline happy again. I *would* do it.

It was near dark when I returned home. I was not surprised to find Marchelline still asleep in bed. I took off my shoes and crept in beside her, laying close to her, looking down upon her angelic face. I brushed a curling tendril of her dark brown hair away from her forehead. How peaceful she looked.

I thought then of her radiant smile, her exuberant spirit – the way I had first seen her on the stage, and afterwards at The Silver Key and Claudine's, when she seemed so happy, so full of life and joy. More than anything, I wanted to see her that way once more.

My opera would soon be staged. I knew I could be the kind of man that she would admire. She would be proud of me then. And how sublime success would be with her at my side. It was all possible, and I had to make it happen.

She stirred, unconsciously putting her arms around me and nestling close. I kissed her cheek and she half-opened her eyes. Her gaze seemed glassy and unfocussed as she looked at me.

"I want to hold you forever," I whispered into her ear.

"I wish you could." Her eyes flashed and she flinched violently in my arms with a cry. "I can see it again – the shadow behind your shoulder."

"Close your eyes, my darling. There is nothing here to harm you. I am here." I held her tenderly and kissed her cheeks, her eyelids, her throat. "There is nothing in the shadows but your own fears. There is nothing in the dark but you and I. I will not let anything harm you. I will show you that the dark conceals no menace but only tenderness and love. These shadows that have come between us, I will banish. This I will do and more, because I love you. Whatever I must do to prove that to you, I swear I will do it."

With her eyes shut fast, she clutched at me, kissing me ardently, clawing and pulling at me with such desperate vehemence that I feared she would crush the air from my lungs. But I cared not for myself. I only longed to possess her, to please her, to make her cry my name that I may have reason to hope that she loved me still and would love me better again.

Afterwards I held her until she fell asleep again. I wandered out into the morning room, where Madame Grudet had lit the lamps and set out a cold collation for our supper. I tried to eat and petted Maxim in his cage. I moved to the window, listening to the sounds of frogs and insects in the still and quiet of the evening. A small fire burned in the hearth and alike in my study, whence I soon found myself drawn, sitting on the chaise, contemplating the list that Dr Palissandro had written up for me.

His explanations had made such sense. The relationships he described between the symbols when used in particular combinations seemed to offer all that was missing from the key in the front of Book of Calling. One group of three symbols promised "to fill the heart with joy." Another tantalized with its promise of "acceptance and admiration." A combination of two other symbols would act "to dispel fear," others yet "to increase love."

Further down the page he had set out other clusters in answer to my other wishes: "to bring adulation and respect," "to ensure success and fortune." And so the list went on.

I could wait not a moment longer. Marchelline had suffered enough from my inept blundering. I cleared a space on the floor and laid out the candles and cast the ritual circle of red chalk. The wind chime in the arbor began to jingle distantly, and I heard the trees give little shivers in the breeze. I completed the invocation, bearing in mind the words of Dr Palissandro, that I approach the book always with authority and certainty of my own will, undaunted by my own fears.

The wind picked up as I filled the raven's quill from my running wounds. Now, again, I fancied that the wind distorted the sounds of insects and frogs until they seemed to speak with uncanny inhuman tones. "Who is to be called?" Her name already written, I merely whispered it aloud, but ere I had begun to speak, that wild, windy massed voice stole the name from my lips. "How to be called?" the voice demanded in a moan that seemed to be coloured with pain and fury. The windows rattled and whistled. I knelt to write, trying to ignore now those illusory shadows that seemed to loom in the periphery of my sight as I formed my blood into the first three

171

shapes. I refilled the quill, ignoring the dark movements I half-glimpsed at the window pane.

It could only be the tree waving in the wind. There was no malignant black figure there – there could not be – it was nothing but an illusion. I would not look at it, any more than I would admit my own fears now. And as I wrote, more of those shadows of my fears seemed to coalesce into the dark corners of the room, swaying, flickering, but I would not look.

The noise of the wind was beginning to alarm me, and those shadows to unnerve me so that I had to focus all of my will on completing the symbols. Logs crackled and shifted in the fireplace and the flames danced wildly. I could not be shaken now; I had to hang on to my determination to master the book, for *her* sake.

I felt perspiration running into my eyes as I marshaled all of my concentration into the bloody shapes that I scratched onto the page. There was a creak behind me. I dared not turn for fear of what my mind might conjure. I had to finish my work.

"Oh dear god in Heaven!" Marchelline's voice cried from the doorway behind me in a tone of shock and despair that struck like a knife in my heart. I could not turn around, I was frozen there upon my knees, caught in the act of bewitching her.

"It is you – you are calling them – see how they surround you, my God! Holy Mother! What have you done? What is this necromancy? It is worse than ever I feared. This can be nothing but damnation – the death of us both!"

"Get out Marchelline! You do not understand!" A searing pain scorched across my chest and up my neck and I shrieked with the shock of it, clutching at my throat and collapsing onto the floor.

"Our Father who art in Heaven," Marchelline cried over the tumult of the wind and my whimpers of pain, charging into the room, shrieking and knocking over and extinguishing the candles in her path and snatching up the book before I could stop her.

"No! Put it down!" I screamed, looking up at her imploringly as she stood over me, staring at the open book in horror.

"This is *my* name, and Émile's!" I could see some thought resolving in her mind. " ... No – no! *You* did it – you did it all," she whimpered. She slammed shut the book, a look of fury on her face. "No!" she yelled, flinging the book into the fireplace. With an explosion of wind and a terrible crack, the book was thrown violently back onto the hearth the instant it touched the flames. At that same instant, some feet away, flames, springing from out of nowhere, burst from the hem of Marchelline's nightdress and licked rapidly upwards. She shrieked and jumped back, but could not escape the fire that was engulfing her. I leapt up, grabbing the rolled up rug and pulling it over her, forcing her down, struggling, screaming onto the floor beneath me.

For a second all was still, then she began to shake forcefully and to cry in pain, hyperventilating as she tried to pray, "Our F–father, who art in, art in H–Heaven ..." I heard running steps approaching and looked up to see Félix's terrified face peering in at me from the doorway, a lamp in his hand. I rose, on shaky legs, seeing Marchelline now below me, shuddering and deathly pale in the chink of light from the doorway. The pain in my neck and chest surged again and for a second I though myself about to lose consciousness. Then with strange relief I felt the flow of hot liquid running from my neck and all across my chest. Félix blanched, horror in his eyes as he looked at me and then at Marchelline upon the floor.

"I – I shall go for the doctor at once, Sir," he gasped then raced back towards the stables.

I pulled the rug off Marchelline and fell to my knees beside her. Her face was twisted in acute pain and her lips were drawn and white. I reached for her, to hold her in my arms and she shrank from me. I looked down at her charred nightdress and her slender legs, now raw, red and blistered:

the skin peeling, bleeding and weeping. I could smell her burned flesh and I felt ill, reeling back as I saw that my own blood was running and dripping onto her open wounds. I could not think what to do: all I had was the jar of salve in my cupboard. I grabbed it and slathered it on wherever I could. But even at the lightest touch of the cool ointment she cried out, screamed with the pain of it. All I could do was try to raise a glass of brandy to her lips and try to get her to drink, as I waited interminably for Félix to return with the doctor. Even then she shook and turned away from me, groaning and gasping in her pain. I paced the room, roughly covering my own wounds for fear of the doctor's questions.

Strangest of all, during that terrible time, was the change I saw in Marchelline's face. As the moments passed, her expression of fear and horror softened into one of eerie rapture, even as she wailed and cried out against her burns. Suddenly she held out her arms to me. I rushed to her.

"Hold me, my love, I want to be close to you."

"Do not worry my darling, the doctor is coming, all will be well."

"I am not afraid," she effused, her words horribly at odds with the strangled voice that produced them. "I am no longer afraid of you, of the shadows, even of death itself. I feel so happy, there is such love in my heart for you. I know what you have done now – how you have killed my own will with your magic. I know you shall kill me too, by and by, but I am no longer afraid. All is well, because I love you." She laughed, her face aglow with delight, as she cried out in agony.

My blood ran cold. I lay down beside her, putting my jacket under her head and holding her. She seized me fiercely and kissed me ravenously, moaning with what might have been pleasure and agony commingled. I pulled my face away from her clutching fingers and hungry mouth, terrified as the wind at last died away that I was about to lose her – that she might be lost to me already.

174

CHAPTER EIGHTEEN

I sat in the morning room, trembling before the fire as I waited for the doctor to emerge. Félix hovered around, busying himself with nothing in particular, clearly in the grip of some great unease, his brow uncharacteristically furrowed. Feeling his agitation only increased my own.

"You may go to bed, Félix, you don't have to stay up on my account, thank you for your kind assistance this evening," I said, my words coming quickly, my jaw tight.

But instead of retiring in his usual way, Félix came to stand before me, his hands fidgeting with a dusting cloth, his eyes downcast.

"I wanted to tell you, Sir, that I shall be leaving your service."

"What? But why, man? You've been with my family for twenty years – no, it must be longer."

"I'm sorry Sir, but my mind's made up. I will stay until the end of the week if you insist but I would rather leave straight away. I will not see Madame de Bresson used so ill. It is not right. I cannot remain where such things occur."

I stood up, unable to contain the disturbance in my nerves any longer, walking around the room in a daze. "But how can you think that I —"

I stopped myself, remembering the things Félix had seen of late; the scandal of the Comte's death, and all the rest. The look in his eyes when he saw me bleeding over Marchelline's prostrate form now struck me with renewed

175

shame and distress. What could he make of all of this except to think me mad, violent, monstrous; that I had abused my poor wife in some vile fashion?

"It's not my place to say, Sir, only you've changed so much of late. It saddens me. The late Monsieur de Bresson would never have ... well, I think it's time I moved on, that's all. I have decided."

I slumped in a chair. Félix and I had always enjoyed a most convivial working relationship. I had come to rely on him so, and found his presence so reassuring: he was a constant living connection to my late father. To lose Félix's esteem cut me to the quick.

"If that is how you feel, Félix, then I am deeply sorry for it. I wish that you would reconsider, but if your mind is made up, I will pay you out, give you a proper letter of recommendation, anything you wish. Only won't you think about it before – things are not what they might appear – surely you know me better than to think me capable of such things?"

But looking into Félix's disappointed eyes I knew that it was too late. He said nothing.

"Very well. You must do as you think best. But you are quite wrong. I never ... I would never ..." I trailed off as he left the room. I followed him to the doorway. Sounds from the bedroom caught my attention and I followed them: the doctor's voice and Marchelline's were raised and overlapping.

As I neared the bedroom door the doctor emerged, scowling and vexed.

"Monsieur, you will have to come and help me, I can do nothing with your wife – she will not lie still, she only wants to go to you."

"Of course, whatever I can do to help – anything."

"Nicolas?" Marchelline cried from behind the door. I heard a stumble then a shriek of agony. The doctor and I rushed in to find Marchelline clinging to the bedpost, struggling towards the door on limbs raw and bloody. At the sight of me she threw herself towards me, catching me around the neck with a strange noise of relief that she sighed again and again. I scooped her up in my arms and laid her back on the bed, but she would not let me go.

"You must lie still, my darling, and let the doctor help you," I soothed, stroking her brow. She stared into my face, devouring every detail, unable to look away. All the while her breaths groaned with that horrible, repeated sound, between torture and ecstasy.

"Has she taken something? Opium?" the doctor pressed bluntly, as he tried to examine Marchelline's restless legs.

"No, no, perhaps a sleeping draught, but I am not sure when, and likely some liquor, but nothing else."

"Madame, you must be still!" the doctor barked crossly, looking at me with sore impatience.

"Lie still, darling, please. You must." Marchelline said nothing, but continued to make that terrible noise, like some tortured bird compulsively cooing. Her fingers pawed at my face, clenched into my hair, pulling me towards her, smothering my mouth with hers, so that the horrible noise continued inside my own head. I tried to pull away, to calm her as the doctor looked on with suspicion and disquiet.

"I might have expected some degree of shock," he said quietly, as at last he was able to begin to clean and dress the wet, red mess of Marchelline's calves and thighs, "but not this. Is your wife's mind troubled, Monsieur? Is she quite sane? Her speech – it makes no sense. She seems quite hysterical – sorely disturbed."

"What? Yes, of course she is sane – but she has had some terrible experiences of late; she has been distressed, not herself. I brought her here for some peace and quiet, to help her recover – and now this. It is simply too much from one person to bear."

The doctor nodded, unconvinced by my words. "Well whatever the case, Madame needs rest now. She *must* not disturb the dressings. Infection is a very real risk here. I need not remind you of how serious such things can be. If your wife cannot be still I shall leave a strong sedative that will help to keep her calm and quiet. These burns are bad, Monsieur, it is no trifling matter."

"Yes, I understand. I will do whatever you say."

The doctor produced a syringe from his bag and filled it from a small glass vial. He tried to take hold of Marchelline's arm but she would let go of me. I clasped her wrist and held her arm down so that he might administer the drug.

"Yes," Marchelline moaned, oblivious to the doctor's ministrations, only staring into my face with her pained and wildly loving eyes that I hardly recognised. "Yes, yes, hold me down, take me, bury me, possess me, my love. I am nothing, only yours, dead and alive for you." Her mouth strained again to reach mine, her back arching, her cheeks flushed with desire.

"Rest, my love, be calm," I pleaded, stroking her cheek.

She kissed me, her breaths shuddering into my mouth, her lips twisting in pain as they pressed against my own. Something in her relaxed as the drug began to take hold and her head fell back upon the pillow, her eyelids growing heavier but her eyes never looking away from me.

"Kiss me," she whispered thickly. "I love you destroyed me. Hold me in your grave forever, my darling. Fill me, devour me, obliterate me." At last her eyes closed and I was able, with a little effort, to remove her fingers that were locked into my hair. I looked up to see the doctor staring at me.

"Your wife's mental condition may be far more serious than you think, Monsieur. Did she do that to you?" he asked, solemnly, gesturing towards the clumsy bandaging I had hastily applied to my neck and chest.

"What? No, no of course not. I had an accident, that is all, in my study. She was trying to help me when – when she got too near the fire. It is nothing of consequence," I blustered, tucking the stray bandage end back between the layers, lest the dressing come loose.

"As you wish, Monsieur." The doctor finished dressing Marchelline's wounds. "Only I should not leave her alone in this state, if she were my wife. She needs a nurse, or a hospital. I shall return tomorrow. You know where to reach me if you should need me before then. Good night."

He turned his back on me, setting a small bottle of sedative on the side table as he left. I heard the front door close and then his horse trotting away into the silence of the night.

I rose from the bed and drifted over to the mirror on the dressing table, taking one of the lamps from the bedside with me. I slumped in the chair before the glass, pulling open my shirt, snatching at my rough bandages and tearing them off. So many new wounds, raw and slowly seeping. A noise of distress caught in the back of my throat. How many new weals had I added: seven, nine? I did not wish to count. I was appalled and mortified at the sight of myself, my flesh inscribed with livid symbols that scattered across my chest and up to the base of my neck: inscribed with my own stupidity, selfishness and sin. I began to weep.

I passed a largely sleepless night, tormented by questions and self-recriminations. Even in her drugged sleep, Marchelline was restless to be near me, to hold me at every moment. I awoke to find her leg entwined with mine, her arm clutching tightly around my chest, her face crushed against me. I could not move for fear of doing further injury to her leg, and so lay for what felt like hours trapped beneath her unconsciously kissing lips, that sometimes found my mouth, and at other times merely moaned and whispered wetly into my ear: "Love me, murderer of love. I must be yours. I am not my own."

Ere the sun rose, I had decided that only one course was open to me. I had to see Dr Palissandro at once. Whatever I had done wrong to cause this calamity, there was no-one else to tell me how it might be put right. I knew not where Gildian Greene might be, nor if I could trust him. But I knew I could find Dr Palissandro, and I had to believe that he held some hope of saving Marchelline from the madness into which I had unwittingly cast her adrift. Knowing that she would try to destroy the book, I could not risk giving it back to her now, when she was so vulnerable and unstable.

At last able to extricate myself, I crept to wake Madame Grudet and advised her of my plan to see this Paris specialist, if she could watch over Marchelline until the doctor could arrange a nurse to come. Hurrying back towards the bedroom I was alarmed to see Marchelline staggering through the door, her arms reaching out towards me, her eyes half open and glassy. I ran to catch her, lifting her up in my arms lest she hurt her legs the more as she stumbled. She pressed her cold lips against my face as I carried her back to the bed, gasping into my mouth, "Take me, I do not want you, you are my blood."

She reached out over my shoulder, stroking the air behind and around me. "Yes, and your shadows too, they are part of you, let them have me too, all of you, all at once, make love to me, I cannot breathe without you inside me. I have no shadow of my own. I am your shadow. I need you, my beloved death."

"Hush, my love, and sleep, I pray you."

I laid her down on the bed, struggling to retrieve the bottle of sedative as she clung to me, squinting to read the dosage on the label in the half-light as she clutched at my hands. At last I poured a little into her throat and held her until she began to succumb. I heard Madame Grudet shuffle into the room behind me, irritation and disapproval huffing in her breath.

"Yes," Marchelline mumbled, pawing the air as I extracted myself from her embrace, "let your shadows ride my bones. The little death or the great one – I thirst for you like water, like poison. Press me down beneath you until the earth swallows us both into our marriage coffin."

"Madame is very unwell," I explained to Madame

Grudet's stony face as I took up a tangled sheet from the bed and tore it in two. I carefully tied the end of each sheet around her wrists, then secured the other ends to the bedposts. "She may try to follow me, but she must not leave her bed. Please take care of her until I return – I will be as fast as I can."

"Very well, Monsieur, *I* will take care of Madame."

My galloping horse, the first train of the morning, my running feet: all seemed so unbearably slow until I reached the Dr Palissandro's house. My furious pounding soon brought him to the door: a look of sleepy, curious surprise animating his owl-like eyes as I panted to catch my breath on his doorstep.

"You must help me, it has all gone horribly wrong! I am desperate!" I cried.

He said nothing but voiced a quizzical "Hmm," and ushered me inside and into the darkened, crowded den where last I had felt so full of optimism and excitement. And somehow, through his steady, calm stare, his penetrating intellect and the quiet assurance of his deep, resonant voice, he restored me to that feeling of hope. Questioning me over the precise sequence of events, my intention, the way I wrote the symbols, he pointed out the mistakes I had made, things he assumed I would know but which, clearly, I did not.

"It was foolish of me not to test your knowledge in more depth than I did yesterday," he meditated. He glided to retrieve another piece of paper from the drawer and deftly wrote some instruction thereon. "I want you to return home at once and perform this rite without delay. The lady's condition is very serious, as you rightly observe. You did well to come to me as soon as you did. It is not too late to restore her mind to its equilibrium, to heal her injuries and bring peace to her heart also." He loomed before me, thrusting the sheet of paper before my eyes. I strained to take in the instructions and symbols and he lowered his chin, peering into my eyes with clinical scrutiny.

"You are very fatigued: dangerously low in your spirits. Before you attempt to follow these instructions, I would like you to take these powders." He turned, his long robe swirling in his wake, as he surged towards the shelves, taking various jars of dried herbs and powders, and pouring a pinch of this and a shake of that into a heavy, black mortar and crushing it swiftly together with a small pestle. This powder he then poured into an empty jar – the whole process was performed with such dexterous speed that I lost track of how many or which items he had used. He placed on the lid and turned back to me, holding out the little jar for me to take.

"Half of this mixture, you must take in water and swallow it. The other half, throw onto the fire in the room where you shall perform the rite. Clarity, focus, strength of spirit: these are what you require now. Go, quickly and do what I have said. Your will brought the current circumstances into being – your will can restore the balance. Do not fear, but trust and know that it can and will be. It has already happened, if you will only believe it so. From the depths of your heart, your blood will rise to make your wishes flesh. So mote it be."

I rushed home to find Félix at the front door, Madame Grudet by his side. They exchanged a look then eyed me coldly as I dismounted my puffing and foaming horse. Félix took up his valise and strode off, nodding towards the gardener, who bowed low to him with a kindly smile, holding his hat over his heart. Tight-lipped and dignified, Félix merely nodded his head at me as I passed him on my way to the door.

"Madame Grudet," I began in a panic as I reached her, "is Madame de Bresson all right? Have you been watching her as I asked?"

"Nothing has changed, Sir," she replied sourly, not meeting my gaze. "The doctor came again and changed the dressings – asked where you were. She still struggles in her sleep and calls out for you – says the most peculiar, obscene things. Perhaps you ought to hire a permanent nurse, as well as a new housekeeper. I'm handing in my notice too, Sir. If Monsieur Félix don't see fit to work for you any more, then I shan't either."

"Fine!" I blurted out in desperate exasperation, unable to deal with one more vexation. "Whatever you wish. Leave an address where I may send your money and your reference and go at once, if that is what you want." With the curtest of curtsies, she was gone.

Little caring, I ran towards the bedroom. It didn't matter. Nothing else mattered now but Marchelline. What a pitiful sight she was, tied to the bed, her delicate legs wrapped in bandages, her brow troubled, her face as pale as death. Without waking, she turned towards me, her fingers stretching, her arms pulling against their restraints to reach for me. I collapsed onto the bed and held her tenderly, kissing her clammy forehead. That dreadful sound passed her lips again, that rhythmic moaning, infinitely pained and primal that tore at my heart and set my teeth on edge. I was dimly aware of some noise from the servants' quarters, then heard the door slam and heavy, intent footsteps on the gravel walking away from the house. So now, at last, we were quite alone.

Leaving Marchelline sleeping, I poured myself a glass of water from the jug and mixed in half of the aromatic powder from the little jar in my pocket. It tasted sharp and indescribably bitter as I drained it down. My palate stung and my eyes watered as I strode from the bedroom towards my study.

In a few moments I had drawn the curtain, set up the candles, the circle and the book. I lit the fire and when it began to burn I sprinkled Dr Palissandro's powder into the flames. There was a hissing sizzle, and fine grey-blue vapours began to rise into the air, snaking out and feeling their way through the room like ghostly tendrils. Something filled my mind, like the faraway music from that dream I had forgotten since Marchelline burned the manuscript. All at once things seemed to sharpen, each detail, each task before me, now grew clear in my thoughts.

I stepped into the circle and lit the flames, Dr Palissandro's voice echoing his instructions in my memory. I had to see it in my mind, to believe that what I desired had already come to be. The music I imagined seemed to swell then and for a second I glimpsed, out of time and out of focus but aglow with light and joy, myself and Marchelline, dancing together in a close embrace, happy and in love. Delight illuminated her radiant, beautiful face, her pink cheeks, and she twirled and flowed, warm in my arms as though we had always been, and would always be together in time. It would be so again. It was almost so already.

My thoughts sharpened, focused on the book before me on the floor. I knew what I had to do now, and deftly, surely, I filled the raven's quill with my blood and made the signs that Dr Palissandro had drawn, holding in my heart the picture of Marchelline and I dancing in that light, blissful in the glow of each other's love. I could almost feel her warmth against my chest, her soft cheek against my own: I could almost smell her perfume, taste her sweet lips.

I set down the quill with a sigh of relief. I lifted my eyes from the book to find the room grown cloudy with the grey-blue vapours. Still they rose from the fire with their bitter, astringent scent. I blew out the candles and stood, unsteadily. My vision seemed narrowed to almost a pinpoint – but that so sharply detailed and supernormal in its clarity, I marveled at it, even as it filled me with a queer, dizzy sensation. My gaze was drawn magnetically to something amiss on my bureau, fixing upon it and pulling me towards it. My letters had been left here in heap, no more to be brought to me neatly on a silver tray by dear Félix.

I seized up the topmost letter, sensing some vital importance in it that my mind could not yet understand. I tore it open, blue-grey vapour swirling around me as I began to read.

184

My dear Monsieur de Bresson,
I can only say how deeply sorry I am: sorry for
giving you the book, sorry that I was not here when you
came to call, sorry I did not get your letter until I came
home this morning. You cannot know how sorry I am, but I
was desperate – I am desperate still. I had hoped that giving
the book away would ease things but they have only grown
worse somehow.
My wife tells me that she gave you the address of Dr
Palissandro and I pray that this letter reaches you before it
is too late. Do not, on any account, make yourself known to
this man or listen to his advice. As you value your life
please – please – heed my warning. You have no reason to
trust me but you must – and I pray that you will, even if
only in this one vital matter.
Palissandro is evil: a servant of the shadows. He
cannot be trusted. I never told my wife that I had stopped
seeing him – I could never have explained why. I hope to
have the chance to explain all to you soon, but for now, I
must keep moving – to protect my wife as much as myself
from the spirits that now pursue me.
I will try to see you when I am able, or write again
when I have more time, but you will understand, my dear
wife's safety must be my first priority.
The more you use the book, the greater the danger.
Do not use it if you can find any way to stop yourself. The
shadows are real, and therein lies the danger.
Yours,
Gildian Greene.

The room tilted and the breath leaving my lips seemed
to shake my whole body. The paper fell from my hand and fog
clouded my vision. I turned around and saw, through the
haze, dark shapes milling in the corners, crawling around the
walls, creeping on the floor around my legs. I gave an

185

exhalation like a silent laugh, and found I could not draw air back into my lungs. I shook, stifling as the shadows all began to move, as one, toward me. I heard a crow cawing outside the window as the grey-blue fog turned to black and darkness engulfed me.

I awoke in blackness, not knowing whether I was still in the thrall of those shadows. I heard a crackle and turned my head to see the dying glow of a fire in the hearth. I was alive, in my study, but night had fallen. How long had I slept?

As my thoughts turned to Marchelline I leapt to my feet, shaking off the dizziness that still seemed to make the floor tilt under my feet as I stumbled, running off-balance to the bedroom. No lamps were lit – no-one was here to light them. In the deep gloom, I lurched through the door. Some small radiance of moonlight shone through a gap in the curtains that had not been drawn. The white sheets of the bed glowed blue against the darkness: blue and bare. I lunged at the bed, feeling with searching hands, hoping that my eyes were deceived. But here, where her warm and tender body should have been; here in the knotted sheets that had held her tiny wrists, here at the pillow that had cradled her divine head, there was only cold and terrible emptiness.

"Marchelline?" I cried into the darkness. The low, distant croaking of a frog was the only reply. I grabbed for the lamp beside the bed and fumbled to light it. I moved from room to room, searching every corner, every space, crying out her name into the empty, echoing house that held no answers save the mocking sound of my own voice and the ghostly sight of my own haunted face in the glass.

I ran outside, searching the front garden, and around the gravel path to the arbor behind and on through the maze of paths between flowerbeds and ancient towering trees. A thousand times I called for her. I wept and trembled for her as I ran back beyond the gardens into the wood.

I rushed on, calling, searching, through the trees,

heedless of the clawing branches that scratched at me. Frantic, my heart pounding, the breath rasping in my throat, I ran on and on.

As the first blush of dawn began to insinuate itself in the sky, I was heading back towards the house. I had left the woods and run back around the other side of the house, along the track that lead to the road. But nowhere could I see any sign of my love. The first bird of morning began to sing quietly. As I trudged on, exhausted, bewildered, other birds joined the chorus. By the time I reached the front garden, the trees were a cacophony of noise beneath the deep blue-pink of the sky.

I was about to go back into the house when I noticed it. Across the lawn, on the pond, the duck and drake were squawking strangely, bunched up together in the reeds at the side of the pond, flapping their wings and huddling close. The lamp fell, smashing, from my hand and I ran to the pond, sending the duck and drake flying away, quacking and hooting in wild alarm. I stopped at the water's edge, gasps burning my lungs as the violently troubled water settled and the ripples began to subside.

Something white glowed against the dark water. Stillness settled and brought into focus a slender white figure, spectral under the surface. Marchelline's arms were extended up towards me, her eyes closed, her lips curled in a smile of unearthly serenity and eternal mystery.

I heard a scream that might have been my own and I crashed through that black, icy mirror into the frigid, swaying embrace of my love. Tendrils of her long, flowing hair brushed my face with their silken, feathery touch as I clutched her to my chest. I pulled her and we twirled together in the water as though we were dancing in that icy, choking dark. I drew her up, gasping as I broke the surface, dragging her to the edge and out onto the lawn. How unnaturally heavy she felt. How deathly cold and leaden were those limbs that should have been warm and alive. How blue and lifeless were those lips that had smiled, and sung and kissed and spoken with such vital force and energy.

I wailed, shaking her fiercely, then cradling her as though she were the most fragile thing in the world. At the sound of my wails there was a discordant massed cry and a violent flapping of wings as the birds took flight and sobbing became the only sound in the desolate garden. My love was dead ...

CHAPTER NINETEEN

How grey the world suddenly became. As though, with Marchelline's passing, all the joy, all the colour and warmth, had simply been drained out of life. I felt so cold and numb, so dead inside. The chill of the water from which I had dragged my beloved never left me, but solidified like ice inside my soul. That water had taken her life and its icy darkness had also sucked the vitality from my very bones.

As I walked from Marchelline's graveside, nothing seemed quite real anymore. Aunt Mathilde-Hélène walked at my side, her face ashen above her black mourning clothes, a black lace handkerchief wiping her eyes beneath the veil she wore. The twins clung to each other in pained bewilderment, reddened, puffy eyes distorting their pretty young faces. Yves said nothing, his youthful bravado for once silenced, and his glib manner of no use to him, for there was nothing at all to be said.

As a suicide, Marchelline could not be buried near my parents and other ancestors in the consecrated section of the graveyard. It was the common section of the churchyard, alongside the unmarked graves of stillborn babies and unbaptised infants, those damned to linger in eternal limbo, where she would have to lie.

The reluctant priest had said as little as possible by way of a service. I had barely heard his words. What was God to me now? What was He to her? I suppose I had turned my back on Him when I sought the powers of the book. I could have

189

understood His punishing me – but why take Marchelline? Perhaps that *was* the cruelest punishment He could inflict upon me. Such religious feelings as I had ever had seemed to vapourise in the face of that terrible thought.

Back at the house, I was all alone. Even Maxim was gone – taken into the temporary care of the twins at my aunt's suggestion. Hubert, the gardener had also departed in sympathy with his colleagues – unable to bear the scandal of a suicide. I had never known the place so silent or so empty, as though life itself had been banished from those once sunny and vibrant rooms.

I felt that I had left something essential to my own survival behind me in the churchyard. Standing by the pond, I wondered if I should follow Marchelline down into whatever peace I hoped that she had found.

Why? Why had she done it? I could only pretend to myself that I did not know. Just as I pretended to my aunt, the doctor, the police and the priest that it was her grief at the death of her former lover that had driven her to such an act. What else could I say? And even in that lie I felt that I was losing her to him all over again: losing her to he whom she had never really stopped loving, even if I had tried to steal her heart for a while. What had all my efforts achieved – they were still together in death. That last ritual – making her love me, when she knew what I had done, had sent her mad. She had escaped from me the only way she could. Had a man ever acted more cruelly to she whom he professed to love? How unforgivably blind I had been to my own base and brutal nature. I wanted to destroy myself, for I had forfeited all right to live among society. I was a killer – no better than those condemned to die under the guillotine's blade.

But could I really chase her into eternity, after all that I had done to her? As much I wanted to die, in that moment, staring into the rippling reedy water, at the duck circling alone through the water lilies, I knew that I must let her go, and leave her to her rest. She had never really been mine, nor could she be again.

I shuffled to the garden bed beneath the window and picked the last of the blood irises whose blooms were fast withering into brown. I returned to the pond and cast it onto the water. It floated and turned slowly, untouched by the insignificant ripples of my tears as they fell into the indifferent pond. The world cared not for my sorrows. Nature continued on, the earth turned even as my own life, my own heart, seemed to have stopped.

What madness had seized hold of me? What desperate, cruel folly had compelled me to destroy the love Marchelline had with the Comte, to crush her will, to twist her heart against itself – to kill? What was this book that had unleashed in me these most dangerous and destructive desires? And the men connected with it, Gildian Greene and Dr Palissandro: I felt now, more than ever before, that I had been merely an unwitting dupe, a pawn in some greater, darker game of which I had no understanding.

If God could punish, so might I. If Marchelline had escaped the chains that I had placed around her heart, then I would find a way to reveal the invisible chains that had been placed around me by Greene and Palissandro, and perhaps, by exposing, shatter them.

I had killed for love. Perhaps I might also kill out of vengeance, if the opportunity came. I had no good opinion of myself left to lose.

It was a grey, late afternoon when I arrived in Paris, a small folding knife secreted in my pocket. I took a cab from the station and instructed the driver to take me to Dr Palissandro's address. How shabby the street looked to me now. How disrespectable the denizens of this neighbourhood appeared as they prowled its narrow sidewalks. Why had I not seen these warning signs when I had first come here?

I instructed the driver to wait while I considered my actions. I had nothing more to lose. The knife that I weighed in

191

my hand could so easily end the matter. But I feared that the mere shedding of more blood might be of little satisfaction to me now. I had to know – I needed to understand who this man was, and why in the name of God he had instructed me to acts which had resulted in such an unthinkable cataclysm. I could not doubt but that he had known exactly what he was doing. What had I ever done to him to deserve such ill use?

I slipped the driver his fare, about to alight and ready to march to the doctor's door and demand an explanation when I froze in my seat. A figure approached the faded black door of Dr Palissandro's house. I drew back into my seat. For a moment I thought it was he, so alike was the long hair and beard he wore, and his bent stature. A hat concealed his features in the gloom of the afternoon. He wore a very long black coat and carried a worn leather bag. He knocked on the door and waited. As he turned to look over his shoulder I glimpsed enough of his face to see that this was not Dr Palissandro. Their faces, in fact, bore no trace of any resemblance and this other man appeared a good deal older.

After some moments the door opened a little and some brief conversation took place. The door closed again and the gentleman turned his face toward the street and waited, discreetly surveying the scene around him with a level of scrutiny beyond the casual. His small eyes narrowed as he glanced toward my cab and I shrank back, hoping that the shadows would conceal me. I reasoned that he could not know who I was, even if he did see me: there was nothing so unusual in a man's waiting in a cab. But some instinct made me fear him.

I pulled the brim of my hat down lower and looked back to see Dr Palissandro now emerging in the street, carrying his own black leather satchel, as the other man continued to speak to him. The doctor merely nodded, his back to me, as he turned his keys in the two locks on his door and then checked it twice with some compulsive impulse. He turned to face his companion and for a moment I thought I perceived his nostrils to flare and his chest to flutter, as though he were sniffing the air. He gave a wan smile to the other shorter gentleman and extended a crooked finger towards the sidewalk at his right in invitation to proceed.

Heavy drops of rain began to fall from the darkened sky as I alighted silently from the cab and haltingly began to follow the two figures in their long, heavy coats as they made their way along the street. How grateful I was for those black clouds that might obscure me as I crept along, turning into narrow streets and deserted alleys, terrified that at any moment the strange pair before me might turn around and see me. Darkness gathered as we walked on and on, through endless streets unfamiliar to me. I clung close to walls peeling with paint and rough with disrepair. I overstepped gutters rank with the stench of piss and alcohol, and jagged with broken bottles. I little knew where we were or whither this circuitous, obscure path might be headed.

I froze as the two men halted, hurriedly trying to flatten myself into a grubby, shallow doorway. I heard their quiet voices conferring and peered out to see them hunched over, both peering into Dr Palissandro's bag as he searched for something within. Satisfied with the results of the search they moved off again. More cautious now, I hung back a little, wary of getting too close. They turned off to the right and I crept on towards the corner, where a small, grimy gas lamp hung from a curling, black iron bracket. A sign on the opposite wall read, "*Rue des Corbeaux*," and I flinched. The Street of Ravens – what were these men in their long black coats, conspiring together in the darkened streets but two great, sinister ravens?

I peered around the corner, expecting to see them further down that impossibly narrow and gloomy alley, but the thoroughfare, shining and oily with rain, was deserted. Tall buildings lined either side of the way, their high walls dotted with irregular black window cavities, here and there showing some faint glow of life within. Some second floor structure overhung the street, only increasing my feeling of claustrophobia and menace.

I walked along, nervously looking for any clue to the men's disappearance. I knew that not enough time had passed for them to reach the end of this alley, as it continued in a straight line for some distance until a sharp curve at the other end promised some escape into more open ground. I was conscious of the sound of my hard breaths echoing between the tight walls and I opened my mouth to try and soften the sound. I crept along further, seeing a narrow, padlocked doorway to my right. All was still, and I was certain I would have heard the sounds of such a lock being opened and removed - aside from the impossibility of the lock being replaced again. I went on, aware now of a tall black opening in the left hand wall some little way ahead.

Here, equidistant between the two small gas lamps that lit the thoroughfare so inadequately, I stopped. It was indeed a doorway, tall but narrow and revealing a door that was set back some way from the street. I passed through ornate, black metal, filigree gates that hung open, and slunk into this dark recess. For the briefest of moments, I thought I detected in the air some very faint aroma of strange herbs or incense. A wind whistled by as the rain grew heavier, and any trace of the scent was banished by the cold, wet blast of air.

The second, closed door was only faintly distinguishable in the gloom against the rough grey walls. I produced the Vesta case from my pocket and fumbled with stiff fingers to produce a flame. In the small, flickering glow I saw a heavy and dark oaken door, evidently of great age, and whose battered boards and panels were banded with strips of black iron that gleamed a little in the light. The ends of these strips were forked into "v" shapes that curled outward. At the right side of the door, at the termination of one of the horizontal bands, was a large curved band of iron, like a letter "c" reversed. I saw then that unlike the other metal bands, with their uniformly forked ends, this rounded shape had a singular difference. While the lower end of the broken circle

194

had the same curved "v" finial, the uppermost end terminated in an inverted "v", so that the broken circle had the form of an arrow curling back upon itself – the symbol of calling.

I extinguished the light and grasped at the heavy iron door handle, giving the slightest tug. It began to open. I paused, checking my pocket once more for the knife, and I tensed myself as I eased the door open wider, dreading that it might make a sound. Silently, the great door opened and I let myself inside.

I stopped short, finding myself upon a little landing at the head of long staircase that descended, vertiginously, down to some great distance. Tiny candles flickered in little, grimy glass holders, set at either side of the steps at intervals. I shivered, my clothes sodden and my nerves taut. The air was warmer here from the heat of the candles, and now I perceived again that strange odour, astringent and stinging to the eyes.

Cautiously I descended step after step, my hands pressed against the cold, narrow walls, for there was no rail or banister. The smell grew stronger the lower down I went, and the walls seemed to shrink in closer. My skin prickled at the suggestion of faint, muffled voices further below. At last I reached the foot of the stairs, turning a corner, past another very heavy door that rested ajar, into a dark passageway whose floor was paved with worn and uneven stones. A little further along another unlocked door to my right opened upon more steps leading further down into blackness. Down this tortuous and claustrophobic staircase, I felt my way, towards the voices and the scent that were both growing ever stronger.

I turned again into a passageway lit by a lantern upon the floor. Rough-hewn stonework suggested I had arrived in subterranean catacombs of some very remote date, like those Roman mines that had been turned into an enormous ossuary beneath the *Barrière d'Enfer*. Tendrils of smoke drifted in the air, guiding me around another corner and into a tunnel where a lantern hung from an alarming archway that seemed to be formed entirely of human skulls and bones. On the aged,

195

white surfaces of many of the bones, symbols from the book had been marked in black. For a moment I quailed at the sight, then tried to steel myself to press on.

I swallowed to suppress a wave of nausea as I detected another scent below the heavy, acrid incense. It was the smell of blood: stale, salty, coppery – a smell bound up with dampness, cold, and the mildew of long, lightless centuries. Through the grisly archway, the lantern's light picked out another gruesome architectural feature ahead. On the left hand wall, set into the masonry, more human skulls formed an inverted crucifix, surrounded by the same shape of the curved arrow, circling back, anti-clockwise: this outer shape being formed by the careful arrangement of innumerable leg bones.

I halted at the sudden proximity of voices, the foul smells now overpowering my senses and making my eyes burn as I hovered near the entrance to some great cavernous chamber. At first, all I could see was that a blazing brazier burned in the centre of the expansive space, beneath a curving, vaulted ceiling that was blackened with the soot of ages. Giant shadows danced on the ceiling and the oddly colonnaded walls, bending and distorting as silhouetted figures moved rapidly around the wildly burning flames.

Thick columns, formed of twisting patterns of skulls and bones, ringed the space, connected by a trellis of artfully arranged bones, forming a kind of screen that, if I were to stoop down, I might easily hide behind. The regular gaps in the geometric skeletal arrangement would provide peepholes enough to observe what was happening. I could only hope that it might offer me sufficient concealment in the low light. Taking my chance, I rushed forward, hiding behind the morbid screen that I might better see what was to happen.

Now I could clearly observe the figures moving around the space. All were clothed in robes of some heavy, dark blue stuff, split at the neck. All carried a small dagger, hanging from a thin leather belt around their hips. And all, men and women alike – for there were several odd-looking women among the assembly – wore very long hair that flowed loosely around their shoulders and beyond. The men all wore long beards. But most striking of all was that not one of the figures was straight of limb or back. I tried to count the revelers as they seemed to wander and jostle aimlessly around the space, each mumbling unintelligible words to themselves through thin, unwholesome smiles. They were thirteen in number. Palissandro and his companion were at first difficult to distinguish among the moving throng of robed, long-haired people, but had perhaps more silver and white in their hair than most of the others – and the doctor's great height, when standing erect, also set him apart.

A cup appeared and was quickly passed from one to another as they moved, each one drinking a draught then passing it forward, and each, after taking his drink beginning to spin and to mutter with greater force and volume. I felt dizzy as they whirled around the room. I wondered that they never collided, as their hair flew out around them in their frenzied dance. Suddenly Palissandro broke out of this peculiar orbiting of the brazier and rushed towards it, wildly casting a great handful of some powder into the flames with a deep, resounding cry of "Diamon!" I jumped as the deafening shout boomed and echoed through the vault.

The fire spat and crackled and trails of blue-grey smoke exploded into the air. The other attendants stopped and contracted into a circle around the brazier, leaning in towards it and filling their lungs with the vile vapours in long, drawn-out, rasping gasps.

Palissandro turned, his huge eyes blazing out through the smoke that bathed his haggard face. "Diamon, we summon thee!" his powerful voice cried again, drawing out his dagger and holding it, flashing, above him. "Open the portal of shadows."

"Diamon," hissed the revelers, likewise drawing their blades with their right hands and holding them aloft.

"With blood we summon thee," Dr Palissandro

197

boomed, slicing into his left thumb and flicking his hand to cast blood into the spattering flames. As one, the others followed suit, the violence of their action sending drops of blood flying into each other's faces.

"Shedu, Shabriri, Asmodai, Azazel!" Palissandro exclaimed with heated excitement. With furious speed and chaotic abandon, the revellers flung themselves into wild motion once more, launching themselves towards the cardinal points of the room, repeating the hissed names of the diamon and flinging their bleeding hands out, casting their blood into the darkness there as they span and lurched. Blood sprayed into the hole I peered through, spattering my face, so that I had to suppress a cry. Suddenly all was still once more, and the circle had reformed, silent around the brazier.

"With a creature of the air we summon thee," Palissandro growled. Breaking from the circle, one of the company reached into the darkness at the far end of the chamber and produced a wicker cage. She unfastened a catch and opened the cage's door. A dove cooed strangely then flew out and up toward the ceiling, it's white wings glowing in the orange light and agitating the smoke haze that hung in the air. No sooner had it reached its apex than it plunged down again, flying headlong into the heart of the fire with not so much as a peep.

A cloud of thick black smoke began to rise from the flapping blackening shape in the fire. Dr Palissandro stepped back in awe as the smoke did not spread but seemed to be coalescing into some monstrously tall shape that I did not want to recognise.

"Master," Palissandro whispered, bowing his head and dropping down upon his left knee as his followers all did the same. "The servants of shadow attend thee."

CHAPTER TWENTY

The black shape seemed to narrow and condense, slowly assuming an enormous, elongated human shape when, with a audible puff, it violently dissipated, spreading out into the smoky air, and darkening it.

"The portal is open," Palissandro whispered. "Let us summon them."

As one, the group stood and pulled down their robes, leaving them hanging around their hips to expose their naked torsos. In the low light I saw at once that each member, now exposed, was covered front and back with silvery-purple scars – as from innumerable weals, long since healed over. Palissandro moved closer to the flame, raising his arms so that his sagging flesh swung.

"Shadows, we summon thee, an offering to make to thee. Come, come Masters – thy servants await."

In unison, the assembly began to breathe, noisily, and with a peculiar lurching rhythm. Some closed their eyes, while others lowered theirs. In the glare of the firelight, Palissandro's huge eyes rolled back in his head, and he gave a terrible, animalistic cry. At that instant, every scarred and dry symbol upon his drooping, bent chest suddenly tore open and began to bleed. Blood ran freely from the weals, and one after another, the weals of the other devotees also began to open and bleed. I shuddered as I felt blood streaming down my own neck and chest, and my hand touched the wetness of my shirt in panic and horror.

199

Then, most terrible of all, I saw that the blood running from Palissandro's chest began to bubble and spatter, and from each wound, dark, smoky vapours began to emerge. All around him the other revelers alike began to be obscured as from every weal dark human-like shapes squeezed and insinuated themselves out, until the smoky air grew thick with flying shadows and the room was nearly dark. I muffled my mouth with my hand as dark, cloudy shapes began to emerge and rise from my own chest, blinding me for a moment until they dissipated. I strained to see Palissandro's face, even as close as he was to the huge fire in the brazier. The white of his owl-like eyes and his large teeth gleamed in a smile of ecstasy through the darkness. His followers seemed to have gathered very close, still breathing in time, but now in slow hissing breaths.

The dark air chilled and swirled and I held my breath as I felt things intangible as wind, as soft as feathers, as black as night itself, brushing past me.

"Masters," Palissandro whispered in utmost reverence, the suggestion of tears sparkling in his eyes. "Thy presence honours us. "

A queer windy noise seemed to echo then through the gloom of vaulted chamber.

"We bring a gift, an offering to thy greatness," Palissandro bellowed.

The windy noise seemed to coalesce into a voice – an airy voice like numerous voices bound together, some high, others low, surging and dying, whistling and rumbling so that my hair stood on end.

"Who is to be offered?" the windy voice asked.

"One of thy sacred nests, Lord," Palissandro hissed, bowing his head.

"And what is the offering?" the windy voice droned.

"A new page, Master, for a new book, that thy nests might increase."

The windy voice seemed to moan at this.

Palissandro nodded and signaled to one of his fellows with his eyes. Someone drew a stick from the fire and moved away with this makeshift torch, but the air was so thick with shadows that I could not see where they went. I heard some sounds from the far end of the room, and thought I perceived some whispered voices under the windy noise, and the sounds of two sets of feet shuffling back over the worn stone floor towards the brazier.

Suddenly a figure was pushed into the small glow of the fire – a man of about five and thirty with short, damp-looking, curly hair and the most woe-begotten, haunted aspect. He shook and struggled to open his eyes. His lips were white and his cheeks shone with perspiration.

"Do you come here willingly to offer a new page to your masters?" Palissandro asked him in a voice of utmost solemnity.

"Y–yes, yes, if it is the only way to free myself, and to release her, then yes ... yes." The wretched man hung his head, stifling a sob.

Palissandro nodded and I saw hands reach for the neck of the man's robe and draw it down, exposing his bare chest. Numerous bleeding weals covered his white, glistening flesh. But something else was very much amiss. This man appeared unbent, well formed, yet upon his chest, clustered around the bleeding weals there were large bulbous protuberances, like virulent tumours growing beneath the skin. The man's shaking increased. "If I do not survive, please send my wife the letter I gave you."

"Purify him," Palissandro instructed. I heard the sound of skin rubbing on wet skin and saw then hand after hand reaching into the light to smear blood over the quivering man's chest, back and neck. His lip curled in revulsion and he clenched his eyelids tightly. Last of all, Palissandro himself walked around the brazier, passed his own hand over his bleeding chest, and wiped the blood onto the wincing face of the tumour-ridden man.

201

"Turn around," Palissandro urged the man in a gentle, soothing voice: that same, paternal doctor's voice he had assumed with me.

The man tried to nod, but his whole body shook so that it was barely distinguishable. His feet shuffled on the cold, damp stones and he revealed his blood-smeared back to the doctor.

"Hold him, tightly," Palissandro cooed. I saw many hands grasp fiercely at the man's arms, his shoulder, even his head. His violent trembling ceased as he was now immobile in the grip of the cult members. Palissandro fumbled for something at his hips, then held up his dagger. The fire light's reflection flashed on the blade.

"Masters, we humbly beg to offer thee a new page for thy sacred Book of Calling."

Palissandro moved and grasped the man's left shoulder with his gnarled hand. His body obscured my view, and I could not see what he did as the man began to scream. I only heard the terrible sound underlying those cries of agony and terror. It was a sound such as is heard when one cuts through uncooked meat with a knife – the sound of fibers being sliced through. The man shrieked again and again as the cutting sound went on, and then a dripping as of liquid spilling onto hard stone. I wanted to stop up my ears. I wanted to run but fear pinned me to the spot: my frozen limbs stiff and unresponsive, as though they were no longer even mine.

A part of me yearned then to run into the circle, to knock Dr Palissandro off his feet and to drag that poor man away from the horrors of this crypt. But he had offered himself to them willingly. What chance had I of escaping the daggers of those madmen if I tried?

The man's screams terminated in a pitiful sigh and I was grateful that he must have fainted at last to escape his torture. Yet the unspeakable slicing sound went on, rasping, wet and relentless. Isolated now from the other sounds in the darkness of this cavern it seemed so much more unbearable.

At last the sound ceased and I heard Dr Palissandro's dagger drop onto the floor with a clatter. A gasp rose up from the company and Dr Palissandro moved, holding up something that glistened wetly in the dull firelight. It seemed flat, rectangular, perhaps more than twenty centimeters across and fifteen high. It was dripping dark drops down onto his face as he held it up for the assembly to admire. He shifted away from the unconscious man and it was then that I saw the hole. The man's head had fallen forward and from his slumping back, between his shoulders, a large rectangle of skin had been excised, leaving a terrible, raw wound from which blood streamed in alarming volume. I could still hear it trickling onto the floor. With a great flurry, a long stream of black shadows puffed and flew out from the hole: I could not guess at how many shadows escaped him, certainly there were dozens of them.

"Lords of shadow," Palissandro intoned with awe, "this is our gift to thee, for thy living book – that bridge between thy world of shadow and our world of light. Let us aid thee to find new nests for thy increase, until thou shalt grow to extinguish the sun with thy eternal shade."

The windy noise resumed and now the air began to stir. The thick darkness seemed to break up into clouds and drifts of shadow that swirled around the chamber. The light increased, and in the haze of blue-grey smoke that churned with dark eddies and black currents, Palissandro and his followers were once again revealed in all their horror. Blood stained, wild eyed, they peered about the great chamber in sharp anticipation. Palissandro walked back before the fire, the sheet of dripping skin still held aloft in his red hands. The unconscious man fell face first onto the ground as the followers released him, only interested now in the clouds of shadow that moved around them in the fog. Some held up their hands, reaching for the shadowy clouds, while others fell to their knees, their palms upturned in some manner of unholy prayer.

203

All at once the nebulous dark shapes sharpened into form – revealing themselves – shadows in the shapes of men, clinging to the walls, crawling over the vaulted ceiling, creeping around the floor, some smaller, some larger, but all alike in kind. They were faceless and utterly black, and their presence at last clearly seen, seemed to poison the air with cold, and a feeling of ancient, unearthly malice. Now revealed, they crept towards their eager servants pressing their featureless faces against those bleeding chests, black, protruding tongues appearing to lick and rasp at seeping weals, at the bloody floor, and most of all, at the hideous flap of skin in the hands of Dr Palissandro. The doctor's face twisted in a rictus grin of ecstasy. He lowered the sheet of skin over his own face, evidently thrilling at the sensation of those many ghostly tongues upon his own flesh.

The man upon the floor seemed to stir, perhaps from the attentions of the shadows upon his own exposed tissue. He cried in pain and tried to crawl away, dragging himself with limbs as weak as a doll's. And as I peered in, absorbed in the horrible tableau before me, the peephole through which I spied went black. I reared back as a shadow slipped through the hole and loomed in my face, its spectral hands feeling for me, and its probing black tongue twisting and curling towards my bloody shirt. I scrambled backwards, into the wall, crying out despite myself, stumbling to my feet and running, mindlessly, wildly, to escape.

Impelled by the most primal of instincts I simply ran – not conscious of where I went. As the shadow hovered between myself and the cavern entrance, I had taken flight in the opposite direction, rushing through the dark skeletal archway at the far end of the chamber, stumbling over empty wicker cages, and crashing through screens on which were stretched taut membranes – skins in varying stages of drying, from the rancid smelling and wet, to the hard and parchment dry.

With my own cries echoing in the dark tunnels I rushed

on blindly, colliding violently with walls, reaching out before me with outstretched hands in the darkness until I tripped on the jagged floor stones and fell, rolling and sliding into some black corner.

I tried to catch my breath, to calm my heart that felt about to burst from my chest. I was still alive – there had to be some way out of this. I could not, could not, be buried alive in this black labyrinth, or worse, fall into the hands of those depraved ghouls and their cult of shadows. I felt around the walls, my fingers sinking into holes, snagging on sharp protuberances, curling around smooth domes that chilled my blood with some primal recognition. I fumbled in my pockets for my Vesta case and frantically lit a match until a flame, small but infinitely warm and welcome to me, cast its meager glow into the void. The chamber I was in was but a small one, yet it lacked nothing in its power to appall.

Before me was a doorway, and the walls around and on either side of this were decorated, or desecrated, with the most macabre mosaic of human skulls. A grimly artistic geometric pattern had been formed by the arrangement of skulls in various attitudes – some showed their faces, others their crania, while others still showed their undersides, alien-looking with their horse-shoe of teeth below the obscene hole of the spinal column. I thought then of Marchelline, buried now in her own world of the dead and felt, in that moment, somehow connected to her once more, underground, in the dark, surrounded by bones. But this thought only filled me with greater pain and despair.

I turned to look behind me and shrank from the alarming spectacle frozen in the masonry. Here was a complete, articulated skeleton, its arms stretched out to the sides, its legs tucked up, and its head turned out. Two sharply pointed birds skulls had been added in front of the mouth, to suggest a beak, and the skeletal wing bones of innumerable birds had been arranged below the arms like radiating feathers. Inserted behind this chimerical monstrosity was a second skeleton, painted or enameled a glossy black, that appeared to be holding the bird-man creature – although whether in an embrace of tenderness or capture, it was impossible to say. I wondered then, how long this cult of shadows had existed out of sight and out of mind beneath the happily dreaming denizens of Paris? And who had supplied the innumerable skulls that covered its unholy walls? I had to get out at once.

I got to my feet and crept out of the chamber holding the little flame aloft to detect any sign of a way out. All I could see was dark corridors and blackness. Not knowing from whence I had come, nor how far into the earth these tunnels might take me, I cursed myself for a fool that I had followed those evil men here. The match burnt out in my fingers.

Realising where my only hope lay, my fingernails biting into the palm of my balled-up fist, I called out in despair, "Hullo?" My voice echoed into the darkness and I leaned back against the cold, stone wall with a sinking heart. It was only a few moments before I heard footsteps and perceived the faint glow of a light approaching. My body tensed. Dr Palissandro's low voice resounded towards me, his tone, kindly and soothing.

"Ah, there you are, Monsieur de Bresson. I had wondered when you might show yourself." The halo of candlelight preceded him as he stepped around the corner, that same thin smile upon his lips. His robe once more covered his bloody torso, but his face was still wet and stained with blood.

"In answer to the question in your mind, there are three ways out of your current predicament. The offering that you just witnessed was one of them. Which shall you choose, I wonder?"

CHAPTER TWENTY-ONE

"Whatever can you mean?" I shouted, following Dr Palissandro as he walked away into the darkness. "I demand to know what manner of game you are playing with me! What is this? You and your wretched book have destroyed my life – taken from me the only woman I have ever loved. All I cared about in this world is gone. Yes, she is dead! But perhaps you knew that already – you seem to know all, *you* seem to be behind all this monstrosity – and I want to know *why!*"

He paused and smiled over his shoulder. "You *demand*? Do you really think you are in a position to demand anything? These catacombs have existed for centuries, unknown and unseen by any but we, the Servants of Shadow. A person might come down here and never, ever be found again. A thousand people might have done just that, before you." He smiled to himself, and his long bent fingers caressed the dome of a skull set into the wall near his head. "If you wish it I shall explain to you as much as a non-initiate is permitted to know. But please remember, you are in our service now. I am your master, just as *they* are my masters. I hold all the keys here. It was I who opened the doors that let you in here. They are locked again now."

I went for the knife in my pocket but stopped myself. Perhaps I *could* kill him, but I would still be lost in this maze, and I needed the answers that only this vile man could give. So I followed like some pathetic puppy dog, as the doctor walked around the dizzying labyrinth of tunnels. Whether he was leading me to freedom or to some oubliette in which I might be consigned to rot forever, I did not know. I clung to the light of his candle as though it were life itself.

"Please then, Dr Palissandro, please won't you tell me what it going on?" I beseeched.

"You bought a book," he began, in a condescending tone, as though I were a dim-witted child.

"No, the book was given to me by Gildian Greene."

"No, you bought the book – without knowing it had a price that you would have to pay."

"Well that is certainly true," I muttered bitterly.

"I suppose you thought that the book existed to serve you, to fulfill your wishes?"

"Yes, yes – that is exactly what Gildian Greene led me to believe!"

"And who did you think would be fulfilling these wishes, performing these services for you? Who did you think you were really calling?"

"I … I do not know – the powers of magic, I suppose – I, oh I never thought of such questions! All I wanted was my love – she was all I thought of. I was possessed by her."

"The book does not exist to serve you, but to serve the desires of its makers. It is their Book of Calling, and it is you who have been called to serve them."

"But who *are* they? *What* are they? What do they want?"

"They whom you and I serve are the dark ones: the Shadow People, the *Tenebrae*," he whispered. We turned a corner and he stopped and unlocked an old door of dark wood – very like the one through which I had first entered high above in the *Rue des Corbeaux*. It was the only door that I had seen since he had been guiding me. He glided inside and used his candle to light other candles that waited for him here – the room was somehow quickly aglow with so much light that it dazzled my eyes.

I cannot convey how precious was the light to me now after being lost in such blackness. And here was light enough to banish all the dark. I tried to breathe it in, as though I could fill myself with it. It appeared that hundreds of candles burned and cast their golden glow upon this strange, dizzying chamber. All around the room, the walls were paneled from floor to ceiling with mirrors, so that on every side the room seemed to stretch off into an infinity of dazzling reflections. I hardly knew how large or small the chamber was. In the middle of the space was a heavy wooden table of medieval workmanship, upon which rested innumerable boxes and great piles of very old books and manuscripts of yellowed parchment.

I tried not to look at myself in the glass, but everywhere, and multiplied into the far distance, that sad, ravaged, dirty and blood-soaked man glared back at me with defeated and accusing eyes. And close by him, that other – that terrible, tall, crooked creature, with his long hair and beard, and his blood-stained face with its huge, blazing eyes – he too was multiplied, so that he seemed to surround and engulf me with a thousand grim doppelgangers.

"Here," he said, opening one of the books and laying it before me. "This is the Daemonicodex of Saganthus – one of the rarest and most fabled books of occult lore – do you read English?"

I nodded and looked at the page. A primitive illustration of a black, featureless form with a raven at its feet was framed by some medieval decorative border of blue and gold, alongside a page of the tiniest black handwriting whose ornate style and archaic language made my eyes swim: all this below a large heading that was written in red, "The Tenebrae."

> *Guard thee against the Men of Shadowe, the Tenebrae, for they shalle bring naught but plague and perdition to thee. Neither daemons nor wraiths be they, but still stranger spirits from a realm unknown to Man, God or the Devyl. Guard thee against the spillinge of blod by magicke, for blod shalle call them to thee.*

209

Dr Palissandro withdrew the book and placed another before me, open to a page marked by a faded red ribbon.

"The grimoire of the heretic, Dr Helvétius-Capriole Mercadeaux," he explained in his slow, deep voice. I scanned the torn, discoloured page before me.

> *It is believed that the Shadow Men use as their lure a Book of Calling. When a rite is performed as the book instructs, a portal is opened by which the Shadow Men may enter our own world from whatever region of Hell they come.*
>
> *Their subjects, unwittingly bound to the talismanic book by the application of their own blood, are then infiltrated by means of an open wound, incised by these Shadow Men into the flesh. These symbolic wounds act as a gateway, for the Shadow Men must reside in living human flesh in order that they might stay in our world, as they so desire – and increase their number. Those in the thrall of the Book of Calling, so rapt in the magic the Book offers, little realise that they are being used as Nests in which the Shadow Men might –*

But here the rest of the page was torn or had eroded away. I gulped, feeling the blood drain from my face so that I had to lean on the table for support.

"A nest?" I asked, trying not to look at the mocking mirrors, trying to pretend that it was all some horrible dream.

"Yes," Dr Palissandro replied with a pleasant smile. "You are a nest, sacred to the purpose of the Shadow People. They are breeding inside you even at this moment. Some might call that an honour to be host to beings of such super-human greatness."

"But that man?" I asked in a small voice, shaking my head in incomprehension. "You said *he* was a nest. Why did he let you do that to him? And those lumps covering his body? Is that what will happen to me?"

210

He raised an eyebrow meditatively as he placed another parchment manuscript on the table. It seemed to be a page torn from some antique book of great size.

A compact made with the spirits of Shadow has a price equal to its value. He who works the Book of Calling will be plagued by sores that shall not heal. But this is a most trivial matter. Watch these bleeding symbols and you shall see, in time, that tumors begin to form around them. These are cancers. The nesting Shadows' larvae poison the flesh, and the mind, and bring painful illness, and untimely death – often preceded by madness.

Alongside these words was an illustration of a man, naked save for a cloth about his loins. His torso was covered in red symbols and large lumps deformed his flesh. His face was sallow and his aspect haunted and pained. His hands clutched at his hair in torment.

I struggled to compose my thoughts. "You told me there were three ways to escape this. You said I had seen one of them tonight, but what you did to that man – you cannot mean that?"

"Oh yes. Yes, most assuredly. The gift of skin to the shadows – a new page for a new Book of Calling: that is one way out of this. The Tenebrae cannot remain in a body thus left open. The promise of a new book, fresh nests to spawn in, will draw them further away from the subject."

"But who could survive such a wound?"

"Some do," he mused, reassuringly. "Perhaps one in a hundred. And from those who do not survive we may harvest the remaining skin to make yet more books. Nothing is wasted. All is as the shadows wish it to be."

I shuddered. "The other ways – will you please tell me the other ways?" My eyes closed against the books and mirrors.

"You just read another way," he explained. I opened

211

my eyes to see him circling the table: his myriad reflections moving around the pale, still man hunched over the table, like a shark circling its prey.

"I did? I —"

"Death." He smiled. "Your own premature death is the second way out of this." His voice was all sweet consolation.

I felt as though the air were being squeezed from my lungs. I tried to inhale. "And the third way?"

"That, you have also seen tonight. Why else do you think we led you here?"

"What?"

"I knew you would return to me, the shadows told me that it would be so. I smelt your blood in the air tonight. I sensed your shadows through the prickling of my hair. It is they who choose whom to bind to their books, whom to make their nests, whom to make their servants, to join their *Ministri Tenebrarum*."

"I don't understand —"

Dr Palissandro moved to my side and spoke into my ear. I cringed, seeing in the glass his proximity and his inescapability.

"We all begin bound to the Book of Calling. I was once as you are now, and would have died, just as your friend Gildian Greene is dying, but the Servants of Shadow found me and told me that I was chosen to become one of their number. That honour did more than save my flesh. For you see, Monsieur de Bresson, the shadows infest the bodies of their nests, but their servants are honoured in a different way. They live in us here," he whispered, stroking his brow, "imparting knowledge, clarity, insights that no-human eye can see alone. They transform us so that we might serve them better. You cannot imagine what it is like - being able to see into the darkness - and knowing that the darkness is looking back into you ... If you could only understand the power of that supernatural communion, you would not hesitate to pay any price to experience it."

I closed my eyes again, clenching them hard against the flickering golden light that illuminated Dr Palissandro's face. "And what is the price of such unholy communion?"

"Nothing so very great, in comparison with what is gifted. One must grow one's hair, one's limbs might become a little crooked ... and there is the small matter of an initiation that carries certain risks to body and soul. But what are these to all that the Tenebrae give us in their bountiful magnificence? You struggle with the Book of Calling because it amuses the shadows to play with you. But the Servants of Shadow have no such struggle. The book gives us all we desire, easily, effortlessly and without unforeseen consequence, because we do foresee. But such petty, worldly desires quickly fall away. The true reward for we members of the Ministri Tenebrarum is in service itself, to our dark masters."

I opened my eyes in anger, and jumped at what I now saw. For somehow there now appeared to be twice the number of reflections of Dr Palissandro in the room. One set still stood at my side, while another moved slowly around the room. I gave a cry, searching the face of the figure at my side, then the face of that other. I began to breathe again when I realised that it was only that same bearded, long-haired man whom I had followed with the doctor earlier in the evening. The man looked me up and down with his narrow, peering eyes.

"Shall he join us then, Brother?" the man asked coldly, as though I were not even in the room. "Is he worthy?"

"Worthy?" I cried, "To serve these demons who destroyed my wife for sport, and who have ruined my life, just as they will ruin my body?"

The doctor and the other man exchanged a smile. "Our masters only followed your wishes, your instructions," the second man explained.

"I never wished for her to suffer like that! I never wished for her to be unhappy, to fear me, to lose her mind and die! I loved her!"

213

"*Did* you?" Dr Palissandro asked earnestly.

"Yes! But that is something *you* could not understand – a mystery into which you are clearly uninitiated!"

Dr Palissandro steepled his long fingers and glided around the room, meeting my gaze only through the mirrors he passed. "You became infatuated with a woman you did not know. You were fixated upon her – upon an ideal of her that your imagination had conjured. You took her away from her lover, in complete disregard for her own happiness, that you might possess her for your own selfish ends. You killed he whom she loved. You turned her against her own feelings, her own heart. You used magic to destroy her will and it sent her mad. Pray, won't you initiate me into what variety of love that is."

"I will not stand here and listen to this foul perversion," I sobbed, my angry voice resounding coldly in the glassy chamber. "You must release me now or kill me, but I will not remain here a moment longer."

The doctor and the other man smirked at each other.

"Just as you wish, Monsieur de Bresson – after all, what is more important than your own desires. But I do not doubt that you shall return here. That too has been foreseen."

"I could never become one of you. Never!"

"No, no, of course not" the other man said evenly to the doctor, tilting his head and staring at me as though I were some specimen to be dissected. He whispered to the doctor, almost laughing, "*Amantes aeterna*, don't you think?"

The doctor smiled warmly at his foul friend as they both regarded me. Extending his long arm towards the door, the doctor beckoned. "Come then, Monsieur de Bresson we must not keep you – I shall show you the way out."

By the time I arrived back at my townhouse I was beyond exhausted. Terror had kept my heart pounding for what seemed like hours. I had run up the innumerable stairs, out of those blighted catacombs and I had kept running for as long as I had been able, through the dark and silent streets of the early morning hours. My lungs ached.

I did not wish to sleep. I could not bear the thought of more darkness. I lit all the lamps in the parlour and turned them up as high as they would go. I tried to distract myself with smoking, drink, playing the piano, reading. But the emptiness of the house seemed like a crushing weight. Here in this room where Marchelline had come, here where we had first touched, first kissed, where the thrill of our love had ignited, her ghost seemed to hover in the air. I could look nowhere without recalling her, seeing her in that same spot. Her warmth and beauty, now removed, had left my home feeling so cold and ugly I could scarcely stand to remain.

I settled close to the fire, hoping that its blazing light and heat might burn away all the black horrors I had seen. Despite myself, I fell asleep.

I was jolted from my sleep late the next morning. The gas lamps still burned but the fire had died. Light filtered in through the heavy drapes and for a moment I wondered where I was. A telephone was ringing and I leapt from my chair and ran to the hall. There I hesitated, not wishing to speak to anyone, but desperate for the noise to stop. I picked up the ear piece but said nothing.

" ... Hullo? ... Hullo?" A familiar voice quavered worriedly down the line.

"Aunty?" I blurted out at last, almost crying to have this contact from someone so beloved to me. I tried to swallow my tears.

"Nicolas, darling," she began, a terrible solemnity in her tone that frightened me. "I ... I do not know how to tell you this. There is no easy way to say it, but you must know: the priest has just been here and in the most terrible distress. It seems that Marchelline's grave has been ... disturbed."

"What? What do you mean 'disturbed'?"

"Please, please, my darling, try to stay calm. We shall find out what has happened. It will be all right — "

215

"Tell me what has happened!"

"The priest was walking through the churchyard when he noticed the ground over Marchelline's grave had been upset – as though it had been dug up. He and his sexton made an investigation and found that the coffin was … empty."

CHAPTER TWENTY-TWO

I stood beside Marchelline's grave – the spot that *had* been her grave – where we had laid her to rest only yesterday morning. It seemed so long ago now. Dark brown earth was scattered and piled all around – its damp scent in the air making me remember the smell of those catacombs. The bouquet of flowers I had left on the grave had been cast aside and was now partially buried by a haphazard fall of soil. Her grave was now only an obscene hole – half-caved in.

I turned my face away from the ministrations of the distraught priest and covered my tears with my handkerchief until I could compose myself.

"Monsieur de Bresson, I have no words to express my sorrow, my – my outrage at this blasphemy. Never, in all my years in the priesthood have I witnessed such an atrocity. That it should happen in my own churchyard, and to you, of all people – I am mortified, utterly mortified and ashamed, and so very, very sorry."

"Are you certain that she is not here?" I asked, wiping my face still unable to believe or comprehend, wishing that it were not so.

"Yes Monsieur, I am afraid there can be no doubting it. The casket, as you may see, is … quite empty. I … should tell you, Monsieur, the police have been here: little good they seemed to do though."

"Why?

"Well this new man, this Inspector Carême, spent many

217

years in Paris I understand. He dismissed the case at once as an instance of grave robbing. I regret to say that it was quite prevalent in the city some time ago - before you were born, of course. It is the first time to my knowledge that it has happened here. The 'resurrection-men' they used to call them, or 'the Ravens,' a name well-suited indeed to their black pursuit."

"What? What did you say?" I exclaimed.

"Please Monsieur, I know this is too much to bear in your grief, but we can only console ourselves with the fact that your poor wife's soul rests safely in God's hands now. No further harm can come to her now. Her immortal souls live on, with Him. We must —"

"'*Ravens*' you said! It cannot be they – what would they want with her now? Why? Why would they take her? Why? For God's sake!"

"Please Monsieur, let go of my arm – try to calm yourself," the priest urged. I hardly realised that I had grabbed his surplice and was shouting into his stricken, white face as I shook him. "Let us pray together —"

"Prayer can't help me now," I growled, clenching my fists as I backed away from him, fearful that I might strike him. I turned my back and stormed off, wild with the fury and pain that struck deep at my heart: tears burning my cheeks. "It is far too late for that," I shouted over my shoulder. "Far too late!"

I could barely think or breathe as I stormed away from the church and down the track to the road. Even here in the sunshine and in the open green fields I could not escape them and their infernal darkness. Dr Palissandro and his *Ministri Tenebrarum* had to be behind this. It could be no coincidence that while I was lost in their subterranean labyrinth my beloved had been taken. But for what foul purpose?

They could not want her skin, surely? "No, no!" I cried out. It was unthinkable. Was this just a ploy to draw me back to them? Some new part of their evil game? I *could not* return to those catacombs. If I was to cling on to the shredded vestiges of my sanity, I must have nothing at all to do with those men ever again. Death was all that waiting for me in those dark tunnels, I knew that with certainty. It might be the death of my body, or of my soul, but I knew that it was there, waiting for me in the dark.

Could I let them have her – keep her? As completely as that thought filled me with horror, I knew that to do otherwise would be to deliver myself into the hands of the blackest of evils. I would not play their game anymore. I would free myself from their chains, never more open the Book of Calling. If I was to die a premature death from the shadows that they said lived inside me now, then so it must be. I would not be drawn further into their black rituals of blood and madness. I would devote my life to music, as I had always wished to do. I would try to pray if I could. I would remain apart from society, hiding my bleeding wounds and my shameful secrets behind closed doors.

Perhaps, in time, all of this might seem like nothing but a terrible nightmare, a delusion to make me wonder whether, one spring, I had briefly lost my mind. There was no body now – nothing to prove that I had ever been married, that any of it had even happened. Perhaps I could try to convince myself that it had not – for how else could I go on, after all I had done, and seen, and lost?

I looked up and saw two pigeons flying at speed through the clear afternoon sky. I followed their flight until the burning glare of the sun made me look away and close my dazzled eyes. I stopped, a thought stuck in mind like that afterglow that lingered in my darkened vision. Had not the grave of Marie-Thérèse Charpantier also been disturbed – her casket empty?

A cold breeze began to gather as the afternoon was cooling into evening. I trudged on, my head throbbing and my eyes sore. I heard a coarse, low calling to my left and turned to see, in the field adjacent to the road, two ravens picking over the carcass of a small hare.

219

I passed an awkward, silent dinner at aunt Mathilde-Hélène's; she had insisted I must come. She and the twins had beseeched me to stay with them so they might take care of me, but as the hour grew late, I wanted only to be alone and in my own home. I put Maxim back in his travelling cage and had Yves drive me back home in the barouche. At least Maxim was pleased to see me – but how uncharacteristically sad he was. Despite the adoring attentions of the twins, I was certain he mourned for Marchelline, just as I did. As the carriage rolled along he chattered and whistled forlornly, climbing around the cage to be closer to me.

"Would you, would you love me then?" he sang, in imitation of Marchelline's voice.

"Please Maxim, shh," I soothed.

"Shh," he repeated, "Would you? Hullo. Time for crackers. Félix!" He whistled to himself, and imitated the sounds of the bell and the telephone, the frogs in the garden, trying to win my attention. "Would you? Would you love me then?"

I rested my head in my hands.

Yves saw me safely inside, as his mother had insisted he do, but left as soon as he could, now more uncomfortable around me than ever.

Finding myself fearful of the dark, I marshaled many lamps and candles around me in the morning room and lit a fire against the evening's chill. I could not eat. I poured a glass of port from the decanter and sat at the piano, trying to exorcise the silence away with music. A letter had been waiting for me, from Monsieur Combet of the Opera, asking if I might extend a section of the overture and add some minor bridging pieces here and there in particular places.

How welcome it would be to have something new to think about, something normal and mundane upon which to try to focus my tortured energies. I tried not to think of Dr Palissandro and his secret society. I tried not to wonder about

Gildian Greene and the mystery of Marie-Thérèse Charpantier. I tried to tell myself that I might never know what had happened to Marchelline's body – and that it would be for the better if I did not. I must forget. I struggled at first to do anything but stare at the manuscript, adrift in currents and eddies of memory.

I forced myself then, simply to play, to play anything. I played the music that was before me, the song of Agnès as she stands beside the river, the words swimming before my eyes as I read them.

> *… Now I shall sink to where*
> *The wrecks of lost boats shall carry me*
> *Down, without light without air*
> *To a land below –*
> *Where all the forgotten fall*
> *Where cold is all.*
> *The river swells with tears*
> *Of the forgotten*
> *And all I held so dear*
> *Shall be forgotten.*
> *Forgotten, forgotten;*

I was only half-present, hardly aware of Maxim's constant twittering and talking as I played. I was unsure if it was he or the voice of Marchelline in my memory that sang the refrain from my "Song to the Unrequitor," but somehow the song from "The Siren's Tear" blended into that earlier song until and I found myself playing and singing softly,

> *To melt into the water and disappear*
> *Would you,*
> *would you love me then?*
> *If time turned its pages and I tried again*
> *Would you*
> *Would you love me then?*

221

Bobbing and swaying strangely on his perch, Maxim echoed my desolate voice in his peculiar tones: a queer mockery of the voice of my dead beloved.

"Would you? Would you love me then? Would you?"

I stopped playing and felt the notes resound into silence.

"Would you?" Maxim repeated, sadly.

Hearing the trees begin to rustle, I shivered.

"Would you?" he repeated with a strange emphasis.

"Maxim, don't," I muttered quietly.

The wind rose again and I noticed Maxim edging along his perch in nervous agitation. "Love me."

"Maxim, please."

"Hullo Marchelline," he cooed, bobbing his head up and down in excitement.

I felt the hairs rise on the back of my neck and thought for a moment I smelled again that cold smell of earth and death that had clung to my nostrils since last night in the catacombs. Something touched the back of my shoulder ever so lightly – like the point of a knife. I froze, unable to breathe.

"Would you?" Maxim repeated uncertainly.

From behind my right shoulder I heard a sound that chilled me to the marrow: a terrible, windy, unearthly voice such as the breath of no living mortal ever made. "Would you? Love me? Love me ..."

I whimpered.

"My love?" the dry, breathless voice rasped.

Overtaken by an impulse beyond conscious thought, I looked over my shoulder, crashing backwards onto the keys at the thing I saw. What had touched me was a kind of claw, with three talons at the front and one to the side. In that moment I thought it the claw of some giant monstrous bird. I fell to the floor, crawling backward like some mindless animal, wetting myself unconsciously and wailing in a voice I did not recognize as my own.

It was not a bird's claw that had touched me, but a

human hand, stripped of most of its flesh: its bones exposed and one of its fingers missing. It was Marchelline's hand reaching out towards me. It was *her* face that stared at me with its dry, lifeless eyes: her face, but hideously changed. Part of the flesh on the forehead near the scalp was missing, and part of the brow and the tip of the nose were also gone, exposing bone and grisly, dead sinew and torn flesh. The white nightgown in which she had been buried was foul with soil and stained with some brownish fluid. Her hair, where it remained, was matted with thick clots of earth. Her purple-grey skin was dirt-marked and misshapen, as though it has somehow shifted from its proper place.

I heard myself scream "No!" as she moved towards me, and now Maxim too began to flap his wings wildly, crying out in alarm.

"Love me," Marchelline wheezed, a scattering of earth falling from her mouth onto the floor. "Make love to me, I need you. I was so alone in that dark. I could not rest without you."

"No, no, no," I sobbed, backing away toward the wall as she crept closer with that stiff inhuman gait. "No, my love, no – this cannot be!" I climbed the wall for I could not stand unaided, lurching away from her, crashing through chairs and upsetting tables and shattering ornaments as I surged haphazardly around the room to get away, trying not to look at her, trying to pretend that she was not, *could not* be there.

"No, I am mad, I have gone mad – this is impossible, unthinkable – no!" I turned around and she loomed into my face, pressing against me that broken, dead countenance so that I felt the sharp chill of her naked bone against my cheek, and froze in the stiff embrace of those arms, feeling the rough scratch of her skeletal hand as it wrapped around my neck.

"Love me," the windy voice whistled into my ear. "I'm so cold. Why did you leave me down there in the dark?"

I tried to twist away from her but she clung tightly, spinning stiffly in my arms as though we were dancing some ghoulish waltz, the points of her bony fingers digging into my throat.

"No, no, my love," I whimpered, trying not to look at her face, recoiling as I grasped her bony arm to try and free myself. "No Marchelline, my darling, you are dead. You must go to your rest."

Her clouded, dull eyes looked up into mine, her dry mouth open, revealing a dark purple tongue as dry as paper. "I cannot. I cannot rest without you. You called me to you, once and forever."

"But ... but you are – you are dead, my love."

"Tell me you love me," she implored, stroking my face with her rasping bones. I stifled a scream that escaped me as an anguished moan. "I am frightened. I do not know what is happening. I feel so strange."

"Of course I love you, I – I will always love you, but ..."

"Then love me. Love me," the discordant voice moaned into my ear. "I cannot feel anything but cold. Make me feel something again. Fill me with ecstasy as you used to do. Warm me with your love, your body. Oh love me, my dearest, my husband. If I cannot have you now I fear that I shall ... I shall ..." All at once she pressed her cold, bloodless lips to my mouth, the taste of dirt and decay filling my mouth as her dry stiff tongue moved against my own. Prickling hands clawed at me as she moved her icy, rigid body against my own.

With a scream I broke free of her, wiping my mouth on my sleeve in a desperate bid to remove the poisonous taste, as if death itself were infectious and she were polluting me with it so that I might join her.

"Who did this to you? Who took you from your grave – who brought you here?"

"It was no-one but you, my darling. It was my love for you, that irresistible impulse calling me to you, as it has from the first. That calling tells me somehow where you are, and draws me to you. I had to free myself from that black prison to be near you. I could not stay there. I fought and I scratched and dug." She held up her damaged hand before her eyes, some dim expression of anguish shadowing her face. "I hurt my hand, and my head." She tried to cover her torn brow with the skeletal hand, as if embarrassed by her appearance.

"You must return to your grave," I ordered, trying vainly to summon some semblance of authority.

"No," she wheezed, the suggestion of displeasure making her monstrous appearance all the more terrifying. "I belong with you. I *must* be with you."

"One day, when I die …. "

"I cannot wait. You must join me now. When you are dead too, we can be together forever – nothing can separate us then. No more blood, no more secrets. Come, my love," she begged, reaching out her clawing hands. "Let me help you to die and we shall be buried together in an eternal embrace. It is easier than you think. Only a minute or two and it shall all be over, then it shall all begin anew." She edged closer to me.

"No … no!" Afraid of what she might do, I sought desperately for some idea. "I do not have to die yet," I began. I swallowed and steeled myself, reaching out to take her hand. My skin crawled to feel those bones moving against the palm of my hand, but I had to go on. "Come, come with me, I shall take you to bed," I soothed, breathlessly.

Marchelline nodded stiffly, her mouth moving in some vestigial attempt to smile. I took up a lamp and led her out towards our bedroom. She followed me eagerly, and with as much speed as her unyielding limbs could manage. "I long for you," that eerie voice whistled behind me. "I think only of you … "

"You haunt my heart at every moment," I murmured as I drew her in through the bedroom door and set the lamp down. I turned it down very low then picked Marchelline up in my arms and laid her down upon the bed.

"I want so to rest," she whispered, "but not alone."

"I know, my love. I am here with you."

I climbed onto the bed beside her, trying not to breath

through my nose as I lay close to her. Her limbs stirred in agitation, her face twisting towards me.

"Love me," she beseeched.

"Let me just hold you," I assuaged, "I am so very tired. I thought you were lost to me and I have been grieving for you. Let us hold each other until sleep comes."

"Yes, my love. Say you love me still."

"I love you, always." I felt a tear roll down my cheek as I held her in the near darkness.

"Yes, you and I and your shadows – we will all be together, forever."

"Hush now … rest a while."

Her longing somehow appeased by my nearness, Marchelline seemed to drift away into some state of torpor. In stillness she appeared to be quite dead. But lying in my bed, holding her corpse in my arms, I was so far from sleep, I wondered how I would ever sleep again.

After some endless time, when I was certain that she was more or less dormant, I began to ease myself from her embrace, as gently and slowly as I could. My arms freed, I slunk from the bed, and taking every caution not to make even the slightest sound, I moved through the door and began to close it, removing the key from the inside lock as I did so. But in closing, the door gave a long, high creak. I fumbled at the lock and turned the key sharply, locking the door from the outside.

At last I could breathe again. I leant against the door, clutching my hands to my face, then recoiling at the stench of death that clung to my skin. I thought I heard a noise and I froze. There was a shuffling of feet from within. Silence, then a sharp, rhythmic scratching and tapping against the door, like the sound of a tree moving against a windowpane.

I had heard the same sound before – that night in Gildian Greene's Paris townhouse. A wave of nausea gripped me as my mind expanded into a dreadful new understanding. I rushed out into the dark garden, falling onto my hands and knees as I vomited, shaking – tears coursing down my face.

CHAPTER TWENTY-THREE

It was late the next evening as I walked silently along the Allée Vivaldi, towards the Paris home of Gildian Greene. Over my shoulder I carried a bag with a heavy iron crow bar concealed inside.

I had passed the remainder of the previous night in securing the bedroom against any chance of Marchelline escaping. If a coffin could not hold her, I feared that a locked door and closed windows would not be sufficient either. In the abandoned gardener's toolshed I had found a hammer and nails, and, by lamplight, I stopped up the bedroom windows and boarded over their shutters. All the while the pitiful tapping of Marchelline's fingers against the glass tore at my heart.

To make sure that my aunt or cousins would not call at the house, I had returned poor Maxim into their care when daylight came, and told them I was going away for a few days. Their horror at the sight of my ravaged and haunted appearance, left them in no doubt that I needed to get away and rest.

I could not stand to remain and see Marchelline the way she was. I simply could not bear to see what I had done to her – the monster that I had made of her. To know that death had brought her no relief from the sufferings I had caused her – to see how my blundering magic had dragged her back from the grave into this hideous travesty of existence – made me wish once more that I were dead myself. If only I could exchange my life for hers. I had broken the most fundamental laws of nature. I had damned my beloved to Hell and myself as well. How could I ever put things right now?

I surveyed the lonely street as I approached number fifteen. All was still and quiet. I smoothed down my black gloves as I walked up the low steps towards the padlocked front door. In the dim gaslight from the street I saw at once that something was different here. The leaves and rubbish that had been piled up on the doorstep had been cleared aside, as if the door had very recently been opened.

I stopped and listened, pressing my ear to the door. I heard nothing. I leaned towards the front window and tried to see in. No hint of any light escaped the heavy drapes that hung there.

Crouching low on the ground, I drew the iron crow from my bag and set to levering off the padlock. I pulled at the iron bar until I heard the creak of the metal bracket being torn away from the wooden door. Another yank broke it free and the padlock fell, swinging against the doorframe with a clank. I tried the door but it was still locked. There was nothing for it but to use the narrow, hooked end of the bar to break the door open.

I winced at the terrible noise of splintering wood as the door gave way under my strenuous efforts and I prayed that no-one heard or cared what I was doing here. With a slow creak the heavy door swung open and a dark hallway was visible beyond. I leaned my hand on the threshold as I searched in the bag for my dark lantern and felt something gritty crunching beneath my palm. I hastened to light the lamp and as its flame bloomed into life I saw that the threshold was crusted in a deep broad line of salt – exactly as I had seen at the threshold of the cellar of the infernal farmhouse. Raising up the lantern in one hand, and the iron crow in the other, I entered.

A sour smell of dust, mould and stale air assailed my

senses and made me cough. When Gildian Greene had first brought me here, I had been near unconscious with drink. All I had noticed was the fire, his face and that infernal book. Now, in a more sober condition, I was stunned to remark the state of the house. Cobwebs hung in great sheets from every corner. Faded paper was peeling from the wall beside a staircase thickly carpeted with dust and bits of fallen plaster. Footprints in the dusty hall floor led through a doorway to the right.

This was the parlour in which Monsieur Greene had entertained me on that accursed evening. The light of my lantern fell upon furniture covered with dust cloths – a room unoccupied for many years. There was the large, black marble fireplace, just as I recalled it – but now I could see that the mantle was grey and densely furred with dust. The armchair in which I had sat was covered up, but the side table next to it still bore the coffee cup I had drunk from. A dark puddle of coffee still remained in the cup – two dead moths floating on its surface.

In the far corner of the room, the tall, sinuous bookcase brooded, its glass door hazy and finger-marked. Remembering my dream, I rushed to scan its shelves. There, high among the neatly arranged rows of books was the void where the Book of Calling had once resided. The adjacent book had fallen over and leaned diagonally across the empty space. I held up the lamp, standing on my toes and pressing my face close to the grimy glass, wishing beyond anything else that it should be that Book Of Release that my dream had conjured. But "Lessons From The Torah," was the title the neighbouring book bore.

I tried the ornately carved door and it swung open freely. Clearly, Monsieur Greene had no reason to lock it anymore. Most of the books treated of religious subjects; others dealt with the cultivation of flowers, the history of art and other mundane matters. I sighed and looked up at the ceiling – a patch of mould darkening the plaster over my head.

I stiffened at the suggestion of some faint sound and

tried to steady my breathing. I had tried not to look at first, distracting myself in details of the room and the pursuit of a non-existent book, but now I had to face it. In the light of sobriety, the peculiar shape of the room was impossible to ignore. In what should have been a regular, rectangular shaped parlour, one large corner of the space had been walled off – as though another, smaller chamber had been formed within the room. One wall of this second chamber – the wall that formed the alcove housing the bookcase – was plastered and finished in perfect harmony with those around it, even bearing an old painting of a hunting scene: but the second face of the smaller chamber, sitting at right angles to the room's tall front windows, was curtained in the same heavy drapes, to create the illusion that behind those soft furnishings was just another window.

The muffled noise behind the curtain grew louder. A hot scorch of fear surged in my stomach as something hard and pointed tapped on glass behind the drape. There was a high keening scratching at the glass.

I held out the iron bar and hooked its curved end around the curtain, raising my lantern as I pulled the faded, burgundy drape aside. At first all I saw was a door. It was made of dark wood and had an oval-shaped glass panel set into it. But this panel was partially obscured by a wrought-iron screen that was bolted to the wood, blocking the blackly shining glass with curving lines and shapes that were suggestive of the eyes of peacock feathers. Despite the fine artistry of its execution, there was no mistaking the intent behind the screen. Its thick ironwork could only be intended as a security barrier to keep something out – or in.

I swept the curtain to one side and edged nearer the glass panel, seeing in it only the lamp-lit reflection of my own gaunt and scowling face. Then something in the reflected face changed and I reared back. There was another face there, trying to see through the glass. Pity stung my heart with a terrible pang to look upon the poor creature before me.

I recognized at once the same stiff and deathly condition, the same awful absences of flesh, the same dry and clouded eyes as I had seen in my poor Marchelline. Here was another corpse, somehow still animated and imprisoned, when she ought to have been in her grave. But this creature was so small, so withered and ancient looking - like an Egyptian mummy I had once seen in the museum - but all the more hideous for the piteous expression she wore. Her countenance was one of ineffable sadness and longing, etched into desiccated flesh. Horrible eyes searched for something through the glass with heartbreaking intensity.

I gestured for the creature to stand back and I broke in the door with the iron crow. I gagged and retched and had to shield my nose at the smell that escaped the room. I could barely begin to describe it. More than mildew and staleness, it was the stench of putrefaction, mixed up with some queer salty smell, as if the taste of tears were a scent in the air that had gone quite rancid. All was darkness within. I intruded my foot across the threshold and felt again the scuffing and scattering of salt crystals under my shoe. The lantern cast its soft glow into the void and what I saw made me want to weep.

The little, desiccated figure huddled in a corner, as though in fear of me. She was so short of stature, little more than five feet tall. The remnants of long blonde hair streamed from her head. Around her tiny neck hung a rosary. She wore a dusty, faded dress, in the fashion of some thirty years ago. But as much as the wretched figure herself, it was the pitiful contents of the room that so stung at my soul: a tiny bed, a crucifix upon the wall, a little chair and a small table with a few pieces of jewellery, a hairbrush and perfume bottle - but no mirror. A yellowed nightgown lay over the end of the bed, unworn, it would appear, for long decades. A hook on the wall supported a heavy, black cloak, stiff with dust. These were all the things she had of her own in her little cell. Everything else in that tiny room belonged, or related to someone else.

On the table and the walls, in simple wooden frames,

232

were numerous photographic likenesses and artist's portraits of Gildian Greene as a younger man: how handsome he looked, and how healthy then. Arranged on two shelves like a little shrine in a corner sat a collection of things I could only surmise had been his: an old pipe, a handkerchief, a battered hat, a pocket watch, a comb, a scent bottle. Then I noticed in the narrow bed a man's suit had been laid out, as though its owner were lying in the bed. Crushed, creased and worn, it appeared that someone had spent years caressing and embracing the empty suit as it lay there.

"Marie-Thérèse Charpantier?" I ventured in a gentle whisper at the cowering figure. She looked at me and shook her head stiffly. Her mouth opened and a noise like cold, rushing air was all the sound that came out, forming almost inaudible words. She struggled to speak – as though she had almost forgotten how.

"Marie-Thérèse Henri," the halting, tortured voice whispered with a queer suggestion of pride. She looked towards the open door in wonder and incomprehension. "Solomon," she sighed with a ghastly wheeze. "I must go to him. I cannot rest without him. I have been trapped here for so very long," she lamented. "I must go to him at once." She lurched towards the door, feeling with her hands, apparently unable to believe that it was open at last.

"Can you tell me, Madame – do you know where your husband is?"

She looked around, frowning, struggling to make sense of my words.

"Always, always. His heart calls me to him constantly. I must go to him. I must be near him. Will he ever forgive me for staying away? It has been an eternity of torture, imprisoned here without my love. There is nothing else."

"Is he far away, can you tell me?"

"In the countryside – a pretty cottage with flowers."

"Is it in Épône, can you tell me that?"

She nodded slowly.

233

"If I hired a carriage, would you allow me to escort you there? I too would very much like to see Monsieur Henri."

"You will take me to him, Monsieur?"

"Yes, yes if you will permit me."

"Soon, soon? Now? I *must* go to him at once."

Unable to lock the doors, as I ran into the streets, searching for any cab or carriage I might be able to hire, I feared the Madame Henri might wander off into the night, so desperate was she to get to her husband. It was with immense relief that I returned, some few minutes later, jumping from the carriage I had hired and running up the steps and into Monsieur Greene's parlour, to find her in a rapture, moving with extraordinary slowness about the room, touching his things as if they were holy relics to be worshipped. From behind, I saw that her tiny frame shook, and a terrible sound escaped her, like dry, wheezing sobs from lungs that were rotten and holed.

"I have a carriage, Madame Henri," I panted, "when you are ready."

She turned to me, her stiff grey countenance grimacing with some strange admixture of sorrow and joy. But her pained eyes were dry as marbles.

I ran to fetch the cloak that hung in her chamber, covering my face as I shook the mildew and dust off the garment. I returned to her side and wrapped the cloak around her narrow, skeletal shoulders. As I lifted the hood to set it upon her head she looked up at me, straining to focus.

"Thank you," her voice whistled. "You cannot know what it means to me. He is all that I think of ... he is life itself ..."

How can I describe the peculiarity of the long, strange journey we took together that night? I tried to press myself into the side of the carriage, fearful of getting too close to this wretched undead creature at my side, who reeked of misery and mildew and long, slow decay. She said but little as the carriage rolled along, only sometimes asking, like a confused child, "How much longer?" "When shall we be there?" – even before we had left the outskirts of the city.

Her silence and the motion of the carriage, coupled with the insupportable strain to mind and body I had endured over the previous days conspired to send me to sleep, and for a while I was able to escape the horror of my predicament. I awoke from a dreamless slumber to the happy bewilderment of one not yet remembering who he is or what his troubles might be.

But the graveyard smell of my companion instantly shattered my oblivion and returned me to the awfulness of reality. There she sat in the light of the early morning. She was as still as death, the motions of the carriage jostling her stiffly like some grotesque china-faced doll.

"Madame?" I ventured as I painfully returned to my senses, curiosity burning in my brain. "Might I ask you a question?"

She seemed to stir, her glazed open eyes beginning to move, taking me in with some momentary confusion, as though she too had been lost in her own kind of sleep.

"If you wish," her windy voice croaked.

"Was your marriage to Monsieur Henri a happy one?"

"Happy?" she replied in evident perplexity. "I loved him utterly, as I love him still. I cannot exist without him. I need always to be at his side or I do not exist. To be near him is more than happiness to me – it is as essential to me as breathing."

"And may I ask – what happened to you? What separated you from your husband?"

She shook her head as if straining to recall or understand. "My beloved was going somewhere ... to do something ... he wished me to remain behind, but I *could* not. I saw him disappearing into a crowd on the other side of the road, and I was compelled to follow. The horse's head struck

235

me here." She frowned and turned her head away from me, pulling down her hood to reveal a horrible crack in the back of her skull, gaping and visible beneath the thin strands of her hair that she moved aside. "And here, and here, their hooves hurt me," she moaned, clutching at her stomach and chest, her fingers sinking into round hollow indentations that her loose dress concealed. "Then I slept for a time, I think. And afterwards, I could not find him. I was trapped somewhere, in the dark. I think some people had taken him away, and confined me too. Somehow we had been separated. I went searching for him, but ... Perhaps I did something to displease him. I was not so pretty after the accident as before, I fear." She pulled up the hood and covered her head, turning her face away. " ... But I know that he loves me still – he must because I love him so, do you see? He must ... must ... he would be with me now if he could. Only something prevents him. I do not know what it is. But we will be together again ere long, I know it ... we must ... "

At last, as the sun was just beginning to rise over the chill of the early morning, the carriage drew up before the deep, sloping lawns and blooming flowerbeds of Gildian Greene's picturesque, high-roofed home. I stepped down and dropped my bag onto the ground, assisting the stiff-limbed Marie-Thérèse out of the carriage, her hood drawn down over her face to conceal her from the driver. I turned back to the driver to pay him his fare and asked him if he might wait.

"Thank you, Monsieur," he tipped his hat before stuffing the generous sum into his pocket. "But these horses need water and feed something awful. There's a coaching inn we passed a mile or two back. That's where I must go now. I'll likely be there for a while if you want me. Or you'll find another carriage there, when I'm gone."

"But can't you wait, I will pay you."

"I'm sorry, Sir, but these beasts are my livelihood, and they ain't used to such long runs. I really oughtn't to have done it at all, only I needed the money so bad."

"Very well then, thank you driver."

I scratched my head as the driver clicked at his weary horses and turned the carriage back up the road. Looking back towards the house I was horrified to find my bag open on the ground and Marie-Thérèse nowhere to be seen.

I padded up the lawn, searching for any clue as to where she might have gone. The gleaming white front door was securely closed, as were the windows. Not a soul stirred. I followed a gravel path around the right side of the house, aware, as I hastened, of a peculiar noise coming from somewhere above me. It was a regular, muffled thumping sound that I could not identify. There was something in the sound that set my teeth on edge and made me run.

In a moment I found the back door of the house – ajar. I burst into the empty kitchen, still hearing that peculiar sound and knowing now that I had to follow it. I found a staircase and bolted up it, taking two and three stairs at once in my frenzy. I ran towards the front of the top floor, the sound growing louder as I approached. Then all at once it ceased. I glimpsed an open door from the hallway I stood in, and lurched towards it.

At first all I saw was a black shape – the small, cloaked form of Marie-Thérèse, standing with her back to me. She was very still, and held something at her side that seemed almost too heavy for her to carry in her fragile arm. Hearing the creak of my step she turned, as fast as she was able, a searching hope in her blood-spattered face. But recognizing me, her countenance fell once more into that pained and longing expression I knew too well. Now I saw that her hand and the front of her dress were dripping red gouts onto the golden wood floorboards. The iron crow was clutched in her hand, its hooked end glistening and wet.

"What have you done?" I hissed, staggering towards the door. My view of the bed blocked by Marie-Thérèse, I could only see pale, yellow-green wallpaper, whose sparse

237

pattern of filigree and flowers was polluted by sprays and flecks of red that did not belong there. Marie-Thérèse dropped the iron bar and stepped aside, looking as frail as a paper doll.

My hand shot up to cover my mouth and nose at what I saw then, stifling myself lest I should scream. A woman lay in the bed, still tucked beneath a white and green coverlet, her elegant hands resting, in perfect stillness, above the counterpane. I recognized them as the hands of Madame Esther Greene, so fine and delicate, those same hands that I had seen caressing the insistent cat and writing Dr Palissandro's address out for me. Her wedding band was adorned with a single drop of blood, like a perfectly round, liquid ruby.

I could not see her face, for that handsome, smiling face was no more. All I saw was a bloody mess where that kindly countenance should have been, and a deep chestnut braid threaded with grey, trailing out behind upon a pillow that was soaked and running with blood. Gildian Greene was nowhere to be seen.

"Why?" I cried, "Why have you done this?"

"*She* did it. She took my love away from me, *she* kept him from me – she is to blame – and I must be with him … Now we can be together. We must … he loves me still … he must … "

"Madame? Madame? Are you all right?" A concerned and confused voice called from another part of the upper floor. Footsteps sounded along the hall rushing towards Madame Greene's bedroom, and my pounding heart flooded with panic.

CHAPTER TWENTY-FOUR

Marie-Thérèse glided out of the bedroom door and I heard the most terrible scream of mortal fear. Then something fell heavily upon the floor.

I rushed out to find Marie-Thérèse standing over the unconscious form of the round-faced little maid – her countenance as white as the nightgown and lace-trimmed cap she wore.

I ran, flying down the stairs, to escape that place – insensible with horror at what had happened and terrified of being observed at such a scene. There was a little stable behind the house and I rushed into it, startling the two black horses that dozed in their stalls.

I snatched a bridle from a hook upon the wall and tried to speak soothingly to the nervous horses, struggling to calm myself sufficiently to allow me to harness one. As soon as the bit was in the horse's mouth and the bridle secured over his head I scrambled onto his back – not waiting to saddle him. I could not linger for even one instant longer.

The horse surged out of the open stable door, shaking his head and circling in agitation as I strained to bring him under my control. At the sight of Marie-Thérèse standing motionless and bloody before him, he reared up with a cry of fright, and it was only by the strenuous grip of my legs around his belly and my arms around his neck that I was not thrown off. Marie-Thérèse stared up at me, those cold dead eyes full of expectancy, her arms reaching up to me to take her with me.

"Where is your husband?" I demanded, my voice breaking, as I struggled to rein in the horse's wildly pulling head.

"A farmhouse in Farceaux," her tiny, windy voice whispered, almost inaudible over the horse's huffing and whinnying. "You must take me to him at once," she pleaded, "you must."

I kicked at the horse's sides and he reared and flung out his hooves towards the wraith before us. For a moment I wished that he had struck her and finished the job that those other horses had only begun decades before. As he took off at a frenzied gallop I did not look back at the tiny, cloaked figure that remained, reaching its arms towards me. But even so, I could not escape that hideous, withered, haunted face that burned in my mind's eye and the gruesome recollection of what she had done.

Little knowing or caring whither I fled, I rode furiously away, sobbing, then wailing uncontrollably, like a lost child. I had pitied her at first, that vile murderous creature – not fully understanding what she was. And now, as much as I abhorred her for the brutal, unspeakable thing she had done to poor, kind Esther Greene, still greater pity and sorrow stung me to the marrow of my bones for what had been done to Marie-Thérèse herself.

What greater torture could be imagined than to love, unrequitedly, compulsively, and with such supernatural intensity that even the finality of death was vanquished by the force of that love? To love eternally in the silent dark, alone and reviled. To know that he whom you loved walked freely and alive in the warm sunshine, in the open air: living, loving again, and aware, all the while, that you were eternally in his thrall, but unwilling and unable to release you, or to ever love you more.

Could she really be blamed for what she had become – for how he had enslaved her to him all those years ago? The full realization of what I had done to poor Marchelline crashed down over my head. And what could I do to save her from this most unthinkable of fates? If I could not find some remedy, I could not go on living. But if I died – would even that release her? Or would she linger on, clutching my corpse until it too rotted into dust? Could her tormented soul ever find freedom?

I had to reach Gildian Greene and learn whatever he knew. I felt the little knife in my pocket bouncing hard against my thigh as the horse ran on. If it came to that, I would not hesitate to force him to finally reveal the truth to me.

Unsure of exactly where I was going, I followed my instincts and tried to divine the way from such scant signposts as I saw. The poor frightened horse ran on, unceasingly, frantic to escape the terrifying creature it had seen and the sobbing man upon his back, who was so filled with self-loathing and grief, and who stank of the blood that seeped through his clothes. At last I saw a road I recognized from before and followed it along to the fork that led to the lonely track that hid the farmhouse.

I scanned along the overgrown hedgerow, looking for the concealed entrance to the farmhouse, as the horse, now foaming and exhausted, lumbered slowly along, his huge chest heaving beneath me. But no great scrutiny was needed, for where I had deduced the entrance lay before, an opening had been hacked and broken through the twigs and bushes, just wide enough for a horse and rider to pass through. Some ineffectual attempt had been made to conceal this gap with long dead branches and broken twigs roughly shoved into the void, but this seemed to have been done in haste and with very little care.

I dismounted, my legs sore from clinging onto the horse, and I held onto the reins as I cleared the obstruction away. The horse's eyes showed white as I tried to lead him through the narrow space and I spoke soothingly to him until he followed, too exhausted to resist me. I tethered him there, where the grass grew long and was wet with dew, and I stole on around the curving track past the dilapidated barn. But my creeping steps were arrested by a terrible sound echoing from within the old farmhouse whose door still lay on the kitchen floor from my last visit. It was the most peculiar sound of a man moaning: half in pleasure, half in pain, but unutterably weary and broken.

"Please," the man's distant voice implored. "Please, let me be. I release you. Go to your rest now." The moaning resumed, coloured now only by torment.

I crept through the door, shielding my face against the flapping pigeons that could little frighten me now, after all else I had seen. Following the sound I stole on, trying not to cough at the foul smell and dust, and at the recollection of the storm of ash and unquiet spirits and shadows that had engulfed me here before.

"I pray you, let me rest," the exhausted voice begged.

It was coming from the little bedroom and through the open doorway I saw that a man's legs lay on the filthy bed, restlessly moving as if trying to struggle free from something. Edging closer I peered around the doorframe, my lip curling at what I saw. There in the middle of the filthy sheets lay Gildian Greene, disheveled, his shirt undone and his chest covered in bandages – dressings which could not hide the innumerable deforming lumps and growths that covered his torso. He moved constantly in some agitation and the sheets around him bunched and ruffled. I was about to speak – to confront him – when I realised that he was not alone.

For even when he momentarily stopped moving, the sheets around him continued to move. The foul dusty bed revealed shallow indentations – as though of other moving bodies who lay beside Greene, unseen. His shirt opened further, and he tried to wrest it back from whoever was invisibly undressing him. His trouser leg creased as if under some undetectable hand, and he wanly tried to bat the phantom hand away, as one would a fly.

"No more, please, I pray you," he cried, and as he turned his head he opened his clenched eyelids and caught sight of me. "No!" he shouted, sitting upright and scrambling back towards the headboard.

"Monsieur Greene," I snarled, "you must tell me the truth – all of it, do you hear – or I will not be responsible for what I might do to you!"

"Monsieur de Bresson?" he gasped, clutching his heart. "Can it really be you?"

"None other, Monsieur." I stepped closer into the dim light of the bedroom.

"With the light behind you, I only saw a black silhouette – I thought you … a shadow." An unseen hand moved his silver hair and he shuddered, struggling to move off the bed against some restraining arms that I could not see, but which tugged at his shirtsleeves and collar. "Please, please?" he beseeched the empty air. "Let me be! I will return to you shortly – just, let me breathe!"

He staggered to his feet unsteadily, clutching at his abdomen: his face twisted and white with pain. He moved close to me as I stood in the doorway, and he took me in with a long, knowing and unimaginably weary look. He laid his hand upon my shoulder. "I am so unutterably sorry. I know that will mean little to you, but – I acted out of desperation. Perhaps now you understand a little of that desperation. It is no excuse, I fully understand that what I have done to you is unforgivable, and yes, I do deserve all of this, and more. Soon enough I will get what is coming to me, have no fear of that. Perhaps you have come to kill me yourself – and I could not blame you for it. Perhaps it would be best for all if you did." He gestured into the air and hung his head, wandering weakly out past me into the long parlour with its darkly stained floor.

"Why?" I shouted, following him, wanting to strike him, to hurt him for all the misfortune he had cast me into. "Why did you choose me? Why destroy my life? Why?"

He looked over his shoulder at me, his red eyes pinched

243

with shame and guilt. He suppressed a cry of pain and his hand gripped the mantelpiece as he reached it. He tried to catch his breath, doubling over in evident agony.

"I saw myself in you," he said quietly, through clenched teeth. "God forgive me. I knew it was wrong, cruel, hateful, but Monsieur – " He tore at the bandages around his chest and pulled them down with an effort that took his breath away. Turning around to face me, his eyes were filled with tears. I blinked at he sight of his naked chest, shocked to see another set of wounds so like my own, and horrified at the profusion of deep, pink, veined, bulbous lumps that clustered like bunches of grapes around his weals. "This is what I am facing – death itself. It is cancer, of the shadows. I have not long to live. The pain is quite unbearable – but that matters not to me compared with the thought of leaving my Esther behind. I thought that if I gave the book away the shadows might follow it and leave me – that the illness might go away. I cannot bear the thought of leaving my wife all alone in this world. I have tried everything else," he sobbed.

"I fell under the influence of that ghoul Dr Palissandro for a time – little realizing at first that his instructions were only making matters worse. I even considered giving them my skin – as he tried to persuade me to do. He tried to mesmerize me into becoming one of their sacrifices. But in my condition, I knew that it would be certain death. I doubt that any of their victims survive.

"Giving the book away was the only thing I could think of that I had not tried. So after I broke free of him some months ago, I decided to find someone. I prowled the bars, stalking the world-weary, the sick of heart. Many times I picked a victim but could not go through with it, leaving them drunk and alone where I had found them. Then you came along … I could say that the shadows chose you. I could say they made me do it, but these are only excuses. I knew you would take the book and use it. I hoped you would use it enough to draw the shadows out of my life. But all I have done is rain misery upon us both – it is inscribed in your face as it is on mine. And my condition has only grown worse." Suddenly, his expression changed and he looked up at me with grave concern. "But how did you know I would be here?"

"Someone told me."

He rushed at me, clutching at my collar in wild-eyed alarm. "Who? Who was it? No-one could have known I was here except – except – You have not been to my house in Paris! Oh please, no!"

"Yes." I shook him off, unsure of how much to reveal to him.

"Dear God, tell me that you did not let her out! Did you? Did you?"

"I opened the door and spoke to her – I had to know. Because of the book my own wife is dead – but undead, she cannot rest – she haunts me bodily. I left her living corpse locked up in my bedroom – like your first wife. You *have* to tell me what is going on – how I can release her from this horror! Tell me!"

"Did you let her out – Marie-Thérèse? Did you?" He searched my eyes, some plan formulating in his mind. "I must fly at once, I have to reach Esther before it is too late. I have to protect her." He rushed to the chair, where his coat and hat lay by his silver-topped walking stick. Snatching them up clumsily in his arms he began to limp, hastily, towards the door.

"It *is* too late," I murmured, to arrest him.

"No." The back of his head shook and his arms clasped tighter around the bundle he carried as he swayed in the doorway. His voice dropped. "No. No, no … "

"I am most deeply sorry for her – I know she was a good woman. She had nothing to do with this and did not deserve –"

" – No!" The tangled mass of coat and hat fell to the floor and the cane rattled on the dusty boards. Monsieur Green's shoulders shook violently. After some moments he spoke, his voice thick with tears and apprehension. "And

245

Marie-Thérèse? Where is she now?"

"I left her there, I presume she is on her way here even as we speak."

Greene turned to face me, his countenance distorted with rage. "Oh God! This is your fault! Yours! If you had not broken the seal," he yelled, gesturing towards the broken doorway I had revealed, scattered now with bricks and rubble, "they would not have come for me, those lustful ghosts – I would not have had to leave Esther then to draw them away. You awoke them! You made me – Your fault – your … " The words stuck in his throat and he fell to his knees, weeping. "Oh Esther, my dearest love – forgive me, forgive me, I beg you. I never deserved you, my love. Oh dear God, may you find rest … oh Esther … "

"And what of her? Is she now doomed to this eternal living death too? Longing for you, unable to die? Another monster to be consigned to a cell forever?"

"No, no. I learned my lessons, God forgive me. I never, never wanted that to happen again. Oh Esther, Esther … "

"Tell me!" I demanded of him, brandishing my little knife towards him with a shaking hand. "Before Marie-Thérèse arrives and some fresh hell breaks loose, you have to tell me what is going on or by God I will kill you myself!"

Greene collapsed backwards, sitting on the floor, hugging his knees, hunched forward. How frail and broken he looked. "I was just a boy myself, only nineteen and so very unworldly, when I first saw Marie-Thérèse. She was so sublimely beautiful, so sweet and good – who can say what it was that stole my heart in the moment I first saw her. Why her and not another who might return my love? I wish now that I had never seen her at all. I loved her with all the fervour of a boy's love – or what I thought was love then. All I knew then was that I had to make her mine. When she refused me, I thought I would die. It only made me want her all the more. I could not imagine how I might ever be happy with anyone else, or how I could go on. I did not want to. And I could not

246

forget her. Why could she not love me as I loved her? I knew I could make her happy if only she would give me the chance. "It was in another sad Paris bar that another kindly old gentleman listened to my woes and promised me the answer to my heart's desire. Of course I did not recognise then the beard and long hair of a member of the *Ministri Tenebrarum* – how could I? All I knew was that the book promised relief from my misery. And yes, I called Marie-Thérèse to me. Yes, I made her love me. And yes, I rejoiced in that love and in the power the book gave me. I thought myself so clever. But even as she loved me, the fear that she had had of me from the start never really left her. And our love never really made her happy. She loved me compulsively, slavishly, desperately – but without joy. Like an automaton, she lived as my bride, and by degrees that forced, unnatural love I had conjured in her breast killed the love I had for her. I was young and selfish. I had thought that the love of such a woman could only make me feel good about myself. But her torments only reflected back to me the wrong I had done her. She suspected that I had something to do with the death of that priest who pursued us. Of course she was right, but I could only deny it. In time, that conflict began to drive her mad.

"I was as fickle as ever youth can be. In time, I simply grew tired of her anguish, tired of *her* – that is the unvarnished truth of the matter. My heart wandered. My imagination took flame with the possibilities the book offered me. I could have any woman I wanted – as many as I desired. But Marie-Thérèse would never leave my side. She could not.

"Another woman caught me eye and I knew I could have her with the book's help. Jeanne Lafitte was everything Marie-Thérèse was not – vivacious, worldly, sensual, a woman ripe, buxom and eager. I was trying to sneak away, to watch Jeanne at the cafe where she worked when Marie-Thérèse followed me and was run down in the road by a carriage.

"Part of me was not sorry to lose her – that is how little I loved her by then. I saw her only as a millstone around my

247

neck when all I craved was the freedom to pursue my desires. That very night I performed the rite and called Jeanne Lafitte to me. This time I did not summon her to love me, but merely to desire me, to want nothing but the pleasures of my flesh. And she came to me then, just as I wished, insatiable for me – willing to do anything, to indulge any impulse ...

"We moved away the next day, before Marie-Thérèse was even cold in the ground. We travelled for a time and then I brought Jeanne here. How different this place looked then, bright with fresh paint in the sunshine, warm with the heat of her desire by day and night. But even that was not enough for me. It was on a lazy daytrip to Forêt-la-Folie that Marthe caught my eye. I did not care that she had a husband, a child. I wanted her. And because I wanted her, Jeanne wanted her too."

He looked up at the ceiling, lost in memories. "It was there in the loft that we summoned her together, Jeanne and I. We thought that all the power and pleasure in the world was ours. Afterwards we made love in the red chalk circle. Shadows, in the form of black snakes, appeared and entwined around our limbs, copulating with us, around us, their touch like some unnatural, icy, scorching heat that mesmerized and thrilled us, even as we were frightened by them. That was the first time I saw fear in Jeanne's eyes.

"Marthe came to us then: beautiful, soft, her great dark eyes so full of desire." The air seemed to stir around him, and he shivered at the caress of unseen hands, stroking his hair and pulling once more at his clothes. "Wait, wait, not now, soon ... " he cooed softly into the air behind him. He turned back to me, his eyes still streaming with tears. "I should not have said their names aloud," he explained quietly. "They think I am calling them again. Yes, I still have that power over them – would that I had the power to send them to their rest."

"But what happened to them? What happened here?" I demanded, mistrustful of Greene. "Did you kill those women? Did you tire of them as well? Was it their bones I uncovered in that cellar?"

Greene closed his eyes and shook his head. "No, no. " He covered his face with his hands. "We were happy here together – more than happy. We did not need the outside world: we found our heaven here. It was Marthe who first saw something wrong – a terrible face at the bedroom window. I went to look but I saw nothing. Later we all heard the tapping on the glass, and a spectral voice like the wind that was always calling my name. Marthe and Jeanne were very afraid. They thought this place haunted. And they were right.

"Jeanne came to me the next night terrified – she had seen a ghostly hooded figure in the barn. I thought it must be her imagination, never dreaming that what I would find there would be no ghost, but the wife I had seen killed and buried, returned to me. When I saw that face beneath the hood I thought my heart had stopped beating. I wondered if I had gone insane. She *was* dead – I could see still the hole in her head, the marks where the horses' hooves had caved in her chest. She was withered, not rotting but desiccated – like a mummy animated by some ghastly desire: the longing I had planted in her had not died. It could not die. And all she wanted was me. I did not understand that then. I commanded her to return to her grave and she left me, distraught and uncomprehending, as she wandered away into the dark.

"She came again the next night, and every night thereafter. We locked the doors and fastened the shutters, hiding from her in terror, prisoners here together. I tried using the book again to send her away, but it did no good. It was Jeanne who suggested burying her again. The next day we dug a deep hole back there in the woods beyond the hill. And when she came again that night, I lured her out there, where Jeanne and Marthe were waiting. I climbed down into that grave and called her in beside me. She threw herself into my arms and I held her down as Marthe and Jeanne began to cover her with boards, with bricks and earth. I prayed to God for her deliverance as that fragile, windy, pleading voice grew

249

ever more muffled beneath the earth. Jeanne and Marthe prayed and sang hymns to drown out the terrible sound of her cries. When silence fell at last, we crept back here, clutching each other, and we drank until we no longer thought of the horror of what we had done. We lost ourselves in wine and in pleasure, here on the great fur rug before the fire, and after, in the bed …

"It was the first proper sleep I had had in many nights. I remember I dreamt I was sitting in a warm bath, as someone chopped wood that lay on the floor, the water lapping and the axe making a rhythmic sound as it struck. But when I awoke, the sound was somehow in the bedroom. The bed was shaking with it. And I did seem to be lying in something warm and wet.

"I opened my eyes to find Marie-Thérèse beside the bed, like a shadow, black with soil and spattered with blood. The axe in her hands was chopping into Marthe who lay beside me." He curved his arm around the empty space and it looked then as though something rushed into the space and embraced him. "Where Jeanne had lain on my right there was only blood. She was still alive then and had crawled out here to escape." Greene looked along the floor of the room, at the dark stains that still marked the wooden boards.

"All Marie-Thérèse said was 'love me, love me. Now you are free, you must love me.' She dropped the axe and climbed into the bed beside me, clutching me in her dirt-encrusted arms that smelt of blood and the grave. It was too late for Marthe. Jeanne died in my arms minutes later. I was so terrified that they too would return from the grave that I built a fire right then in the yard, and I burnt their sweet, beautiful bodies – burnt them to ashes while Marie-Thérèse clung to me and I howled in rage, pain and terror, knowing even then that they might come back. But I thought that if their bodies were destroyed before they 'awoke' then perhaps they could not return at all.

"So I gathered every bit of ash, every bone, every

fragment of them, and I sealed it all up in there, desperate that what scant knowledge of occult lore I knew might be enough to contain them, to let them rest. But I never ever forgot them, nor the price they had paid for my desires. Even sealed up as they were, their memories haunted me: the ecstasies we had shared, and the horror that overtook us here. For a time I stayed here with Marie-Thérèse, paralysed with despair, my life a waking nightmare with my corpse bride clinging ever to me. And nothing I tried could ever lay her to rest – no rite, no symbol in the book.

"At last I could stand it no more. I knew there must be someone, some expert – priest or necromancer, I cared not – who could help me. I took her to my Paris home and did all I could to keep her confined there. That was when I first found Dr Palissandro – or he found me. It was he who told me what to do, the dimensions the cell should be, and exactly where it must be placed within the house – what kind of door must seal the room, and what to place in the room with her. At last it seemed that she was safely held in that room, surrounded by my things. He said that, in time, and without me near her, she would settle into a kind of sleep. It seemed to work. I trusted him then.

"So I went away, travelling, still in a daze of grief and self-loathing. I changed my name in the vain hope that that would free me from the book's chains – but of course, it did nothing at all. The book knew who I was. It would not be fooled, nor outsmarted. I vowed never to love again – nevermore to use the book in that fashion. For years I was alone and meant to stay that way. But on that ship to America, Esther saw me and she decided." He smiled through his tears. "She pursued me, broke through the walls of my solitude and misery. And on that long voyage, I grew to love her, not with a boy's infatuation or a youth's unbridled desire, but with a man's love – mature, steady and true. We knew true happiness and we loved each other freely, willingly, joyfully. I did not need to use the book to call her to me, so I never did. I only used the book to ensure that she would always love me as I loved her. But it was quite unnecessary. My one consolation now is that those who are not called by the book do not return as Thralls."

"Thralls?"

"That is what Palissandro called them, the living dead whom the book has called and will never release. They are eternally in our thrall, like these restless spirits of Jeanne and Marthe that you awoke. I called them to desire me and even now, without bodies, those desires that can never ever be satisfied torment them and they cannot let me alone. That is why they sought me out the other night – that is why I had to flee my home – for how could I ever explain to Esther these ghosts that want nothing but to make love to me? Palissandro said that if I joined his damned cult then I would gain power over my Thralls, and could use them as instruments to do any bidding. I could think of nothing more cruel than to further abuse those wretched unfortunates."

"So there is no remedy? Nothing at all I might do to release Marchelline from this?"

"No. If there were, Palissandro would never reveal it to one who was not an initiate of the *Ministri*. Unless your wife is securely and permanently contained, you may never love again – for the love that calls her to you will impel her to destroy whomever else you love. And the shadow people help the Thralls in any such gruesome endeavour. The book attaches shadows to those we call as much as to ourselves."

"No, that cannot be true! There *must* be another way!"

"If there is, I have not found it." Greene bent over, his face blanching in a grimace of agony as he clutched his abdomen. "And I have learned better than to think that I can ever outsmart the book. As far as I know, the only ways to undo the book's effects are to die, to join the *Ministri Tenebrarum*, or to offer your skin in sacrifice for a new book. The choice has been made for me. I shall very soon try the first way." He cried out and panted to catch his breath against the pain that wracked him. "I pray God that it works, and that the four of us shall all find peace at last."

His hair moved again under invisible fingers and he moaned and writhed under caressing hands that seemed to alleviate his pain.

"Is there really nothing else I can do? Please? Please – I will try anything!"

Gildian Greene looked at me through narrowed, reddened eyes and shook his head.

Both of us turned then at the sound of my horse whinnying and stamping the ground outside in alarm. A cool whistling wind began to blow through the broken windows and open doorways of the ruined farmhouse. Was it my imagination that detected some mildewed smell of the charnel house in that cold air? Faintly perceptible, a tone in the wind seemed to form a sound full of longing and despair. "Solomon …"

Gildian Green tensed and crouched up onto the balls of his feet and fingertips, his brow contorted in anguish, his voice a hissed whisper.

"She is here!"

Chapter Twenty-Five

Some invisible tumult churned the air around Gildian Greene, and the atmosphere seemed to bristle with a strange, violent intensity. Greene shrank from whatever surrounded him and pressed his back into the wall, his hand clamped over his mouth, his face grey.

A shadow crossed the threshold of the kitchen and with a great commotion, panicked pigeons fled into the daylight. I backed away, around to the side of the fireplace. Wind gusted into the dusty room and seemed to blow with it a cloud of some dark matter that swirled and hung in the thick air as Marie-Thérèse walked in, stiff and searching. At the sight of Gildian Greene cowering against the opposite wall, her face transformed, that look of immortal longing replaced by a rictus grin of bliss.

"Solomon," she sighed reaching out her skeletal arms towards him, "my love, my love. I have found you. I have waited all this time, only for you."

At that moment, the air crackled and some fierce movement agitated the dark atmosphere of the room. Something flew at Marie-Thérèse – two somethings – buffeting and assailing her so that her long pale hair flew up around her, strands of it gusting away into the foul, stirred-up air. Marie-Thérèse's frail hands covered her head and she tried to move a step closer to Greene, but she seemed held back by the dirty, compact whirlwind that raged around her

"No, no," Green muttered in panic through his hand,

his eyes searching and wild.

"What is happening? What is this?" I hissed at him across the room, drawing further back from the horrible scene before me.

"Jeanne and Marthe," he wailed, unable to take his eyes off his wife as she twisted and struggled before us, "they must remember Marie-Thérèse and what she did to them. They recognize her as wanting to take me away from them. Oh dear God, this cannot be happening. The dead are fighting over me."

At the mention of his lovers' names, some peculiar change came over Marie-Thérèse and her besieged look was replaced by a countenance dark and full of anger. No longer trying to protect herself, she began to strike out, clawing and batting at the churning air as one might at vexatious insects, but with fearsome rage. Something appeared to pop with a dusty little explosion on the side of Marie-Thérèse's face; then on her neck, then her arm. It was flesh, or what remained of it, dried and withered, being chipped and broken away by ghostly, clawing hands.

"Solomon!" Marie-Thérèse begged, "As you love me, help me!"

"No! No! Jeanne, Marthe, I implore you – stop this!" Gildian cried out, lurching forwards but halting before he got too close.

"Let them destroy each other if they can," I urged, "and perhaps that will be an end to the matter."

"No!" Gildian shouted, hugging himself with clutching, twitching hands as he edged around the terrible scene towards me. "While Marie-Thérèse is intact there is at least some hope of containing her. If her body is destroyed she will become as they are – inescapable!"

Nebulous shadows swirled around Marie-Thérèse as she lashed out into the air and more sprays of powdery flesh erupted from her frame. Then a larger chunk flew off and I thought I heard the almost imperceptible laughter of two

255

voices that seemed to echo dimly from very far away.

"My loves," Gildian ventured, his voice breaking, "pray do not fight, it displeases me so. If you love me at all, you must cease this violence!"

"You do not love them," Marie-Thérèse cried as a long strip of flesh appeared to be pulled off her bony forearm. "You love me – only me! Send them away! Destroy them – so that we can be together, alone." Her head jerked as something grabbed a hunk of hair behind her left ear and pulled it hard. Flesh crumbled as the hair came away and with it a broad band of withered tissue and muscle that peeled down her fragile neck to the jugular notch between her collarbones, from whence it tore free. The long torn flap was flung out at Gildian Greene and he struck it away in revulsion, burying his head in his hands and shaking his head in terror and dismay as yet more tissue continued to be stripped from the raging skeleton of Marie-Thérèse.

I covered my mouth with my sleeve as the swirling air grew thick with the dust and flakes of her flesh. I did not know what to do, and could only look on in horror as the ghosts of Gildian Greene's lovers continued to fight for him. And in the thickening grey haze I could see them at last, the vague, nebulous shapes of those poor women whose bodies Marie-Thérèse had destroyed, but whose tormented existence knew no end.

Long, sticklike arms, that appeared to bend and sway as no human arms could, scratched and gouged at Marie-Thérèse. Elongated, translucent faces bit and leered at her as they circled in the air. And swirling around them like black clouds I caught glimpses of the shadow people reveling in it all: sometimes supporting the long arms of Jeanne and Marthe as they struck out, sometimes leering over the narrow, ghostly shoulders of those jealous, vindictive wraiths.

Unable to bear the sight of it any longer, Gildian Greene gave a pained cry and threw himself forward, into the melee. Dust and inchoate forms engulfed him as he seized Marie-

Thérèse in a protective embrace. Oh, to see her face then, freed in that moment from her pain and delivered, as she thought, into the arms of love. A loving smile softened those terrible features, and an arm, its bone exposed by her tormentors, reached up and she stroked Gildian's face with indescribable tenderness, cherishing his nearness with the supremely intense fervour that only her condition could endow.

"My love, my love," she whispered sweetly to him as the spirits of Jeanne and Marthe continued to tear the flesh from her bones. She did not care. All she wanted in this world, or the next, was now in her embrace. But this only provoked her attackers to renew their violence. One of them stripped her scalp almost entirely away, exposing the smooth creamy white of her cranium and sending a mass of hair flying into the air. She faltered in Gildian's arms as her leg was snapped off and flung away. He cradled and supported her tenderly, trying to draw her away towards the bedroom, but Jeanne and Marthe would not be denied so easily, and continued their assaults.

Ghostly hands seized the arm with which Marie-Thérèse caressed her husband's face, and the dark hands of shadows aided them to wrench it from the socket and fling it away. It landed on the floor with a dreadful clatter and skidded to halt against the wall. How pitiful she looked now, her fragile corpse decaying before our eyes, her bones spare of flesh: limbs, hair, chunks of her substance cruelly torn away. But her face, still largely intact, only smiled that strange rapturous smile. Nothing else mattered to her but Gildian Greene. The fevered longing of decades was satisfied at last. Only the hands of those vengeful spirits could take the smile from her face. As she reached up to kiss the agonised face of her love, her dark, withered lips were torn away, flying, spinning into the air like brittle autumn leaves. Undeterred she pressed her exposed teeth against his grimacing mouth, and I heard him groan then with a pain that could never be spoken in words.

Overwhelmed with horror, Gildian Greene let go of

257

Marie-Thérèse and jumped back from her. Poised on one frail bony leg she reached out after him and toppled to the floor, striking the ground with such impact that her fragile besieged frame snapped in two at the waist. Unable to rise, she could only twist stiffly where she lay, her bony fingers scratching at the floorboards as her lipless mouth tried in vain to form words. "Tolonon," her tiny rasping voice pleaded to her lover, "lud ne … hold ne … "

Gildian turned away, falling to his knees and weeping into his hands. The turmoil in the air seemed at last to subside, and the dust began to fall, like a carpet of pale, dirty, pink-grey snow upon the floor. His hair moved under spectral hands and he shook his head violently and barked, "Get away! Get away from me! You disgust me!" I had to turn my face away at the spectacle, as he sobbed and wailed, and the remains of Marie-Thérèse flailed weakly upon the floor. But after only a few moments he fell silent and I turned to see why. He nodded to himself, oblivious to the hands that pulled at his shirt and ruffled the fabric of his waistcoat.

"Yes," he said quietly to himself and with a strangely calm resolution in his voice. "That is what I must do. Yes. Thank you." He looked up to the ceiling, his eyes closing and his face easing with the smile that spread over his white lips. He sighed. "Ah, yes, yes, I see now. Wait for me Esther. I pray you will wait … "

Filled with a serenity that seemed, miraculously, to wash all of his previous torment away, Gildian calmly wiped his eyes with his handkerchief and stood up. He walked to the end of the room and stood before the pile of bricks and broken masonry that led to the cellar, slowly nodding his head.

"I have a favour to ask of you, Monsieur De Bresson. I realise I have no right to impose upon you so, after all the misfortune I have brought you, but perhaps, for that very reason, you will not find the task I propose an objectionable one."

"What? What more is it that you want of me?" I asked,

still angry at all he had put me through.

'It is nothing so very great." He explained, stooping over with painful exertion to pick up a brick from the floor, and easily brushing away the crumbling mortar that barely stuck to it. "I had meant to make the repair myself," he explained, gesturing at some dirty old buckets upon the floor that I had not previously noticed. One appeared to hold a quantity of sand; the other held a grey powder that might have been lime. Against the wall a little further along sat a small dusty bag labeled "salt."

"I had hoped to coax Jeanne and Marthe back to their rest somehow and seal this doorway again forever – but all my efforts to lure them failed. It was hardly surprising. But now my plans have changed. You must make the seal, Monsieur, for I shall be inside that cellar, down there, with the ghosts of my loves."

"What?"

"I have nothing to live for. My will to go on died with Esther. It is my fault that she is gone. My fault because I never dealt with these terrible things I have done. I only hid them, buried them, hoping that they would never emerge. My first wife, my lovers, I called them to me and then I abandoned them. Now at last, I shall give them what I made them desire. They can have me, forever, and together – I pray – we might all find some peace at last."

"You cannot intend to – "

"What else should I do? Tell me. What other options do I have?"

I said nothing.

"No. This is the only way. I must give them what I owe them. It is … right."

I nodded, and despite myself a tear came to my eye – but whether it was for Monsieur Greene, or for some similar fate that I feared awaited me, I could not say.

Gildian Greene found the stubs of some old candles and together we descended into that cold, stale cellar. The floor all

259

around was scattered with ashes, fragments and pieces of bone that had been sealed in the green wooden box until I had disturbed them. Gildian had brought with him a worn out broom, and a brush and shovel from the fireplace, and together we carefully swept the remains of Jeanne and Marthe and gently returned them to their tiny coffin. Birds cooed softly in the loft high above us. A curious tranquility had descended upon the farmhouse, broken only by the occasional sounds of Marie-Thérèse moaning in the room at the top of the stairs, her words indistinct through her broken mouth.

Once or twice, as we handled the remains, I thought I felt the feathery touch of something brushing past me in the air. As we worked, I felt that the atmosphere of the room grew still and heavy with sadness that was not my own.

Gildian replaced the knotted red cord around the box and prayed quietly over it, in the language of his own religion.

"Come up the stairs with me a moment," he urged softly when he had finished, and I followed him, halting behind him when his pain forced him to pause, leaning heavily upon the handle of the broom that he carried. He went on, and I walked behind him to the bedroom, careful to walk around and not to look too much upon the broken form of Marie-Thérèse.

Greene opened a low drawer in the bedroom and pulled out a folded pale blue blanket, thick with dust. He turned his face away as he opened and shook it. Together we emerged back into the long parlour and he gestured to me to take one end of the blanket.

"Let us lay it out carefully beside her," he murmured, and I obliged him. He knelt on the blanket beside Marie-Thérèse and with infinite gentleness he put his arms around that broken torso and cradled her in his embrace. "There, my love," he soothed at that gaping, incoherent mouth with its hideous permanent grin. "A blanket to make you more comfortable."

"I lud yu, ny dearet" the mouth strained to say.

260

"Yes, yes my love," Gildian reassured as he laid the torso down upon the blanket, clasping the one arm that remained as it reached for him. "And I love you too. From the first moment I saw you." A tear rolled down his face. "Rest here, you are very tired and weary. I shall take care of you now. I was very wrong to leave you. I hope you can forgive me. You are not alone anymore." The skeletal face nodded slowly, the dry eyes following Gildian's every movement as he reached over to gather up the lower torso and leg that had been left behind.

"There," he said softly as he placed the pieces back where they had once belonged with the rest of Marie-Thérèse on the blanket. "Will you lie here and rest a moment while I fetch your … things?" he asked her.

With eyes full of love, Marie-Thérèse watched as her husband limped painfully around the room, gathering up her arm, her leg, swatches of her long, pale hair, pieces of withered skin and dried muscle that lay scattered around the dirty floor. All of these he brought back to her, carefully restoring them to their former positions. "There," he said, "just as you were. Just as lovely as you were when first we met."

He held her hand and gestured to me with his eyes towards the broom. I understood at once and as quickly as I was able, I carefully swept the floor until all the dust that might once have been a part of her was collected in a little pile. Greene scanned the room, and not finding what he desired, he pulled the handkerchief from his pocket and laid it out alongside the pile of dust. It was the work of a few moments to sweep up the dust with the old fire implements and to transfer it into the handkerchief. Greene let go of her hand and patted it, then set to gathering up the corners of the handkerchief and tying them in a secure knot so that not a spec of her might be lost again.

"Marie-Thérèse, my dearest," he said, holding the little makeshift urn gently before her, "may I ask if you be so kind as to mind my handkerchief for me? You were always so good at looking after my things, not losing your handkerchiefs as I so often do." He smiled down at her and she nodded, eagerly holding out her hand to take what he offered her. "How very good and loving you have been to me," he said, touching her face lightly, "I wish I had been more deserving of you."

Greene looked at me from under those sad, silvery-white eyebrows. "Now Monsieur, if you would be so kind." Together we folded and wrapped the blanket around her tiny frame, until at last it enfolded her securely, and it appeared as if an unbroken body was swaddled within, with only the ghastly head visible. Greene gathered her in his arms and lifted her as he stood. "Light as a feather," he smiled at her, "as you always were."

I ran ahead and kicked and cleared the rubble from his path as he returned to the cellar stairs and carried her down them into the gloom. This time I did not follow him. "Will you wait there a moment my dears," his quiet voice echoed up to me. "I shall return to you presently, I swear it on my life."

Gildian Greene's white, perspiring face reappeared in the doorway and he hastened to retrieve a leather satchel from the bedroom. He tucked it under his arm as he returned to me.

"Do you know what to do?" he asked.

I nodded.

"And after, when the room is sealed, you must lay a line of salt here." He gestured at the threshold. There is a small bag of it over there. But I hope that will be an unnecessary precaution." He frowned to himself in thought, then looked at me again and smiled. "Very well then – I shall say goodbye to you now. And once again, I can only apologise from the bottom of my heart for what I have done to you. No words are sufficient to express the sorrow I feel. When you are finished would you call out to tell me so, or perhaps knock twice upon the wall, so that I might know it?"

"Yes, yes of course," I assented, feeling now that I was leading this man to the gallows.

"Good, good ... " He looked about the room, taking in

the late afternoon light that flooded in from the kitchen and the broken parlour window, knowing that it was the last light he would ever see in this world. He held out his hand tentatively, seeming unsure of whether I would wish to shake it. Of course I took it. Somehow all the anger and blame I had felt for him seemed to have melted away. Above our heads the pigeons cooed louder, as Gildian Greene dropped his gaze to the floor and walked through the broken doorway, his satchel tightly clenched under his arm. I watched his silhouette descend into the dimly candlelit dark, then hastened to start my work.

It was not so very long afterwards that I smoothed a final, thick layer of lime mortar over the bricked up doorway and set down the trowel. I poured a thick trail of salt along the threshold, pressing it into the mortar that had dripped onto the floor there, before brushing the sticky grit of sand and salt and wet cement from my hands.

"Monsieur Greene," I called out, my face leaning against the cold brick wall alongside the new wet surface. "It is done." I heard no reply. I knocked hard upon the wall, certain that he would at least hear that. I waited again and heard nothing save the eternal cooing of the pigeons in the loft. "Goodbye," I murmured to myself as I turned on my heel and left that house.

With immense relief I emerged into the daylight. I saw Gildian Greene's horse tethered in the dilapidated barn and I untied him. Saddled and rested as he was he would make a far better mount than the other exhausted horse with its frayed nerves who grazed nervously at the far end of the curving grass track.

I mounted into the saddle and set off into the coming evening. As I trotted down the track into the long wet grass, I was violently startled, and felt the horse jump in fright – the report of a gun emanated from the farmhouse behind me. I spun around in the saddle in the direction of the sound and saw   four   grey   pigeons   flying   up   into   the   sky.

CHAPTER TWENTY-SIX

I pointed the horse in the direction of home and let him walk. The relief I felt at escaping that farmhouse and its horrors was tempered by the despair that welled in me with every step that took me closer to Giverny and to the living corpse of my love that awaited me there.

What was I to do? Now there was no-one left to help me – no hope of finding any more solutions to the cataclysm I had made of my life, and of Marchelline's. I was utterly alone.

It had been so long since I had changed the dressings on my chest; my shirt and waistcoat were soaked through with blood. I could not escape the smell of blood, the sight of it: blood stained my thoughts, my memories. Even the future that I had once thought so rosy seemed darkened beyond all recognition or hope.

How could I live with Marchelline as She was? How could I live with myself if I shut her up in some cell – like an eternal, living coffin? The pity I felt for poor Marie-Thérèse would never permit me to force such a cruel fate upon Marchelline, understanding now what it entailed. For a moment I toyed with the idea of running away, travelling overseas, as Gildian Greene had done, but that would only delay the inevitable. The thought of spending the rest of my life as a fugitive and never escaping this feeling of guilt and pain … it was unthinkable.

I little noticed where the horse walked nor how much time had passed as we went on. For in my mind, I travelled only in tiny, inescapable circles, trying in vain to find means of escape from the terrible options that lay before me. Suicide, or a premature death caused by the shadow people, the sacrifice of my skin – and most likely my life with it – or becoming one of those hateful ghouls as a member of the *Ministri Tenebrarum*: these were all the choices I had to free Marchelline and myself from this hell.

At length I came to my senses with a shiver and found it was growing dark. The horse had meandered from the road and we were now entering into a little wood I thought I recognized from childhood wanderings. Twigs and leaves crunched and crackled under his steady, plodding feet, and the cacophony of twilight's birdsong was subsiding into lone cries and solitary calls of one bird to another, in the cold, blue half-light. But there was no peace here.

I thought at first that it was the fading light that made the shadows of the tall trees appear the sway and move. I wondered then if it was deer or wild boar I thought I glimpsed, as darting shadows in the gloom. The wood grew denser and darker as we walked on, and the old and well-worn bridal path that the horse followed led us down into a low gully whose banks at the sides were crested with rows of trees. It was then that I saw them clearly.

Against the darkening, deep blue of the evening sky, the outlines of the trees were at last clearly defined: long, straight trunks, slender boughs and skeletal branches. But that same pale light silhouetted other shapes that should not have been there. Black, human-like forms, silent and featureless, stood hunched and swaying almost imperceptibly among the tall trees. Some stood alone, some huddled in groups, but all facing me with those black, empty faces, watching. Now and then some obscure movement in the gully caught my eye, and I feared that they were moving around me, almost invisible in the undergrowth. They were toying with me, openly now. They had been toying with me all along.

The gully itself seemed frozen with cold and despair. I

felt my broken heart sink then into abject desolation. They had me just where they wanted me. I was theirs – just one more nest, a worthless vessel to increase their unspeakable hordes. What could I do but destroy myself? At least then they could no longer use me. The thought of actually doing such a thing turned the blood in my veins to ice, but now it seemed there was no other way for me to escape them.

I had felt that cold, evil desolation that their presence evoked before, when the shadows were summoned in the crypt. And with every step I took, as they surrounded me now, that same feeling seized me tighter and tighter, until the thought of my own suicide seemed like something to be greatly desired. I wondered then that I could entertain thoughts so alien and abhorrent to my own nature: I wondered if they were my own thoughts at all? They were inside me as much as around me. How could I trust even my own impulses when I knew that I was but a plaything of these beings of darkness? In cold and low places it seemed they liked best to gather. How could I trust my own thoughts here in this god-forsaken gully that teemed with them? How could I know that whatever I chose to do would not be what they had made me choose? My heart sank.

I had to get out of this place, this darkness. The bridal path rose before me and I spurred the horse on to ascend it. But just as I looked up to the summit, a queer presentiment made me gently pull the reins of the horse. At that very instant a red stag glided silently, calmly, across the path at the lip of the gully, his fine, long antlers reaching up toward the sky like emaciated arms and clawing hands. The luster of his coat shimmered in the failing light and for a moment he turned his noble head and looked toward me.

Something stirred at my memory and the horse gave a quiet huff and a slow nod of his head. Not in fear, but with agile animal grace, the stag darted away into the wood and with him he took the terrible burden that had been oppressing me so grievously. All at once I knew what it was that I must

267

do.

There was a fourth way. I need not die. I would not die. I would live again and be free of this darkness. I turned my head and scanned the tree line. The shadows had disappeared. I gave a sharp exhalation that was almost a laugh and spurred the horse onward and beyond the crest of the rise.

He who shalle be called can never be released save by the giving of this book, and thereby thine own fate, into his hands.

I had rejected that idea when Marchelline was alive, for I had feared most dreadfully what she might do to me then in revenge. But now – she was dead, desiccated – blood no longer flowed through her veins. She *could not* use the book against me. If I gave it back to her, the spell might be broken and the Book of Calling might be buried with her forever: no more to bring harm to myself or any other.

Hope ignited in my breast like a life-giving flame, and warmth and light seemed once more within my reach. I rode on as a huge white-grey moon rose above us. I cantered through open fields under the soft glow of the moon's watchful eye. We picked our way through trees and on into the narrow spare wood that connected with the wood at the back of my home. Now it was with eagerness rather than dread that I hastened back to Marchelline.

The song of a nightingale echoed through the slender trees, whistling and trilling with solitary beauty. I thought then of Marchelline as I had first seen her, singing on the stage with such incandescent joy and loveliness. In the distance before me, a spectral white figure moved into a chink of moonlight, frail and stiff, as she shuffled slowly in my direction. I knew it was her long before the horse traversed that long, moonlight-scattered path. And likewise, Marchelline knew it was I. Fragile arms reached out to me, a broken skeletal hand clawing into the air to pull me closer.

No longer afraid or filled with dread, I rode on urgently to meet her.

"Where did you go? Why did you leave me?" her ghostly voice implored as I reached her. Her visage gave me no less pain now than when first I had seen it, but the panic and terror that had overwhelmed me then was now washed away by a flood of pity and sorrow for this poor girl, whose life and death I had corrupted.

"All that matters now, is that we are together again," I smiled at her, reaching down to take her hands. Without effort I lifted her into the saddle before me.

"Yes, yes," her airy voice whistled in rapture.

"I have come home to look after you and take care of you, my love," I reassured her.

"And will you promise, Nicolas, that you will never leave me again?"

"Never, never," I murmured as I spurred the horse on. I passed my arms around her waist that was sunken and stiff, like an old leather bag filled with bones.

"Oh, my love," she sighed, stiffly leaning her head back against my shoulder. I looked down upon her broken face with its missing skin and its odour of the grave.

I whispered through my pain. "All I ever wanted was to love you. I truly never meant you any harm. I tried so hard to win you – and only succeeded in failing you, time and again. Let me take you home and make amends, as far as ever I can to you."

She seemed happy then in my arms as we rode together back to the house, under the haunting serenade of the nightingale. I lifted Marchelline down from the horse and she held my hand and followed as I hastened inside. I lit a lamp in the cold, dark house and drew her after me towards my study.

With bliss on that tortured dead face she followed me – she would have followed me anywhere. I put a match to the fire and bade her to sit upon the chaise longue. She was peaceful as I moved to my desk and withdrew the Book of

Calling from the drawer.

How had something so small, so inconsequential as a book, caused all of this? All the most fervent and florid hopes of my youth had turned to ashes under the book's influence. All the lofty ideas I had had about myself had been blackened under the pall of its shadows. But I could be free of it again. I would give her the book, and with it, give away all the foolish dreams and illusions that had led me to this.

I drew a deep breath and went to sit beside Marchelline. She stared into my face with adoration in those dry eyes.

"I have a gift for you, my love," I began, my voice trembling and weak.

"I need no gifts, only your love."

I nodded and looked down at the book. I watched her face as her eyes moved slowly down to see what I pressed into her hands. Some cloud passed over her countenance, the firelight illuminating the papery texture of her discoloured skin. She laid the book upon her knees and opened the cover with her claw-like hand. For a long moment she said nothing and I was unsure if she understood. Could those eyes even read anymore?

"This is the book with which you bewitched me, is it not, my love?" she asked, her voice filled with scratchy wonderment.

"Yes. I am most desperately sorry for the great wrong I have done you. I am sorrier than you will ever know. Will you accept the book?"

"But … but … you still love me, don't you? You must!" Her hand clutched my arm in terror.

"Yes, my love, now and always. I just wanted you to have the book, as a present from me, as a token of how sorry I am – that is all. And with it, I humbly beg you to forgive me. I love you."

She nodded slowly, as if struggling to comprehend.

"I will cherish this always, because it came from you."

She hugged the book to her sunken chest and leaned

forward to kiss me. I thought of her as she had been in all her glory, and I closed my eyes and kissed her for the last time.

She rose then and moved to the desk where she laid the book down once more and sat as she leafed through the pages until she came to my page, with its raven quill as a placeholder. She picked up the feather and turned it in to light.

"Would you? Would you love me then? ... " her airy voice wheezed absently and her dry lips formed a kind of smile. She seized up the silver letter-opener that lay on the desk and plunged it into her chest, dragging it down with a noise like tearing fabric. The blade clicked against bone and dried flesh crumbled onto the floor.

I leapt to my feet, bellowing at her in horror, "What are you doing?"

She only smiled as she looked down into the cavity the knife had opened. She reached in through the torn fabric of her nightdress and her own tissue, feeling around inside her abdomen. With a sound like ripping paper, she tore something out and held it in her fist so I could not see. Her claw hand hooked one of its bony fingers into a glass half filled with water that still sat on the desk from days before. She squeezed the thing in her hand and a blob of very dark gelatinous matter oozed slowly out of it and into the glass. Threads of red began to insinuate into the water as the blob of dark matter sank to the bottom of the glass.

"You *cannot* use the book!" I cried in disbelief. "You *cannot!*"

"It was yours and now it is mine, it is ours. I shall write my name in it, as you have written yours." She smiled, as she began to stir the glass with the point of the letter-opener and a red tint stained and deepened the water. "And I shall use it for us – so that we can always be together – always. You gave me another gift, the gift of death – and death took away all my fear. Now I only love you and want you the more."

She dipped the quill into the red water and began to

271

write on the page after mine.

"What are you doing?" I rushed forward. "No!"

"I love you, I love you," she whispered, over her shoulder, then returned to her writing. "Now our names are here together, forever."

"Please, Marchelline, stop! You should rest now, my love. You must rest. Lay down the quill."

"Yes," she said at last, setting down the quill with a nod. She turned in the chair and at last I could see what she had written. Under her own name at the top of the page she had formed the symbol of calling, not with a line, but with her own name and mine. Inside this large, written symbol she had formed another, smaller sign, the flame of love.

"Yes, I will rest now," she said slowly, picking up the book and cradling it like a baby in her arms. "And you must rest too my love – you look so very tired … Soon we shall rest together … "

Some change appeared to have come over her then. It was in the expression of her face, the flat weak tone of her voice, but mostly it was evident in the deathly slowness of her movements. Like an automaton whose clockworks had run down, her energy seemed to be dissipating by the moment. Her attention, formerly so acutely concentrated upon me, had now wandered into some strange reverie. She no longer looked at me – I wondered if she even knew that I was there.

Her head drooped in exhaustion as she rose and walked slowly from the room. I followed, some paces behind, as she. moved down the hall and out of the front door. "I love you," her voice whispered absently, but she never turned back towards me as she walked out into the moonlit garden and across the lawn in the direction of the churchyard.

I locked the door and wandered through the house, not sure exactly what had happened.

She could not have used the book on me. It could not work. That dried and blackened substance in her vein was no longer proper blood. And the rite – lighting the candles,

272

summoning the diamon, the ritual with the blood in the flames – she had done none of what the book demanded to call the shadows. I had seen no shadows in the room, heard not the wind, nor the voice of the wind that spoke whenever the book was being used. It was utterly impossible.

The fact that she had left me seemed the most telling thing – that gave me reason at last to hope, and to dismiss those other fears from my mind. Here was proof that the spell I had cast upon her had indeed been broken. Whatever pantomime she had performed with the book was perhaps just in imitation of me. Clearly she had not understood how to use it – the way she made the symbol of calling had demonstrated that.

I walked to my bedroom and found the formerly locked door broken and ajar. A smell of the grave hung in the air there. If I could sleep at all, I could not sleep there tonight. My chest itched and I was suddenly reminded of the appalling state of my clothes, stained with blood, cement, horse sweat, and the dust of travelling. Exhausted, I grabbed a fresh nightshirt from my drawer and hastened back to my study.

I tore my clothes off in front of the fire and cast them into it. The wet and stinking dressings and bandages I likewise pulled off and threw into the flames. If I were not so exhausted, I would have heated some water and bathed. But I was so utterly enervated by my ordeal: it was all I could do to remain upright, leaning my arm upon the mantle for support. As the fire warmed my skin, I became aware that something was amiss. My chest – it felt dry, and it tingled in a most curious way.

I straightened my back and looked into the mirror. My chest was caked with dried blood. Yes, it was all dry – not a single drop of fresh blood seeped from the weals – not even a suggestion of moisture could my searching hand detect. I seized up the decanter of port from the shelf and splashed it over my neck and chest. It did not sting. I wiped and scrubbed roughly with my hands, then seized up the nightshirt and rubbed my chest with it. There was no mistake. My eyes widened in the glass as I saw that the many weals that had scarred me were all now dry, silvery-purple scars that seemed to be fading even as I watched them.

My life might be my own again. This terrible crushing secret shame and guilt might be lifted. I would return to my music – my first love – and try to make something good out of my life. I would do it. I took a drink from the decanter and resolved to rest my weary head and try to sleep at last.

My eye fell then upon the glass that still sat upon the desk, the liquid within now clear at the top, but reddening to black at the base of the glass. Throwing open the window, I flung the contents of the glass out into the garden. If I never saw another drop of blood it would be too soon. With a heavy clunk I set the glass back down, turning away when I noticed that a thick lump of dark matter still clung to its side, slowly sliding down the glass, leaving a thin trail of red in its wake.

I wrapped myself in a rug and collapsed upon the chaise longue, and into the heaviest of slumbers.

CHAPTER TWENTY-SEVEN

It was birdsong that awoke me the next day. A high trilling exquisite song had inveigled its way into my dreams, repeating its enchanting melody and drawing me out of my slumber.

My study was bathed in golden light and warm air drifted in from the open window, making the sheer curtains softly wave and flutter. I breathed in deeply of the air and of that captivating, joyous melody and I felt my heart swell.

I rose and caught my reflection in the glass. There he was, that self I thought I had lost all those months ago. How calm and pleasant seemed the fair face that smiled back at me from under his light brown hair. There was happiness in those clear hazel eyes. It was the song that made me smile. It made me think of Marchelline. I had to go outside, to follow that song. I rushed to pull on some clothes and ran from the house into the garden that seemed alive and florid with effervescing vitality and excitement.

How queer it was to find myself so happy. Even the strange aching longing that fluttered in my breast was tinged with joy, for that longing was a sacred expression of the love that filled me. How could I have sent her away? Who was I yesterday that I could commit such abominable cruelty to the woman I loved beyond all measure. I had to find her. I knew I could, for – like a magnet – my love and the song that danced through my senses seemed to be pulling me onwards.

Even the two ravens that stood together cawing in the

275

arbor seemed to have no fear of me as I ran by them – such was the change that had overtaken me. Whatever I had been before – however selfish, cruel and thoughtless – I was such a man no more. My mind raced only with thoughts of Marchelline – how much I worshipped and adored her, and what I might do to show her all the love that burned in my heart for her. That love consumed me like a fire sent from Heaven. It struck me then with a pang that the years of life that remained to me might not be sufficient to do all the honour and service that I wished to bestow upon my bride – but with every fibre of my being, I would try.

I ran on, down to the end of the garden and beyond, into the wood, where that sublime song seemed to ring through the trees, and all the other sounds of birds and wild creatures were but a muted counterpoint to that one melody that put them all to shame with its angelic magnificence. I could not lose another minute. I needed to be with her so badly.

But even the worry and urgency I felt seemed to melt away as the song caressed my soul. How could it be that a songbird could form the semblance of words as it sang? And yet I heard those words sharpening into clarity now, and I knew that I must be drawing close.

Birds flew wildly around me as I ran through the trees and the crunching twigs of the forest floor. Bright sunlight filtered, dazzling, in a myriad chinks and rays through the canopy of leaves and branches. The tweets and cries of the startled birds around me swelled to a cacophonous crescendo as the steady voice continued its song, pure, clear and joyous.

Well, my sweetheart and I, we went walking,
Out in the country one day
My dearest, he said, here's a sweet little bed
A pillow of flowers for your pretty head.

It was then that I saw her, her slender frame crouching

beside the trunk of a tree. Even with her back to me, I could never mistake her, that Nightingale who had from the very first note, bewitched me with her sweet song.

'Come lay down beside me,' he beckoned,
'Away from the world's prying eyes,'
But we weren't so alone as he reckoned
In a branch up above us a birdy did cry

Tears of joy streamed down my face at the sight of my love.

It was Heaven I found with my true love ...

"Marchelline, my beloved," I called to her, falling to my knees in thanks that I had found her. Slowly she turned her head to look over her shoulder at me. She was even more beautiful than I had remembered her, like some unearthly, divine bird. Dark eyes peered at me seductively from under chestnut curls that were adorned with leaves and feathers. The sunlight glinted golden off the creamy white of her bones where they showed through. Beside her, on the ground, lay the Book of Calling. She extended a hand to me, more beautiful and slender than any mortal hand. As elegant and fine as a bird's foot, it reached out to me, and I rushed forward on my knees the kiss that hand, and to fall at her feet in adoration.

"Love me," I wept, beseeching her with tears that fell, glistening, onto the bones of her feet. She took my face between her hands and drew me up towards her. How my senses thrilled at the sweet perfume of her skin as I held her in my arms.

"Yes my love," her musical voice murmured as I caressed her face with a thousand kisses. "I am yours and you are mine, forever, my sweetheart ..."

We kissed then, rolling in that bed of leaves and

277

wildflowers. I had never dared to imagine such rapture as I knew then, simply to be close to her, to hold her slender form in my arms.

"What can I do? Anything in my power to please you is yours, if you will only name it, that I might show you how much I love and adore you."

"Paris," she whispered in my ear, as we lay entangled in each other's arm. "Take me back to Paris."

"Yes, yes, anything. Nothing would please me more than to return to Paris with you, my love."

She picked up the book in her delicate hands and I swept her up in my arms and carried her, light as a feather, as I ran back to the house. I dressed her in her finest gown of red and black striped silk. She pinned up her hair and set upon her gorgeous head that little red hat decorated with a tiny stuffed finch of red, black and golden yellow, drawing down the gathered up red veil until it covered her lovely face against the bright sunlight.

I aided her into red satin gloves, and tied a black velvet ribbon around her sinuous throat. I left her attending to her toilette as I dusted off the trap from the stable and harnessed the two chestnut carriage horses into it, pulling down the hood for shelter on the long drive ahead.

What bliss it was just to sit beside her for those blessed hours as the horses walked on. Through the late afternoon and twilight we held each other close, each enraptured in the other, wordlessly reveling in the love that we shared. All I wanted to do was to look at her, to gaze into those mysterious, dark eyes. I little noticed where we went as she directed me to turn the horses this way or that.

At last she bade me to stop.

"We are here," she announced, smilingly.

"I do not care where we are," I cooed, "as long as we are together." I clasped her hand and gazed into her eyes, seeing nothing but her.

"We are just where we belong," she answered, her voice echoing off high walls.

I looked around and saw that we were in a long, narrow laneway, illuminated at either end by a small gas lamp, hanging from a curved hook of dark metal. I recognized it at once as the *Rue des Corbeaux*.

Marchelline leaned towards me and touched my face, kissing me through her veil. "We have been called here, all along."

I nodded and smiled at her.

Alighting, I moved swiftly to aid her from the carriage, lifting her down beside me and taking her hand. Together we walked into the darkness of the deeply recessed doorway and I opened the heavy door for her. Tiny candles once more lit that steep and narrow stairway, and I walked ahead, with the Book of Calling tucked under my arm as I guided Marchelline down so that she might not fall.

Step after step we descended, gay and laughing at the curious dance we danced upon those never-ending stairs, down through further doors and yet others, until at last we came to the archway made of skulls, and saw firelight playing in the brazier of the cavernous chamber within. Hand in hand we advanced towards the welcoming light.

There, behind the fire, stood Dr Palissandro and his companion with the narrow eyes from the other evening. Both were smiling, almost laughing, as we were.

"Just as I told you," Dr Palissandro's companion nodded, staring fixedly at us. "*Amantes aeterna* – eternal lovers. Does it not warm your heart, Johannes?"

"Indeed so. There is little that is more pleasing to an old man then to see young people so very much in love."

Marchelline squeezed my hand and we exchanged a secret smile.

"Welcome," Dr Palissandro's deep voice resounded through the chamber as he advanced to greet us, his arms spread wide, "to your new home. An apartment has been

279

prepared for you, with servants, and every convenience that you might require. But this apartment, however modest, has one thing that no other home might offer you. It is the one thing that lovers so devoted as you are crave most – peace and quiet, where you may be together, quite undisturbed."

"Yes, yes," Marchelline nodded eagerly.

"That is just what we desire," I concurred.

"And I see you have brought the book back to us. Shall I take it from you?"

Happily I handed Dr Palissandro the Book of Calling, and he passed it to his companion who smiled at the tome with great fondness, and stroked its cover with warm affection.

"Come then, friends," Dr Palissandro beckoned, taking a torch from the wall and lighting it in the fire. "Won't you follow me?"

Eagerly we walked behind him, through the cavern that echoed with our footsteps, and the archway beyond. Past innumerable screens stretched tight with skin that glowed warmly with the lamp's light we walked on, and along labyrinthine corridors, sloping down, down into yet deeper chambers far below the city.

At last we came to a long corridor set with wooden doors at lengthy intervals along its expanse, stretching off into the distance beyond the meager light of the lamp. And from behind some of these doors, as we passed them, we thought we heard quiet muffled voices, weak and airy voices, some talking quietly, others laughing. Further still we passed many silent doors, until Dr Palissandro produced a silver key and opened the door to his left.

With a quiet creak the door swung open and Dr Palissandro's lamp cast its throbbing light into the chamber. How prettily the room was furnished, with furniture whose ornate, antique forms glowed a worn, pale gold. With macabre elegance, a great chandelier formed entirely of human bones hung from the vaulted ceiling. The doctor touched it with his torch and it took light, so the white skulls and bones of the chandelier, and the multitude of others that ornamented the walls, also took on a golden luster.

"And see," Palissandro urged, moving to the far corner of the room, "we have thought of everything you might require."

We followed him to see a fine old harpsichord, upon which two skulls formed eccentric candle holders.

"And beyond, you will find your bedchamber and other rooms, clothes too, we have furnished for you."

Marchelline smiled at him. "You are most kind."

"These apartments are yours, forever. We ask nothing in return, except that perhaps once in a while, we might request of you some small favour or other: to go aloft into the city on some trifling business or other, little errands, nothing more. Or perhaps to assist us in some little ceremony or other."

"Of course," I assented.

"And if you require anything, you need not even do so much as ring a bell. You have only to think about what you wish and a servant shall come. Go on, Madame," Palissandro urged Marchelline. "Try it."

Marchelline went to touch her hat then stopped, thinking. At that moment the wall before us darkened and the shadow that appeared coalesced into a human shape. It drifted over to her and dark fingers lifted her veil and took her hat, wafting it over to a marble topped table with gilded, ornamental legs.

"You see," the doctor continued. "It is that easy. And if the shadows wish sometimes to dress you in some particular way, or to rearrange your furniture as it may amuse them to do – if they wish to play with you as a child might play with dolls in a doll house – why, you would not think anything of that, I imagine. It is just their little game."

We nodded our heads, Marchelline laughing gaily.

"Or if they wished even to perhaps borrow some little

bone from you that you could easily spare – that would be nothing so terrible, in return for all of this."

"No," I replied, lost in the wonder of our surroundings, my heart thrilling to the prospect of uninterrupted solitude with my dearest beloved.

"Good, good," he nodded, smilingly. "Then I shall leave you to your privacy. I hope that you shall be very happy here."

With a bow he withdrew, and we heard the silver key turn in the lock behind us.

Marchelline swept around the room, her bony hand brushing admiringly over fine ornaments and beautiful antiques, until at last she came upon a lovely music box, made of polished rosewood, inlaid with swirling, elaborate patterns and bands of ebony. She wound the handle and lifted the lid, revealing two tiny clockwork figures that twirled and danced in perfect miniature. In tinkling tones that echoed and rang around the cold stone walls, a familiar waltzing melody chimed into life. But how much sweeter it sounded now than ever it had before.

I took Marchelline in my arms and slowly we danced, under the light of the pendulous chandelier to that song that we both remembered so well, that first song I had written just for her. As she gazed into my eyes, her divine voice began quietly to sing to the music.

If you could see my heart
If you could feel the love it bears
If you only knew –
Would you
Would love me then?
If you knew I was yours
If you only saw me as I am
If you could hear my song
Would you
Would you love me then?

Oh would you
Would you love me then?
If time turned its pages and I tried again
Would you
Would you love me then?

Delight illuminated her radiant, beautiful face, her elegant hollow cheeks, and she twirled and flowed in my arms as though we had always been, and would always be together, dancing in time, in perfect synchrony, bound by the spell of love. And thus it will be so with us, here forever, among the shadows and the dead.

TANIA DONALD

Acknowledgements

Grateful thanks to Stephen Bates for his tireless and generous assistance in bringing this project to completion. Special thanks to Richard May for going above and beyond the call of duty. Thanks also to Peter Holmes and Erin Vine for continuing encouragement and feedback, and to Dr Dan Vine for Latin expertise. Thanks to Henry Mayo for his invaluable suggestions.